Writing Can Be Murder

Writing Can Be Murder

A Can Be Murder Novel

By

Marilyn Rausch and Mary Donlon

Published by
Red Quill Press
Minneapolis, Minnesota

First Edition: October 2014
Printed in the United States of America

Dedications

For my dear sister Carole, red shoes and blue shoes together forever. MJR

For Bob, Tom, Bill, Jane and Larry, my original brothers and sister in crime. Thanks for making room for one more in the club. MJD

Acknowledgements

Our gratitude to Pat Frovarp and Gary Shulze, owners of the marvelous ONCE UPON A CRIME bookstore, for their permission to be included in this story and for their support and encouragement to us and so many other crime writers.

Thanks to those who have so graciously shared their expertise: John Kess and Julie Saffrin, for publishing advice, Eric Ernst MD and Eloise Loeffler MD, for medical advice and Colin T. Nelson, for legal advice.

To our fellow writers who have offered their insights and provided guidance throughout the writing of this trilogy, many thanks to Kathy Nelson, Linda Pinnell, Lesley Ackerberg, Nico Taranovsky, Deb Mackay, Elise Schadauer, Jane Beauchamp and Maureen Kelleher.

Appreciation for their professional service to Judy Bullard, cover designer, and Ethan Boatner, photographer.

Love to our cheering section, Peter, Jessica, Rachel, Ted, Ela and Jon and our extended families and many terrific friends.

Chapter One

Iowa
Early September

Cʜɪᴘ ᴄᴏʟʟɪɴɢꜱᴡᴏʀᴛʜ ʜᴀᴅ ᴡʀɪᴛᴛᴇɴ about murder…victims shot, brutally mutilated, suffocated, poisoned. But that was all fiction. He hadn't seen a real murder scene until he stood and stared at the inert body.

The man was dressed in jeans, a purple University of St. Thomas sweatshirt and Nikes. He looked as if he had fallen asleep while reading the book that was open on his chest. But his face was ashy and his body stiff-looking with what Chip assumed was *rigor mortis*. A thin trail of blood seeped beneath the pages of the book. It pooled on his left side, a dark red, sticky puddle. There was little doubt that he was dead.

A knot of nausea formed in Chip's midsection and started to rise up his chest, his gag reflex forming a bitter taste in his mouth. He quickly turned aside and took a deep breath, then another.

It was his friend Patrick Finnegan.

***

Early that morning Chip Collingsworth drove from Turners Bend, Iowa, to Minneapolis. For as far as he could see, orange cones blocked off one lane of Interstate 35. He thought of himself as a fairly intelligent man. Yet, the workings of the Department of Transportation were beyond his understanding. There were no signs of any work being done, no workers, no heavy equipment, no torn-up asphalt, only a long line of slow-moving traffic inching north at 35 mph. *The road crew is probably off drinking coffee and eating donuts waiting for their lunch break.*

Chip had recently traded in his Volvo convertible for a new state-of-the-art hybrid, a Ford 2014 C-Max with a SYNC voice-activated system. He hadn't tired of ringing all the car's bells and tooting all its whistles.

"Call Jane," he commanded. "Hi, darling. How's my blushing bride?"

"I'm in Hjalmer's barn treating a nasty case of scours. Neonatal calf diarrhea is no fun. Being a vet is not all cute kitties and puppies, you know. Are you in Minneapolis yet?"

"Not even close. I'm caught in road construction traffic. Being on the road trying to promote my books is no fun either, especially when it takes me away from you. If it doesn't let up, I'll be late for my signing at ONCE UPON A CRIME bookstore. What's that bellowing I hear?"

"It's the calf, Chip. Have to go, love. Sell lots of books and drive safely."

That's the same thing Lucinda said to me...only with venom not sweetness in her voice.

Lucinda Patterson Williams was his literary agent. She always found time to promote his career, as well as make his life hell. For a brief period Chip thought romance and marriage might soften her, but he was sadly mistaken. She wanted him in the public eye making appearances and promoting his crime novels. And, as if that wasn't enough, she was pressuring him to sign another three-book contract.

"Play Lorde." Strains from "Royals" filled the car's interior and Chip sang along... *"I've never seen a diamond in the flesh..."*

He was on his way for a joint signing with a fellow crime writer, Patrick Finnegan. Finnegan was moderately successful, while Chip's books were hugely popular. *There's no under-estimating the reading public's desire for tall, handsome doctors and strong, sexy female FBI agents!*

He liked Finnegan. They had met in New York at ThrillerFest, a writer's convention, and discovered they both lived in the Midwest, Chip in Turners Bend, Iowa, and Patrick in Minneapolis, and that they both wrote police procedural novels. Shortly after, they started sharing and critiquing each other's work, emailing chapters back and forth. Chip trusted Patrick's opinions and respected his writing skills. He was pleased to be seeing him again in person and sharing a signing event at ONCE UPON A CRIME.

Chip placed a call to Patrick, but got his voice mail box. "Hi Patrick, this is Chip. I'm meeting Pat and Gary at Common Roots before the store opens. Meet us there, if you can. Otherwise I'll see you at 11:00."

The bookstore was a popular site for mystery readers, and author signings drew large crowds. Jane's son, Sven, was a student at the Minneapolis College of Art and Design. MCAD was within walking distance of the store, and Sven had promised to bring a bunch of his college friends to the book signing.

Chip had done some research on the college when Sven first expressed an interest in the school. He thought it would make a great location for a crime story, or better still, a ghost story. The Minnesota Paranormal Society reported that a student who was raped and murdered haunted the school, and students had claimed to be awakened in the night freezing and hearing screams.

"Call Sven." *Sven would say this voice-activated system is "sick."*

"Sven, it's Chip. You hear any ghosts screaming in the night yet?"

"Nah, I sleep with ear plugs. This on-campus apartment is noisy until the early morning hours. It's usually two or three in the morning before the partying stops."

"Still plan on coming to the signing today?"

"Sure, and we've decided to all come as our favorite detective. I found this dirty, rumpled trench coat in a thrift store; I'm coming as Colombo."

"How in the world do you know Colombo? That show was off the air before you were born."

"We studied it in our Television History class. My friend Bart has a shaved head so he's coming as Kojak."

"I can always count on you for added entertainment, Sven. See you soon."

Chip's mind turned to Jane's kids, Sven and Ingrid. He had grown fond of them, but he tread carefully in his relationship with them. They had both suffered from their parents' divorce. Now their father was a fugitive from the law. Not easy for teens to cope with. Both kids had seen a slew of federal agents hunting for their dad and had their own brushes with crimes, Sven as a perpetrator and Ingrid as a victim. Sven had proven to be resilient and seemed to be enjoying college, but Ingrid had become fearful and withdrawn.

Chip left Iowa's wind farms behind and passed the **Welcome to Minnesota** sign. The orange cones disappeared and traffic began to

3

flow at or above the posted 70 mph. He would arrive just in time to meet the bookstore owners, Gary and Pat, for coffee at Common Roots. He was badly in need of a cup of coffee to quell his traffic-jangled nerves.

Chip admired the bookstore owners. Gary was tall and slender with a wry smile and quiet demeanor. He usually hung out behind the sales counter. Pat was petit and intense. She scurried around amongst the book cases and racks, always busy. They were a perfectly matched couple of opposites, and they ran a thriving business in an economy that was not kind to independent booksellers.

***

Chip walked with Pat and Gary to the store thirty minutes before opening time. He took along a large cup of dark roast, enough to get him through the two-hour session of meeting and greeting his readers. A line of customers was already forming along the sidewalk. Chip scanned the group. He waved to Colombo and Kojak and a pair of girls who looked like they could be Cagney and Lacey.

"Wow, that's a pretty impressive turn-out," said Chip.

"Oh, we expect you and Finnegan will draw a constant stream of buyers. Minneapolis is one of the best mystery markets in the country," explained Gary. "Maybe it's the long winters. All I can say is our little store has survived for twenty-six years, and we sell only one genre."

The garden-level store was in an old apartment building. It was about as far from a big box bookstore as you could get. Chip felt like he was back East, maybe in Brooklyn or Cambridge or his hometown of Baltimore.

They descended five steps and Pat unlocked the door and flipped on the lights. The main room had floor-to-ceiling books along the walls. Tables and low shelves crowded the cramped space so that there was barely room to walk. It was a little dated, but charming and inviting, a book-lover's haven.

Pat moved toward the back of the store to set up a table for signing. Chip heard her gasp, and he and Gary walked toward her. She was on her knees next to a man lying on the floor.

"Gary, quick. Call 911." She reached out to feel the man's neck and quickly withdrew her hand. "Oh my God, oh my God, he's cold, I think he's dead."

***

Not long after the first MPD officers arrived and called for assistance, Dr. Samuel Cooper, the Hennepin County Medical Examiner, and Homicide Detective Mario Franco, who eerily reminded Chip of his fictional detective, Mike Frisco, were on the scene.

"The cause of death is clearly a single gunshot wound to the chest," the ME said to the detective. "The TOD is probably at least twelve hours ago. Weapon was a small-caliber handgun of some kind. I'll have more definitive info for you after the autopsy. When the crime photos are done, send him over to the lab. We have a full house today, two shootings on the Northside last night."

"Thanks Doc. There's no sign of a struggle in the store. The back door was broken into. He wasn't murdered here. The way he's positioned with the book on his chest indicates the body was staged," said the detective. "The perp wanted to send a message. We just have to find out what and why. The choice of that book is a good place to start."

He turned to Chip. "The officers told me this guy was an author and you're an author, too, Collingsworth. You read his books?"

"Yes, I've read them all. He was a damn good writer."

"What about the book on his chest? It's one of his, right?"

"Yes. The book was Finnegan's latest thriller, *Shanghaied*, a story about Asian gangs in St. Paul. It contains a lot of factual information about gang culture and criminal activities, and exposé of sorts."

"I'd like to talk with you later, find out what was in his books. Don't have time to read when I've got a murder investigation on my hands. For starters I'll need to know what the victim wrote about as a possible connection to his murder. Of course, that's only one angle we'll have to pursue."

***

At Franco's request, Chip checked into the Hyatt on Nicollet Mall, just a short distance from ONCE UPON A CRIME. He would spend the night, make a statement at the First Precinct police station the next morning and then return to his home and Jane. This was the first night away from her since their wedding in Las Vegas last year, and he would rather have been going home.

He was shaken and spooked as he walked down the deserted hallway to his hotel room. He needed a drink to calm his nerves and wrap his head around the death of his friend. *Hopefully this place has a well-stocked mini-bar.*

The bar had his brew of choice, Sam Adams. With a bottle in one hand, he placed a call to Jane with the other. When he got her voice mail, all he could think to say was, "Where are you, honey? I'm missing you something fierce. Call me."

Then strangely, if he couldn't be with Jane, he wanted to be with his characters. They had become so real to him that he felt a need to communicate with them. He had brought along his new toy, a state-of-the-art tablet. He set up the stand and keyboard and started the first chapter of his next book, flushing out an idea sparked by the experiences of his most unusual day and welcoming the return of FBI agent, Jo Schwann, and Dr. John Goodman, neurosurgeon. He was pretty sure the two of them could look at a brutal murder scene without getting queasy.

Chapter Two

Untitled
By: Charles Edgar Collingsworth III

St. Paul, MN
Late October

IT WAS WHAT RICK WILSON didn't hear that mattered in the end.

If only he'd been able to hear the lock being picked, the stealthy footsteps of the killer as he entered the apartment, he might have been able to do something. He might have called the cops, or hidden away, or even found the courage to go after the bad guy with the Louisville Slugger he kept under his bed, if he was feeling bad-ass enough.

But he'd worn the neon-green earplugs to bed, so he wouldn't wake up later to hear his roommate Kyle fucking Anna, the girl he'd been in love with since freshman year. He knew they'd stumble in after another night of partying at the frat house and he couldn't bear to hear their sexual escapades one more time.

The earplugs silenced everything except the pounding inside his head. That is, until the bullet furrowed its way through his skull. Then all sound ceased.

He didn't hear Anna's cry of ecstasy crescendo into a scream of terror, nor the abrupt halt of her breath with the spit of a silenced gun. He didn't hear the whimpered pleas of Kyle, begging for his life before it, too, was gone.

He didn't hear the sounds of the apartment being torn apart, of his laptop being smashed, all his meticulous notes ripped from the notebook, crumpled up and set on fire. He didn't hear the killer leave.

He didn't hear the shouts of Grant, the hipster who lived two doors down, when he snuffed out the fledgling flames with a blanket.

He didn't hear the EMTs shove everyone aside to work frantically on his body that was desperately trying to mend itself.

He didn't hear the siren of the ambulance or the beeping of the instruments as he was whisked away to the hospital.

As it was, he was blissfully unaware of it all. He didn't hear a thing.

Chapter Three

Hyatt Hotel, Minneapolis
September

IN HIS ROOM CHIP WORKED on his opening chapter for over three hours. He was in one of his rare writing zones where ideas came quickly, and he shut out the rest of the world. His fingers tapped out word after word, sentence after sentence as his new story came to life on the screen. He had a vision of Sven in his campus apartment, an intruder coming in and shooting him in the head. He couldn't think of anything worse for a parent. Should he start his book this way? Jane would be horrified, and it might frighten Sven and his friends. But, it certainly would get a reader's attention.

He called Jane again, hoping to catch her at the vet clinic. She answered with "Dr. Jane speaking."

"Hi Jane, you're not going to believe this."

"Let me guess, ONCE UPON A CRIME sold 100 copies of your book today."

"No, the total sold was zero, but the dead body count was one. We found Patrick Finnegan dead on the floor of the store. The signing was called off and the police want me to stay in Minneapolis."

"Oh my God. Dead? Was it a heart sudden attack?"

"No, he was murdered, shot someplace else and deposited in the store. Frisco and Dr. Goodman showed up. It was surreal."

"Chip, you're talking gibberish. Frisco and Goodman are characters from your books. Have you been drinking?"

"Jeez, Jane, I haven't had anything to eat or drink today except for a couple cups of coffee and one beer. I'm a little freaked out, I guess."

"Why would someone kill Finnegan? You don't think there's a maniac running loose who kills writers, do you?"

Chip broke out in a cold sweat, and he felt dizzy. "That hadn't even crossed my mind. You've been reading too many crime novels lately. Now I'll be seeing murderers behind every bush and standing in every dark doorway."

"Chip, I didn't mean that. Relax."

"I have a room at the Hyatt. It's not too far from the Minneapolis College of Art and Design. Sven and his friends were outside the store. I'm sure he's heard about the dead body and will be eager for the details. I'll call him, and invite him out to dinner and Kojak and Cagney and Lacey, too." Silly or not, he realized he wanted to assure himself that Sven was okay.

"Who? Chip, you're not making sense. Get something to eat and clear your head. You've obviously had a traumatic day. Call me after your dinner with Sven. I'm worried about you, honey."

Chip wiped the sweat off his forehead with the sleeve of his shirt. "I'll be fine, Jane, I'm just a little shaken by all of this. I'll call again later. Love you."

He pondered his confusion between the characters in his book and the detective and medical examiner he had met at the crime scene. Franco for Frisco was obvious…the name similarity for two homicide detectives. But, it was more than that; it was the guy's manner of speech, his gruffness. When Franco entered the store and said, "Hey Pat and Gary, hear you found a stiff in the stacks. Hell of a marketing ploy," Chip had immediately looked up, expecting Frisco.

But what about the medical examiner? What was it that made me confuse him with Dr. Goodman? Chip thought about Dr. Cooper, recalling his appearance and how he examined Finnegan's body. Tall, handsome, physically fit, impeccably dressed, highly professional. *Yes, most definitely the dashing Dr. Goodman-type.*

He felt relieved to have sorted out the real people from the fictional ones. His two worlds had intertwined ever since he started writing crime stories. At times it benefited his creativity, but on occasion, it could be disturbing. Today was one of those days.

***

Sven and his friends eagerly accepted his invitation to dinner. They suggested a place called Brit's Pub on Nicollet Mall. From the rooftop veranda they could see the newly renovated Orchestra Hall and Peavey Plaza, even hear the tinkling of the fountain. Under different circumstances Chip would have relished an opportunity to explore the city's attractions.

He told the kids to have whatever they wanted, and they ordered Bangers & Mash, making a series of silly jokes about the name. He opted for fish and chips and a glass of Surly Furious, a locally-brewed ale.

"Shut up," said Sven, when Chip described the scene inside the bookstore. "A dead author inside a mystery bookstore, that's so cool. Well, not for the dead dude, but you know what I mean."

Chip observed Sven. Unlike his sister, who was the spitting image of Jane, Sven had brown hair, not red. He was tall and lanky, not burly like his father, Hal. Chip had been told Sven looked a lot like his grandfather, the vet whose practice Jane took over upon his death. The boy seemed happy, he had friends; he was in his element studying film-making. Jane would be pleased to hear her son was doing well. She had wanted him home for the summer, but he had opted to take a summer class. Chip thought it was a good idea, but it had led to a dispute with his wife. When it came to discipline or decision-making about her children, Jane insisted she have the final say-so.

"Well, Sven, any exciting projects coming up?" Chip asked.

"Yes, I just heard about an opportunity to spend next semester shooting a documentary on the new Wild West," Sven said, as he grabbed the dessert menu. "Places like North Dakota, where they're fracking for oil. And filming gold miners in Alaska and cattle ranchers in Wyoming. Drillers, prospectors, cowboys."

"Very exciting. I think you should go for it." As he said it, he wondered if Jane's apron strings would reach to Alaska.

***

The walk back to the hotel refreshed Chip. It was late to call Jane. She usually went to bed early and rose early, often arriving at a client's farm by 5:00 a.m. Yet, he called her knowing she would wake with no complaint. She answered quickly.

"Sorry to wake you, Janey. I just wanted to assure you that I'm fine."

"I couldn't sleep. I'm painting the kitchen...tomato red."

"Red. Are you sure you want a red kitchen?"

"No, I'm done with one wall and now I'm not sure. With the white cupboards the room is starting to look like a huge can of Campbell's tomato soup."

"Ah, you could be the Andy Warhol of Turners Bend."

Chip shared his dinner conversation with Sven and his friends, and the two ended their call with phone kisses.

11

Chip's thoughts strayed to his new novel. No title was coming to him, but it would. His titles always seemed to pop out at him, usually in the middle of the night.

His thoughts then switched to Finnegan. *What kind of research had he been doing? Did it get him killed?*

Chapter Four

Untitled

Minneapolis, MN
Late October

Dr. JOHN GOODMAN IGNORED the slight pull at the scarring on his right thigh as he climbed the steps to the back door of the south Minneapolis house he now shared with Special Agent Jo Schwann. The gunshot wound to his leg was in its final stages of healing. Morning laps in the university pool had restored it to almost complete mobility, and the limp was barely noticeable to anyone but John.

Caddy, the retriever that had become his – now theirs – when he and Jo had met on a case, greeted him as he entered the kitchen. She licked his cheek eagerly as he set down his packages to scratch her behind the ears. Cleo, their black cat, was more aloof, but purred appreciatively when he rubbed his hand along her back. She sniffed delicately at the paint can on the floor at his side. "Hello, sweet girls. Where's your mom? Still painting?"

John picked up the paint can and the bag of paint roller refills, and took the steps, two at a time, up to the second floor. As he walked down the hallway, the slightly sour, chemical scent of fresh paint assaulted his nose and he could hear loud music coming from the spare bedroom where Jo was working.

He stopped at the doorway, taking a moment to admire the view of Jo balanced on a rung of the step ladder. Fully focused on painting the walls and singing along with the music, she was unaware of John's scrutiny.

Her red hair was pulled back into a ponytail, and splatters of green paint clung to the ends of a few errant curls. In spite of the chill in the air outside, inside the house it was warm and her toned legs stretched out from cut-off denim shorts. A maroon and gold University of Minnesota t-shirt clung to her in all the right places.

From her I-Phone connected to speakers, Grand Funk Railroad urged everyone to do "The LocoMotion." Jo, a classic rock fan, obliged by swinging her hips atop the ladder as she sang along to the music with gusto, occasionally reaching out to a distant spot with her paintbrush. Her face radiated joy. He loved seeing her so relaxed; in his opinion, her job with the FBI made her too serious most of the time.

The realization of how much he loved her at that moment caused John's chest to tighten and a thought came to him in an instant. *It's time.*

He dragged his eyes away from her and turned his attention to the progress she had made since he had left for the hardware store. His grin grew wider as he scanned each wall in turn.

Forcing a straight face, he called out, "Is it just me or has this room gotten smaller in the last couple of hours?"

Jo started at his voice and John reached out to steady the ladder as she shifted her weight. A rose flush spread across Jo's cheeks, as if she was embarrassed because he had witnessed her performance. She said, "Sorry...what did you say?"

John turned down the volume of the music and repeated, "The room. It's smaller."

A confused look appeared in her green eyes. "Smaller?"

Unable to contain his amusement any longer, he grinned. "You've changed the color of the room so many times. I think all the layers of paint are shrinking the room."

Jo's eyes scanned the room, looking from one colored wall to the next, each a different shade of green. She burst out laughing. "I guess I have been a little indecisive. Jeez, I can take down a bad guy without a second thought, but I can't make up my mind on a paint color for your home office."

She wiped her hands on one of his old t-shirts she used as a paint rag and eased down the ladder. "I just want it to be perfect for you. I want..." She paused, and then finished, "I want this to be *our* home."

He set the paint can and bag on the tarp spread over the hardwood floors, and reached out, pulling her to him. Studying her face for a moment, he thumbed the fresh smear of paint on her cheek. "This is my favorite shade of green." John gently turned her around to face the wall by the door. Pointing, he said, "That is where I'll put my dad's old desk tomorrow. Sitting in his creaky chair, I will look around and think of this moment, and this dab of color on your cheek. It will always remind me of how lucky I am to share a life with you."

Her eyes grew bright and she blinked a few times. "I feel the same way. I…"

John interrupted her by holding her slightly away from him and looked around the room again. "Ok. Enough goofing off for me. What can I do to help?"

"Well, you can start by taping off the wood trim on that wall over there."

John looked at the wall she had just completed and noticed the trim was not protected with painters' tape. Not a drop of wall paint had strayed to the white woodwork. "But you don't tape off the woodwork…." His eyes narrowed and, with mock indignation, he said, "Hey, wait a minute. Are you just giving me busy work so I'll stay out of your way?"

Jo's grin was sheepish. "Guilty as charged. You know I painted houses to put myself through college, so I can practically do this in my sleep." She nudged him, and continued, "But I love it when we work together."

"Well, there is that." They worked for another hour, until John went downstairs to make a late dinner of spaghetti and salad.

As they sat at the kitchen table, John refilled Jo's wine glass and cleared his throat. He needed to say what was on his mind before he lost his nerve. "You still have one more important decision to make, you know."

She peered at him from across the table. "Oh, yeah. And what's that?"

"Will you marry me?"

Jo went utterly still. For one awful moment, John felt queasy. *Shit. Too soon. I scared her off….*

15

His mind was searching for something to say, anything to fill the empty silence in the room, when she stood up from her chair and came to sit on his lap. She kissed him until she robbed him of breath. At last, Jo pulled away and said in a slightly shaky voice, "Yes! Oh, yes." Tears filled her eyes and she swiped at them with the edge of her t-shirt. She chuckled through the tears. "God, for a moment there, I thought you wanted me to make a hard decision, like what color to paint the wood trim."

They both laughed until they almost fell out of the chair, and then John was kissing her hard. He picked her up and carried her to their bedroom.

***

Jo woke up in the darkened bedroom a few hours later, with a sense of panic. The dream that had awakened her was rapidly dissolving into a gossamer mist, but she recalled walking down a long church aisle, one that never seemed to end. She had called out to John, but he couldn't – or wouldn't – answer her. There were no guests, no one but her.

The residual feeling of uneasiness from her dream made her wonder if she had made a mistake accepting John's marriage proposal so quickly. Looking back over the evening, she couldn't quite believe her own reaction, the fact that she hadn't the slightest doubt in her mind when she said yes. She had never been more certain of anything in her life. Even the job offer from the FBI had cost her a few nights of sleep before she accepted.

But what if I screw up the marriage? Her father had not remarried after her mother had died when Jo was a toddler, and so she didn't have a significant role model of how to be married. Before John, her previous relationships had burned out quickly. Her life with John was perfect now, just the way it was. Did they really want to mess that up?

She rolled over on her side, craving the comfort of curling up to John's muscular back. Her hand encountered nothing but cool sheets and a slip of paper. Jo flipped back over and turned on the bedside lamp, reading the note he had left her.

So sorry to leave you tonight, of all nights. My pager went off for a severe head trauma case and I didn't want to wake you. I hope to be home in time to serve you breakfast in bed, but I'll call if I'm running late.
Love, J.
P.S. Thanks for saying yes.

Jo sighed, missing him already. They had so much to discuss. However, to be honest, she was relieved to have some time to herself to sort out her feelings.

She looked at the clock and saw it was 1:16 a.m.

Hearing Caddy scratch on the closed bedroom door, she slipped her shorts and t-shirt back on and padded over to the door to let her in. Caddy trotted in and, without waiting for an invitation, climbed up into their bed. Cleo followed suit and curled up next to the warmth of the retriever.

Jo laughed. "All right, you two. Just for tonight. Guess I'm too wound up to sleep anyway, so I might as well finish painting John's office. A good way to work out my nerves, right?"

***

John arrived at the hospital and quickly slipped into a set of scrubs. When he hung up his sweatshirt, he caught a whiff of Jo's perfume that clung to the fabric from the last time she had borrowed it. He sighed and closed the locker door.

As he prepped for surgery, the emergency physician peppered him with the case details. "We're in Trauma 2. Patient's name is Rick Wilson. Male, age twenty-one. Shot a little over an hour ago. Entry wound is to the left occipital lobe, with the exit wound just above the left eye. The bullet's path appears to be limited to the left hemisphere."

"We may have caught a break there, if the bullet avoided the large blood vessels down the middle and didn't ricochet around the skull. What are the vitals?"

"As stable as can be expected. Blood pressure is at 150, heart rate is 100, temp is at 100.7, respiratory is at 25." The emergency physician's face was grave as he gave the final statistic. "The ICP is 21."

"The intracranial pressure is at 21?" He shook his head. "Well, first order of business is to get that down." John snapped on a pair of gloves and pushed his way through the operating room doors with his forearms.

John's day had begun.

Chapter Five

Hyatt Hotel, Minneapolis
September

Cʜɪᴘ ᴀᴡᴏᴋᴇ ᴀᴛ ᴛʜᴇ ʜʏᴀᴛᴛ in a tangle of sweaty sheets with disturbing images from a dream in which he was being pursued by a killer who did not like his books. He felt exhausted rather than rested, unsettled and anxious. The events of the previous day had taken their toll, and he was unsure of what this day would bring. He called Jane again.

"Morning, sweetheart. How did you sleep?" he asked.

"Crappy, I missed you. How was your night?"

"Ditto for me."

"I got a text message from Sven. Seems you scored with your dinner last night. He said it was 'ridiculous.' Oh, and Ingrid asked when you were coming home. She wants you to help her with her English essay."

"Wow, that's huge, right?"

"Yes, I think she is finally coming around. It's been harder for her than for Sven. So, when are you coming home?"

Chip crawled out of bed and headed toward the bathroom, cell phone in hand. He was longing to clear his head and revive his energy with a steaming hot shower.

"I have to meet with the homicide detective and then I plan to head out of town. I'll be home for supper. Oh, and Jane, last night I wrote a chapter you'll like. Jo was painting a room and John came home and proposed to her."

Jane laughed. "It's about time. For some reason I want Jo and John to be as happy as we are. Was Jo painting the walls tomato red?"

"No, she settled on green."

"Well, the red in our kitchen is growing on me. We'll see what you think when you come home. I'll throw a roast in the slow cooker before I head to the clinic, so we can have a nice dinner tonight. Love you."

"Thanks, sweetie. Love you, too."

Chip still got that newlywed rush when he heard those words, marveling at the thought of someone waiting at home for him and with dinner planned, to boot.

***

After his hot shower, shave and a cup of weak coffee brewed in his room, Chip was ready to face the day. He checked out of the hotel and headed to the hotel's parking ramp.

The parking ramp was dim and damp. Chip got turned around and it took some searching to locate his car. He spotted a huge black Escalade with dark-tinted windows idling not far from his car. He noticed a car rental sticker on the bumper. For some inexplicable reason it gave him an eerie feeling; he increased his pace to the Ford and used his remote key to unlock the door as he neared. It beeped and the running lights came on. He quickly opened the door, and as he slid into the front seat, he heard a roar from the Escalade as it started to move toward him, the engine's sound echoing throughout the ramp. Chip instinctively ducked down and a split second later the driver's side window exploded, sending shattered pieces of glass cascading down on him like a meteor shower.

He froze, unable to move out of fear. He strained to hear the vehicle's engine fade as it exited the ramp. From his cramped position he slipped his cell phone out of his pocket. His finger fumbled and he misdialed, tried again and finally reached a 911 operator.

***

By some divine intervention, he was taken to the Emergency Room of Hennepin County Medical Center rather than to his eternal resting place.

Hours later he sat in Franco's office. He watched the detective open the bottom drawer of his desk and extract a bottle of bourbon and a not-too-clean looking lowball glass. The detective poured a generous amount of the amber liquid before handing it to him.

"Here drink this. Think of it as medicine. It'll do you good."

He gingerly took a sip and felt the heat slide down his throat, closed his eyes and took another. "Holy crap, that's the second time I've been shot at in the past year. At least this time, I only got a couple of nicks." The ER doctor had extracted a few shards of glass, doused the cuts with antiseptic and applied butterfly bandages. Then she had sent him off with prescriptions for an antibiotic and a pain killer, telling him he might experience some discomfort in the next few days.

"If you wouldn't have ducked, your brains would have been splattered all over the inside of your car. What made you sense danger?"

The thought made his stomach lurch, and he felt faint. Franco's face wavered in front of him, and he was forced to put his head between his knees. *Jeez, I can't believe what a wimp I am.*

"Honest to God, I don't really know." His voice was muffled by his pants. "There was just something ominous about that SUV idling in the empty parking ramp. It made my skin crawl."

"Can you describe the driver or the vehicle?"

Chip raised his head slowly. "It was an Escalade, big and black with tinted windows. I couldn't see the driver at all. I do recall a rental sticker on the bumper, green and white. National, I think."

"We'll run a trace on it. Shouldn't be too hard to track down. The bigger question is why would someone be shooting at you?"

Chip finished the bourbon and was indeed feeling better. He tried to conjure up potential enemies, but came up empty. "I haven't got a clue."

"Could be a random drive-by shooting. They're a pretty common gang initiation around here lately, although not usually in upscale hotel ramps," said Franco as he opened the bourbon again and took a swig, replaced the cap and returned the bottle and glass to his bottom drawer.

Franco opened a file on his desk and scanned it. "You know a writer named Margaret Murphy?"

"I never met her or read her stuff. Isn't she that true crime writer who committed suicide about two weeks ago, self-infected gun shot?"

"Yup, she's the one. The newspapers said it was a suicide; forensics wasn't sure. Homicide is still considering it an open case."

"Are you suggesting it wasn't a suicide, that she was murdered?"

"What I'm saying is I've got two dead crime writers and another one who's damn lucky he's not dead. Maybe it's just a coincidence, but I'm not a big believer in coincidences."

He continued. "Finnegan wrote three books and was apparently researching a fourth. I figure he pissed off someone in one of his books, maybe uncovered someone's shady past. As I said before, that book on his chest was selected for a reason."

"Well, the book on his chest was *Shanghaied;* he wrote about Asian gangs in that one. In addition to Asian gangs, he wrote about crooked politicians, police brutality, corporate embezzlers, just to name a few. Many of Finnegan's characters were thinly disguised local newsmakers. There was a crooked businessman like Tom Petters, that guy now serving a fifty-year sentence for a Ponzi scheme. The hockey-playing governor in one of his books is a dead give-away. And, he had a story about a murdered young woman, kidnapped from a mall parking lot, wasn't there a local case like that?"

Franco answered. "Yes, sounds like the Dru Sjodin case, but we put that perp away. Real creepy little guy."

"I don't know who the crooked police officer in his last book might be, but I bet you have an idea." Chip waited for a response but did not receive one.

The detective hesitated as if he was weighing his words. "Could be Finnegan and that Murphy gal might have pissed off the same people. Any connection between you, Finnegan and Murphy?"

"No, only in that Finnegan and I read each other's work. To my knowledge we weren't writing about the same topics, and I have no idea what Margaret Murphy may have been digging up."

Franco took off his rumpled suit jacket and loosened his tie. "Then again, I could be wrong. Maybe he was cheating on his wife and she popped him or he owed a bookie a wad of cash, or was mixed up with drugs, but I doubt it. My gut tells me he was offed because of something he wrote, and I've got a pretty good record by following my gut."

Chip felt another wave of nausea and he broke out in a sweat. "Okay, now you're scaring the crap out of me, Detective."

"In this case, scared is probably good. I advise you to be vigilant until we know what's going down here. You packing, Collingsworth?"

Chip gulped. "You mean a gun?"

Franco didn't answer, just rolled his eyes and shook his head.

"No, I don't own a gun, never shot one in my life, unless you count squirt guns and arcade ray guns." His attempt at humor fell flat.

"You may want to consider it. For your safety, I suggest you go home to Iowa and lay low. Unfortunately, forensics won't be done with your vehicle until later today. They have to retrieve that bullet. Once it's released, you can take it to a body shop for repair."

Franco picked up a pencil. "You got a decent police chief in Turners Bend?"

"Yes, Chief Fredrickson is a pretty good law enforcement guy, why?"

Franco wrote down the name. "I'll be transferring your protection to him soon and sending you on your way tomorrow. I appreciate your willingness to cooperate in the Finnegan case, but we're going to have to get you out of Dodge as soon as possible. I don't want another dead author on my hands."

***

Unable to drive home until the police were finished with his vehicle and the window was repaired, Chip re-registered at the Hyatt. He called Jane and told her about his day.

"It was just a big city, drive-by crime. I was merely in the wrong place at the wrong time. Just a few scratches and a broken window."

"First poor Patrick and now this. I was teasing earlier when I asked if someone was gunning for authors, but now..."

Chip interrupted her. "Really Jane, this had nothing to do with Finnegan's murder. I'm fine and I'll be home as soon as my car is ready to drive."

He didn't want her to worry, but she didn't sound convinced and neither was he. The whole thing was starting to freak him out, and Franco's words about coincidences kept replaying in his head. He read recently that coincidences lead to messages. *Is someone sending me a message?*

He took two pain relievers and a dose of antibiotics, and to divert his attention from the events of the day he called his brother. The call wasn't to share the shooting or his fears; he didn't have that kind of relationship with Parker. He wanted to consult with him about his character's brain injury. Parker, like their father and grandfather before him, was a neurosurgeon in Baltimore. It was late but he placed the call anyway.

Parker answered in a wide-awake voice. "Hey, bro, I was up and just about to send you a copy of the article about me in this month's *Lancet Neurology*. They named me the world's leader in deep brain stimulation for Parkinson's. Just carrying on the family tradition in neurosurgery."

Parker never missed an opportunity to remind Chip he was the black sheep of the family, the only male who was not a neurosurgeon. The remark pushed Chip's button, but he swallowed it and played the bigger man by congratulating his brother and moving on to his questions about head injuries.

After he hung up, Chip made a conscious decision to cast Dr. John Goodman as a compassionate surgeon and a man with a tender side, not a prick like his brother.

Chapter Six

Untitled

St. Paul, MN
Late October

DR. JOHN GOODMAN TILTED his head one way, and then the other, attempting to stretch out the stiff muscles in his neck. The surgery to save Rick Wilson and repair the damage to his brain from the bullet had taken long hours of close, careful work and John felt the tension up and down his back. He was pleased with the results of the surgery, but it had been a long night and he longed to climb back in bed with Jo.

However, that would have to wait until after he spoke to his patient's family members. He strode through the swinging doors and his tired eyes swept the room.

A woman with short, spiky gray hair stood as he entered. John took in her reddened eyes and walked toward her. Just as he reached her, he was startled to see Detective Mike Frisco stand up next to the woman.

John said, "Detective…this is a surprise. I assume you are working Rick Wilson's case?"

Frisco indicated the woman by his side. "Yes, I had some questions for his mother. Dr. Goodman, this is Caroline Wilson."

Before John had a chance to say anything, Caroline blurted out, "Doctor, is my son going to make it? How bad is it?"

John reached out and gripped her hand in both of his. "Ms. Wilson. Your son did very well during the surgery and we are cautiously optimistic at this point. We were able to relieve some of the pressure inside his head. He is in intensive care now, but you will be able to see him in a few moments. I want to assure you we are doing everything possible for your son."

She pulled her hand away from his and took a deep breath, leveling her brown eyes at him. "Don't take this as a sign of disrespect, but let me be blunt. I lost my husband to cancer last

25

year. I found knowing the details of his case gave me a sense of control; when God knows, I obviously had none. The minutiae gave me something to focus on, rather than just sit and watch my husband of thirty years waste away in front of my eyes. Something to hate, rather than to hate him for leaving me behind. So, while I appreciate your sensitivity, please just tell me exactly what's happening to my son."

John was taken aback, but found himself respecting the woman's strength. He looked at Frisco. The detective shrugged slightly. "She's handled all my tough questions. Tell her; she can take it."

Taking a deep breath, John said, "Very well. Your son sustained a bullet wound to the occipital lobe, at the back of the head. From there, the bullet traveled the left side of the brain, exiting out the frontal lobe." John pulled out a sheet of paper and pen from his pocket. Quickly, he sketched a rudimentary diagram to show her the path of the bullet.

"I know it doesn't sound good, but the path the bullet took actually gave us a fighting chance. Because the bullet exited the head and didn't cross over to the other side of the brain, the damage was minimized."

John saw the woman's shoulders relax a fraction, and then he continued. "That's not to say your son is out of the woods yet. As the bullet passed through the brain, it sheared off small blood vessels. The bleeding caused increased pressure within the skull. If left unchecked, it will damage the brainstem and quickly lead to death. Therefore, our number one priority was relieving the pressure on the brain."

John watched Caroline Wilson carefully, ensuring she understood his explanation. Even though her eyes had widened at the extent of the damage, she nodded her understanding. Satisfied, John continued, "First, we removed a section of Rick's skull to relieve the swelling and to save the brainstem. Next, we put him into a medically induced coma, so that his body has time to repair itself."

Caroline paled a bit. "So, he's in a coma...that's bad, isn't it?"

"No, not at all. As I've said, we induced the coma to give his body a chance to recover from the trauma. It's a necessary part of his recovery. We'll continue to monitor the pressure on the brain and control it through steroids. We'll also use a concentrated sugar solution called mannitol to draw out the excess fluids."

"What...what do you think his chances are?" Caroline Wilson's voice was thick with emotion.

"Your son is a fighter and he did very well throughout the surgery. If he makes it through the day, he has a chance, perhaps a good one. Only time will tell, of course. Rick has a long journey in front of him, but he's young and strong. We'll know more tonight." John laid his hand on her shoulder. "I know this is hard, but try to get some rest. You look like you could use a break."

Tears flowed freely down the woman's cheeks. "Thank you for your honesty and for all you've done to help Rick."

Frisco spoke up. "Rick's in good hands, Ms. Wilson. Doc Goodman's the best at what he does."

John felt his face flush at the compliment. "We've got a great team here, all doing their best for your son. We'll keep you informed of any new developments. Call me personally if you have any questions." He recited his cell phone number and she scribbled it down on an envelope she had fished out of her purse.

As a nurse directed Caroline Wilson to her son's room, John turned to Frisco. The detective frowned slightly as he watched her leave the room. John said, "Quite a strong woman isn't she?"

"Yeah. You should have seen her answering my questions. Wish all the families I dealt with were as helpful."

Frisco reached his hand out, and John gripped it tightly. "Good to see you, Mike. It's been awhile."

"Not since I saw you and Jo in the hospital up in Grand Marais, I think. Great to see you looking a little healthier."

"That's an understatement." John chuckled at the memory. *He* had been the patient then, suffering from a concussion and a bullet wound to the leg, the result of a madman who had been obsessed with Jo.

John's thoughts turned back to his patient. "Any progress on finding out who shot Rick Wilson and why?"

The detective shook his head. "Not yet. Wilson's roommate and his girlfriend were home as well, but they didn't make it. They were both DOA by the time help arrived. The killer tried to cover his tracks by starting a fire. At that point, the neighbors called 911. Looks like the killer trashed the place, looking for something. Sure would love to know what that something was."

"A burglary gone wrong?"

Frisco shrugged his shoulders. "The thought crossed my mind, but we have some evidence that suggests Wilson was the intended target. Could have something to do with a fracking documentary his mother said he was working on."

John raised his eyebrow. "You really think that could be at the root of all of this?"

The detective shrugged. "Trust me; people have been killed for a lot less."

Frisco looked down at his watch. "Say, doc. I'd better get going while the trail is still relatively warm. Give my best to Jo, will you?"

John smiled. He was bursting to share his news with the detective – and everyone else, for that matter – but he knew Jo would want to tell Frisco of their engagement herself. So, instead of what he wanted to say, he replied, "I certainly will. And let's get together when all this settles down. It's been too long."

"It's a plan."

***

Jo was awakened the next morning by a light kiss on her lips. She grinned and opened her eyes to see John leaning over her as she lay in bed. He looked tired, but his smile was warm.

Propping herself up on one elbow, she felt the room tilt slightly. Glancing at the clock on her nightstand, Jo saw it was nearly 9:00 a.m. She lay back on the bed, surprised at how tired she felt. Painting John's office had kept her up until two in the morning, but this felt like a different kind of tired. *Damn! Feels like I'm coming down with the flu again....second time this fall.*

Not wanting John to fuss over her, she managed a small smile. "Wow. I was really out. Glad to have you home."

He bent down and gave her another kiss, this one lingering a bit longer than the one that woke her. He sat down on the bed next to her. "The surgery went better than I expected."

"What type of head trauma was it?"

"A gun shot. Some college kid, asleep in his apartment."

Jo's inquisitive nature kicked in, and she ignored a sour taste in her mouth. "Wow. Wrong place, wrong time?"

"Not really sure."

"Amazing he survived. Did they catch the shooter?"

John shook his head. "No suspects yet, from what I gather. By the way, guess who was assigned to the case? Frisco. I ran into him after the surgery. He was just wrapping up an interview with the kid's mother."

"Well, I'm sure Frisco will figure it out." Jo rubbed her chin and stared off into space. Her discomfort temporarily forgotten, her investigative brain whirled around a case that wasn't hers. "Wonder what the motive was?"

John grinned, "Now you sound like the FBI agent I first fell in love with. Frisco thought it might be related to some documentary the kid was making on fracking, although I don't know why someone would have killed him over that."

"I keep forgetting you haven't lived in the Midwest for long. Fracking has become a real hot-button topic, especially in North Dakota where the oil fields are located."

John stretched his long arms upward and then smothered a yawn. "What exactly is fracking, anyway? I know it's a process of removing oil from the ground, and it's been all over the news lately, but can't say I've paid much attention."

"From what I understand, it involves creating fractures in rocks formations by forcing fluid into smaller cracks to make them bigger, making it easier to extract the oil."

John frowned. "Seems like that would make people happy, bringing more jobs into the region and making the U.S. less dependent on foreign oil."

Jo shifted slightly to make more room for him on the bed. "There *is* a lot of support for it, especially because these fields could be the largest source of oil discovered in the U.S. But there are a lot of 'fractivists', who worry about the environmental impact of the process itself. Several countries have already banned it, as a matter of fact."

John studied her for a moment. "You're intrigued. Are you disappointed this isn't your case?"

Jo felt a sheepish grin creep across her lips. "Well, no, not exactly. It's just that I've been following this in the news lately, so it's an interesting topic. I wonder what your patient found...." John was right; Jo *was* more than just a little curious about Frisco's case. Her nimble mind sorted through scenarios, based on what she had read in the newspapers.

Jo was stirred out of her musings when she felt John's weight shift off the bed. He removed his sweatshirt, and draped it across the chair in the corner. "Well, my job is to make sure the kid recovers. With any luck, he'll be able to answer those questions himself."

John moved back to the side of the bed. "Scoot over. I'm climbing in with you." He let out a loud yawn. "God, I'm exhausted."

She obliged as he slipped off his shoes. He crawled in next to her and turned her around, so her back was against his chest. She felt the weight of his arm settle around her waist as he pulled her closer. Grateful her bout of queasiness had abated, she sighed in contentment.

Tugging at his shirt, she said, "Aren't you going to undress? You're still wearing your street clothes."

"Nah, I was kind of hoping you'd help me with that later." He nuzzled her neck and she felt her pulse race. She knew he needed sleep, but she was definitely looking forward to "later".

After a moment or two, Jo said, "This is my idea of a perfect Sunday morning."

She felt his warm breath on the back of her neck as he stifled another yawn. He replied, "Mine, too, although I wish I had some energy. I'd really love to...."

Waiting for him to finish his sentence, Jo felt him relax against her and soon she could feel the deep rise and fall of his chest against her back. She sighed and closed her eyes.

***

Jo awoke a second time that morning, this time to her cell's ringtone. Worried it would wake up John, she snapped fully awake, carefully slid out of his embrace and snatched the phone off the nightstand.

Jo felt a flash of irritation when she saw her boss's number on the screen of her smartphone. She answered the call with a whispered, "Hang on a minute, will you?" Before he had a chance to respond, she moved into the hallway, carefully closing the door behind her.

Resuming the phone call, she said, "Good morning, Tom. You do know it is Sunday, right? Traditionally a day off from work."

Jo heard the deep chuckle of Tom Gunderson in her ear. "Well, it's a good thing I don't stand by tradition, since this isn't a social call."

"I was afraid you were going to say that. What's up?"

"The St. Paul PD called me bright and early this morning. They need our help with the investigation of a shooting of a twenty-one year-old college student, near the St. Paul campus of the University. Also found dead at the scene were his male roommate and a young woman."

"Why bring us in on a local murder case?"

"It looks like the investigation will spread outside their jurisdiction. The kid was shot in the head, but survived. We can't talk to him yet, but his mother said something about him working on a documentary of some sort..."

Her heart pounded as she recalled her earlier conversations with John about his patient. "Wait. Are you talking about Detective Mike Frisco's case? John was the surgeon and ran into Frisco. So, they are serious about investigating the fracking angle?"

31

Jo heard Tom's gasp of surprise. "You already heard about that, huh?"

"Frisco mentioned it to John. This could take us into other parts of Minnesota and North Dakota, correct?"

"You got it. Right now, the documentary is just one of the angles they are looking at, but it's the strongest so far. They want the Bureau involved now, before it spills into a broader geographical area. Of course, I thought of you, since you and Frisco have worked so well together in the past. He's at the crime scene now."

Jotting down the address Tom rattled off, Jo remembered John's earlier teasing that she envied Frisco's involvement in the case. *That'll teach me to watch what I wish for.*

She glanced at the closed door of her bedroom and thought about John sleeping on the other side. Feeling exhausted and wishing she was still dozing next to him, Jo blew out a puff of air. "I'm on my way."

Chapter Seven

Downtown Minneapolis/Turners Bend
September

CHIP RETRIEVED HIS CAR from the body shop where his window had been replaced. He knew he should head straight home, but he had two stops he wanted to make, first back to the bookstore to check on Gary and Pat and to see if they had any news about Finnegan's murder. Then he wanted to visit Maureen, Finnegan's widow, to offer his condolences and help.

He parked in one of ONCE UPON A CRIME's three parking spots in the alley. He elbowed his way through the crowd of people standing on the steps outside the doorway, much to the irritation of those in the line that snaked down the sidewalk.

Gary was behind the check-out counter ringing up sales with a harried look on his face. Chip gave him a wave and mouthed "Pat?" Gary nodded to the back of the store.

Chip found Pat in the back hall storeroom, unpacking a case of books. "Holy mackerel, Pat. What's going on?"

She jumped and emitted a little yelp. "Sorry, Chip, guess I'm a little edgy. It's one thing to have a store full of books about murder and an entirely different thing to find a dead body in your store. Being back in business has me freaked. It didn't take forensics long to finish, and they said we could re-open the store. I don't think they found any prints or clues."

She loaded a stack of books into her arms. "To your question, it seems we are a hot tourist site today. Lots of crime scene gawkers, but at least most of them have the decency to buy a book. We've almost sold all of Finnegan's books we stocked for the signing and lots of your books, too."

She shook her head and blew out a puff of breath. "Just seems wrong to be profiting from Finnegan's murder. We're donating the proceeds from his books to a fund for his family. Gary and I want to see his murder solved."

Pat took a close look at Chip. "What in the heck happened to you?"

"Just a minor mishap. I'm fine."

Chip worked his way to the back of the store and stood near the area where the writer's body had lain. Pat had placed a draped table stacked with Finnegan's books over the spot, but it couldn't erase the scene from Chip's memory. It gave him goose bumps. He bid the owners farewell, promising to return for a signing before the end of the year and walked back to his car, stopping to check for anything or anyone suspicious, reminding himself to be vigilant

He headed to Prospect Park and the address on Sharon Avenue he had found in the phone directory in his hotel room. He crossed the Mississippi and caught a glimpse of the new 35W bridge that had replaced the one that collapsed and killed thirteen people in 2007, then passed the University of Minnesota campus.

As he approached Prospect Park he saw a strange looking water tower with a top that looked like a witch's hat, the landmark he was looking for. He exited the freeway and wound his way through the residential area stopping in front of a classic 1920s bungalow, a story-and-a-half stucco house with a dark green canvas awning over the front window. There was a toddler's riding toy on the front walk. He double checked to make sure it was the Finnegan's address.

He had not met Finnegan's wife, but Patrick had frequently talked about his family. Seeing the bright yellow tricycle, it struck Chip that two little children would be without the father who adored them. He took a deep breath to steel himself for the visit, sighed and got out of the car.

***

Maureen Finnegan was an attractive thirty-something with short black hair and fair skin. She sat on a leather sofa, propped up by her parents on either side. Her eyes were puffy and blood-shot, and she clutched a soggy tissue.

Chip greeted them and Maureen's father introduced himself as David Edwards and his wife as Diane; they all shook hands. "What happened to you?" asked David Edwards. Chip again explained. His face felt hot and swollen, worse than the previous day. I must really look ghastly, he thought.

"The kids are at my sister's, Chip; they're too young to understand what's going on, Sean is three and Abby is ten months," said Maureen. "As soon as Patrick's parents arrive from Boston, we have to go to the morgue and the funeral home." Tears welled up in her eyes and her father put his arm around her; she leaned her head against his shoulder.

"I'm sorry for your loss, Maureen. This is an unimaginable tragedy. Patrick was a wonderful writer and I valued his friendship. I'll miss him greatly."

She broke down in soul-wrenching sobs. Crying women always got to Chip. Maureen's sobs were on a whole new level for him. They were beyond heart-breaking; they were devastating. He was frozen, unable to decide what he could do or say to comfort her.

After her crying subsided, she said, "My husband was looking forward to the signing with you, Chip. He admired your work."

"It was mutual. I was impressed with how much research he did and how he could create so much suspense in his stories." Chip took a business card from his wallet and gave it to her. "Please let me know if I can ever be of help."

"Chip, Patrick seemed very agitated about his new book. He said he was on the trail of something disturbing, but I don't know exactly what it was. He told me he was going to discuss it with you after your signing."

"Did you mention that to the homicide detective?"

Maureen shook her head. "I just realized it could be important."

"It might be. Do you know of anyone who would want to harm Patrick? Anyone who had a grudge against him?"

"No, I can't imagine who would do this to him. He was a good husband, a great father. All he wanted was to be an author, and his books were doing so well."

"When did you last see him?"

"On Saturday morning. He left with his laptop to go to the Loft Literary Center in downtown Minneapolis. During the week I work and he stays at home with the kids. On weekends I take over with the kids, and he rents a little writer's room at the Loft. Saturday he left at about 10:30 a.m., just like always. Sometimes when he was in what he called a zone, he'd write all day and far into the night. I didn't worry until I woke yesterday morning and realized he hadn't come home. I called the Loft, but it wasn't open. I called his brother and a few friends to ask if he was there. When I couldn't locate him, I called the police and Father Mike, our parish priest over at St. Francis of Cabrini."

Chip politely refused an offer of coffee from Maureen's mother and after again expressing his offer of help, departed and left for home with a deep yearning to be with his new family. He also made a mental note to call his own parents to check on their welfare and tell them he loved them.

***

Chip headed back to Turners Bend with mixed feelings. He wanted to stay and try to find out what Finnegan was on to, what he was about to share with him. But, he wanted to go home, too. He was concerned about his own safety but was having a hard time believing he was in any real danger, that he could possibly suffer the same fate as Patrick Finnegan. Still he was feeling vulnerable and kept looking in his rearview mirror checking for the black Escalade from the parking ramp. He didn't see one, but somehow that failed to calm his nerves.

Just after he spotted the **Welcome to Iowa** sign he looked ahead at what appeared to be miles of orange cones. In the time he had been in Minneapolis the cones had been moved from the northbound lanes to the southbound lanes, again with no apparent road work in progress. Single lane traffic stretched ahead for as far as he could see.

"Call Jane," he commanded his car phone.

"Hi, sweetie, where are you?" answered Jane.

"In road construction hell."

"How are you holding up?"

"I visited Maureen Finnegan and it was tough. What are you doing?"

"I'm on my way out to the Schmitt farm to put Radio Frequency ID chips in his herd. Poor Tom, he thinks cattle rustlers have snatched two steer. He's got Chief Frederickson on the case. Never a dull moment in Turners Bend."

"You mean like Old West cattle rustlers? In Iowa? In the 21st century?"

"Yes, it does happen. Unbranded cattle are taken across the border into southern Minnesota and sold at sales barns. It's happening more with the bad economy. The RFID chips will help Tom track his cattle.

It's similar to the chips we have in our pets. Sorry, I've got to run. Love you."

"Play Josh Groban." Chip hoped that hearing the tenor sing Italian love ballads would ease his mind, which it did for a few miles, until his thoughts returned again to Finnegan's murder. *What did he uncover? What, if anything, did Margaret Murphy have to do with it?*

He checked his rear-view mirror. *That poor chap in the red Chevy Suburban has been stuck behind me for miles. Avis rental car sticker on the bumper. Must be someone on vacation or business who is not going to get wherever he's going any faster than I am.*

***

"Oh my God, Chip, you look like someone went at you with a weed whacker," said Jane gently touching the side of his nicked and bandaged face. "You can't go out meeting your reading public looking like that. Plus someone shot at you. What are you going to do?"

"Franco, the homicide detective, said drive-by shootings are often gang initiations. It's made me a little nervous, but I think I'll feel safe now that I'm home. Try not to worry too much. I'll be fine."

"It's a wife's job to worry. What, if for some reason, you were the intended target, not just a random victim? First Patrick and now this. I'm glad you're finally home. You'll be safer here than in Minneapolis."

Jane kissed him lightly on his nose, made him tomato basil soup and sent him to bed...alone. When he awoke, he discovered he had slept through the night and Jane had joined him at some point with her back to him. He reached his arm over and pulled her toward him, spooning her. He kissed her neck, catching a whiff of the citrus-scented shampoo she used.

***

Later the two were in their kitchen, Jane scrambling eggs for their breakfast. "What are you going to do about your tour? I think you should cancel the engagements for a while. Didn't you say the homicide detective told you to lay low and be careful? It's just not safe for you to be out in public, plus you look a fright right now. Lucinda won't fuss; she has other things on her mind."

Chip poured himself a glass of orange juice. "Lucinda. I almost forgot about her. I can't believe she hasn't been hounding me. What does she have on her mind, other than my next book contract?"

"Babies. After a year of trying her biological clock is taking over like a ticking bomb."

Chip guffawed and spit out the coffee he had just sipped. "Lucinda with a baby? Really? I can't picture it."

"That's unkind, Chip. Many women, who you wouldn't expect, have strong maternal desires. I do admit, however, it's kind of difficult to imagine Lucinda changing diapers."

Jane served his eggs and toast and poured coffee in her thermal mug. "Baby pigs are calling me. I better run off to Hoffman's farm. Try to rest today, dear."

He looked around the kitchen with its one red wall. It was the most-used room in Jane's house where he now lived with her and Ingrid. On the counter were the proofs from Ingrid's senior pictures. He had heard Jane and Ingrid discussing the pros and cons of each as they tried to select a head shot for the yearbook.

Shuffling through the poses he mentally attached a label to each...sullen, worried, intense, sad, distant, hurt. Ingrid was going through a tough period and was still dealing with the aftermath of several traumas, the worst being a kidnapping. Her expressions conveyed her pain.

The photographer must have had a hard time getting a genuine smile out of her, he thought. That is until he came to shots of her with Sugar, her prized Appaloosa. Ingrid's face had a peaceful glow in those photos. One of them would get his vote if he were asked.

It came to him in a flash, the long-elusive title for his newest novel...*Head Shot*.

Chapter Eight

Head Shot
St. Paul, MN
Late October

Jo PULLED UP BEHIND Frisco's car, in front of Rick Wilson's apartment building. She verified the apartment number and climbed the steps to the third floor. Pushing aside the yellow crime-scene tape, she turned the knob of the apartment door and her nose was immediately assailed by the combined smells of smoke and blood. Jo's stomach protested and she swallowed a few times to push back the bile that had risen in her throat.

She steadied herself and went in. Her eyes watered at the acrid odor and she coughed. Breathing through her mouth to avoid the smell, she called out, "Frisco. You in here?"

Jo heard him reply, "Yeah, first bedroom on your right." She gingerly stepped around an overturned kitchen chair and wove her way through the crime scene.

Entering the bedroom, Jo recognized Frisco's dark hair as he crouched low over the bed. She looked around the destroyed room. "What a mess."

Frisco straightened up and Jo could see the blood stain that covered the upper part of the bed. He said, "No kidding. Glad to be working with you again, Jo." He looked down at his gloved hands. "I'd shake your hand, but these latex gloves are a bitch to get back on."

Jo felt the roiling once again in her stomach. *I don't have time to have the flu.* She fought to keep her composure and mentally counted to twenty before she trusted herself to respond, "Not a problem. So, bring me up to speed."

Frisco studied her. "You feeling ok? You look a little green around the gills."

Jo waved a hand. "I'm fine. It's just a bit rank in here. So, tell me what you know about the case."

The detective pulled out his note pad and flipped to a page. "About midnight last night, Grant Humphreys, a kid who lives two doors down, smelled smoke. When he came out into the hallway to investigate, he saw the door was wide open and there was a fire blazing on the floor of the living room. Humphreys said it looked like a stack of notebooks and a pile of printer paper. He grabbed a blanket off the couch and started slapping the fire, screaming for help."

"Didn't Humphreys think it was odd no one in the apartment helped him out?"

Frisco chuckled. "I don't think he gave anything much thought except putting out the fire. Turns out, Humphreys has some priors for possession of marijuana. He was scared shitless the whole place would go up in flames, spread down to his apartment and he'd lose his latest crop growing in his bathroom under heat lamps. It was only after the flames were out that Humphreys went to investigate the bedrooms and found our vics."

"Well, thank God he called 911. He could have been more concerned about getting caught with another batch of weed than saving their lives."

"Yeah, good thing for Rick Wilson. Talk about one lucky bastard. I saw Dr. Goodman after the operation. John said the kid might actually pull through." Frisco frowned. "The other two vics ran out of luck, however. The roommate..." Frisco paused to consult his notes again, "Uh, Kyle Marshall, and the young woman, Anna Wroblewski, were found naked in the other bedroom. Evidently they were in the heat of the moment and didn't hear the killer come in. Both vics were shot in the head. The EMTs said both were DOA."

"I'm assuming you've ruled out a double murder-suicide scenario, with our surviving vic being the jealous type."

"He was shot in the back of the head. Ain't no way that was a suicide shot."

"Tom said you were leaning toward the fracking documentary as possible motive. Why not just a simple burglary gone bad? This place is a wreck."

"Ah, but it seems a little extreme to set a fire to cover up a burglary. Also, the medical examiner found very little gunshot residue around the wounds, even though the shots were clearly up-close and personal. So I'm thinking the killer used a silencer…"

Jo finished his thought, "…because most of the gunshot residue would be caught up in the silencer."

Frisco nodded. "Not only that, but no one heard the shots. There were several neighbors home last night and no one heard a damned thing. So, what kind of burglar uses a silencer? Looks to me like the shooter planned the murders and then hunted around to find something and/or to destroy it."

Jo rubbed her jaw for a moment, deep in thought. "If the killer simply wanted to steal whatever he was looking for, why wouldn't he wait until no one was home? Not a lot of security in this building that I could see when I walked in. It wouldn't be hard to figure out a college kid's class schedule and pick an opportune time to sneak in."

"Assuming it was the documentary information he or she was after, then just destroying it wouldn't be enough." Frisco tapped his forehead. "The information would also be up here, in Wilson's head."

She thought about Frisco's theory. It sounded plausible, but she wasn't totally convinced. "Tell me why you think it has to do with Wilson's documentary and not something his roommate was into."

"We're checking into all possibilities, obviously. My new co-worker, Riley Simmons, is following up with the roommate's family and acquaintances and we'll compare notes." Frisco waved his hand around the bedroom. "But, here's the deal. This is Wilson's bedroom. Take a look around. This place is trashed. Big time. It was *his* laptop that was smashed. I found a scrap of the burned notebooks out in the living room. Wilson's name was on the scrap."

He showed Jo the piece of the notebook he had placed in a clear evidence bag. As she examined it, he continued, "If you go into the other bedroom, you'll see not much is disturbed." The detective smirked. "Well, except for the mess you'd find in any college guy's bedroom."

"I guess we weren't lucky enough to find finger prints, witnesses seeing the killer walk in…anything like that?"

"The crime scene techies were in here earlier, combing the place for clues, so maybe they'll have something for us later. They found tons of prints, but I'm not holding my breath. If the killer was smart enough to use a silencer, then he or she was smart enough to wear gloves. The cops have canvassed the neighbors. So far, no one saw the killer enter or leave the building."

"So, where do we go from here?"

"Let's you and I focus on the documentary angle and let Riley work her side of the case. We need to find someone who knew more about that damned documentary. I called up Wilson's mother and tracked down the name of the professor who advised him on the project. Maybe he can help us, or another student. I'm thinking it might be a good idea to get our hands on a copy."

Jo's mind was already cataloging all the avenues to search. "We have a lot of work to do."

Frisco smirked. "Yeah, sounds like job security to me."

***

The sky was a brilliant blue by the time Jo and Frisco stepped outside. Jo was grateful her earlier queasiness had faded and she inhaled deeply, taking a moment to enjoy the fresh, crisp air. The fall colors were past peak, but a few stubborn leaves clung to the branches, flickering in the light breeze. The leaves on the ground crunched beneath their feet as they walked toward their vehicles.

Frisco turned and waved a hand at the apartment building. "You know, even after being a cop for all these years, I still find it hard to believe there were multiple homicides in there when it's so beautiful out here."

Jo nodded and lifted her face toward the sun, knowing in another month or so, she'd be raising her face to snowflakes. "Hard to believe there is any kind of violence in the world on a day like today."

The detective sighed. "Well, guess we'd best get back to it." He patted his jacket pocket. "Got the name and address of Wilson's professor at the university right here. Let's start there."

He indicated his vehicle. "Why don't I drive and you navigate. I'm still finding my way around."

Once they were in the car, he fished out a slip of paper with the information from his pocket and handed it to Jo. She glanced at the address and commented, "Looks like a Crocus Hill address. Pricey real estate."

They arrived at Professor Michael Mazlo's house several minutes later. Frisco pulled in front along the curb and put the car in park. Jo looked toward the mammoth red brick house, with an impeccably manicured front lawn.

Frisco voiced her thoughts when he remarked, "Looks like the professor does okay for himself."

Jo waited for Frisco to join her on the front stoop and then rang the doorbell. An elegantly dressed woman answered almost immediately, as if she had been waiting all day for them to arrive at her door.

Her voice was low and slightly husky. "May I help you?"

Jo held up her badge. "My name is Special Agent Schwann with the FBI and this is Detective Frisco, with the St. Paul PD. We're here to speak to Professor Michael Mazlo."

The woman arched her eyebrow. "My name is Candace Mazlo. May I ask why you'd like to see my husband?"

Frisco said, "We're here to ask about one of his students. Is he around?"

The woman looked them both up and down for a moment. As if deciding something, she finally stepped aside to let them into the spacious foyer. "Of course. Let me get him for you."

They waited while the professor's wife disappeared into a room off to the right. A few moments later, a slight, be-speckled man she presumed to be Michael Mazlo entered the foyer without his wife. He appeared to be in his early fifties and his salt-and-pepper hair touched the collar of the green tartan plaid shirt he was wearing.

He squinted at them through artsy eyeglasses. "May I help you?"

Frisco said, "Are you Michael Mazlo ... *Professor* Mazlo?"

"Yes, well, I'm an adjunct professor, but yes, that's me. What can I do for you?"

Jo raised an eyebrow. A house in this neighborhood meant that either Mazlo had quite a lucrative job outside his meager adjunct professor salary, or he came from money. She tucked away the thought for the moment. After the introductions were made once again, Jo said, "We're here to speak to you about one of your students. Would you mind if we asked you some questions?"

Mazlo's eyes darted between the two of them. "Of course, of course. Please, follow me." He led them across the black-and-white marble tiled floor of the foyer into a wood-paneled library. After they had settled into stiff red leather chairs in front of a massive desk, Mazlo began, "So, I'm curious. What kind of trouble could a student of mine be in to warrant the attention of the FBI?"

Frisco cleared his throat. He sidestepped the question and asked one of his own. "We understand you are currently advising Rick Wilson on a special project."

A frown line formed between the adjunct professor's eyes. "Um, yes."

The detective said, "And what sort of classes do you teach at the U?"

"Business. Look, what does that have to do with..."

Jo asked the next question before he could finish. "Is it common for business students to create documentaries?"

She noticed a red flush creep up the neck of the professor. "Yes...I mean, no. He recently switched his major from business to environmental sciences. Rick was a student in one of my international marketing classes a few semesters ago. We hit it off, so when he asked me to be the advisor on a project, I agreed."

Frisco said, "That special project wouldn't happen to be a documentary on fracking, would it?"

Michael Mazlo's eyes widened slightly. "Now how would you know that? Seriously, I'd like to know what this is all about before I say anything else. Is Rick in some kind of trouble, because...."

Jo interrupted with a wave of her hand. "Professor, I'm afraid we have some bad news. Rick Wilson was shot yesterday."

Mazlo turned pale. "Wha...What do you mean, shot? Is he dead? Oh, no....."

Jo said, "As of now, he's in critical condition. The doctors are doing everything they can for him, but he's not out of the woods yet."

The adjunct professor's color was returning to his face and he swiped a hand across his eyes. "What can I do to help?"

Jo turned to Frisco. He said, "We're hoping you can give us some information about his project."

"Yes, yes, of course. But wait, you don't think the documentary has anything to do with his shooting, do you? Couldn't it have been just a random thing?"

"We haven't ruled anything out yet. I'm not at liberty to go into a lot of detail about the crime scene, but it appeared as if someone intentionally tried to destroy some paperwork and computer files."

Michael Mazlo clapped his hand to his mouth. "Jesus Christ! You mean you think someone tried to kill him for his work on the documentary? Well, then it would have to be the Frackers. Those bastards! Wouldn't surprise me a bit if they were involved."

Frisco glanced at Jo. His look said, "Now we're getting somewhere." He turned to Mazlo. "What makes you say that?"

The professor leapt up from his desk chair and began to pace, his arms flailing about. "They threatened to sue Rick, me, the U...anyone they could think of. Got a couple of injunctions to bring filming to a standstill. Of course, they couldn't stop people from talking. But they just kept coming after us." He tugged on his earlobe. "Shit."

Frisco raised his eyebrow. "Professor, we'll need a list of the individuals and/or companies involved."

"I can do you one better." He walked back to his desk and pulled out a sheaf of papers. "Here, you're welcome to it all. It's a copy of the legal filings. Rick was scared out of his wits when he saw his name at the top of the filing. I can't say as I blame him, but my lawyer has been helping us out with the legalities."

Jo read the name of the company at the top of the document. It read, "Wellborne Industries". After flipping through a few sheets, she came across the management team, with the CEO's name in bold lettering, "Jonathon Wellborne".

Jo flipped through more of the document before setting it back on the desktop. "Seems like a big fuss for a little documentary project."

Mazlo smirked. "Yeah, well, they've had many people questioning their tactics. From what I heard, they've sent these filings out - like scattershot - to anyone who got a little too nosey." The smile abruptly disappeared from his face, as if he suddenly remembered why Jo and Frisco were here to see him.

He lowered his head. "I swear, I never thought they'd physically harm anyone."

Jo patted his shoulder. "We still don't know who did this and why." She changed the subject when he gave a brief nod. "Do you have a copy of his documentary? It might shed some light on whatever he'd discovered so far. It appears anything he might have had at the apartment was either destroyed or it disappeared."

"No. Rick was pretty cagey about his research. He didn't want me to see it until he was ready with the final product."

Frisco said, "Was he working with anyone else on this project? Another student, maybe?"

The professor frowned. "I'm not quite sure. Rick didn't mention anyone else to me." He shrugged. "Could be wrong, though."

Jo and Frisco rose to leave. Jo grabbed the stack of injunction documents the professor had left on the desk for her. Out of the corner of her eye, she noticed a flyer, with the picture of a fresh-faced, attractive young woman on it.

Curious, she tilted her head and began to read the flyer. It was an announcement for a vigil for a student who had recently disappeared from the University of Minnesota's Minneapolis campus. Jo remembered reading about the case in the local papers.

Mazlo pointed to the flyer. "Shame about Claire. Wandered away from a party one night and never returned to her dorm room." He shook his head. "I can't imagine what those parents are going through. She was a smart, beautiful young woman."

Frisco said, "So you knew her?"

"Yes, she was in my intro to marketing class last fall." He pointed to the flyer. "I plan on going to the vigil tonight; it's the least I can do. I sure hope they find her."

Jo felt a stab of pity for the man. He obviously cared about his pupils. Jo said, "So sorry to bring you more bad news about another one of your students."

"Thank you, Agent Schwann. I appreciate that."

Jo turned to Frisco. "Do you have any more questions for the professor?"

The detective said, "Nope, guess that's it for now." Jo packed up the copy of the injunction and Michael Mazlo escorted them to the front door.

Glancing around the spacious foyer, Jo remembered a final question on her mind. "You have a beautiful home, Professor Mazlo. What do you do for a living?"

Mazlo's smile was self-deprecating. "Is that your polite way of asking how an adjunct professor can afford a house like this?"

Jo smiled. "The thought *had* crossed my mind."

"I'm in the import/export business, mostly native art."

He paused, and tilted his head, studying Jo for a moment. "You're wondering why a successful business person would bother teaching classes. Well, at the risk of sounding pompous, I've been very fortunate in my career. However, I had help along the way. Teaching business classes to young people is my way of giving back. It brings me immense satisfaction and I like to think it keeps me young in the process."

Satisfied, Jo handed Mazlo one of her business cards. "Call me if you think of anything else."

The adjunct professor stared down at the card for a moment. "Will they let me see Rick? At the hospital, I mean."

Jo said, "That's not up to us, but I'm sure you could talk to Mr. Wilson's mother about it."

His eyes were closed when he said, "It was just supposed to be a college credit project, for God's sake."

Frisco said, "Yeah, well, it looks like someone took it a little more seriously."

Chapter Nine

Chip READ OVER THE CHAPTER of *Head Shot* he had written the previous day. He was pleased. He opened a new file for the next chapter, placed his fingers on the keyboard and…nothing. He stared at the blank screen. Writer's block, the frustrating but common ailment suffered by most writers at some time. He got up and fixed himself a piece of toast with crunchy peanut butter and blueberry jam, fresh from his friend Mabel's kitchen. Still nothing.

The house was empty and so quiet he could hear the clicking of the wall clock and the humming of the refrigerator. Not a damn word was coming to him. Callie, his calico, jumped onto his lap and proceeded to curl up on the keyboard. It was Chip's cue to quit for the day.

It was a one of those lovely, late September mornings with bright sunshine, a China blue sky and a light breeze. Just like the day he had written about in his last chapter. The leaves on the maples were just starting to turn orange. The apple tree was laden with ripe fruit, so heavy the branches almost reached the ground. Chip grabbed a grocery bag and went to the side yard to Jane's Wealthy apple tree. He plucked an apple, rubbed it on his shirt and took a bite; a little juice ran down his chin. He filled the bag half full with bright red apples and folded down the top.

The apples were perfect for desserts and would make a nice gift for Bernice, the waitress at the Cinnamon Bun Café, who was on a kick of experimenting with new bakery delights. He grabbed the keys to his Ford from the house and headed for the driveway. Runt, his golden retriever mix, beat him to the car, sat by the door wagging his tail and barking. Chip sent him back to the yard, the dog's tail drooping. His animals had ruined his previous vehicle and he was determined to keep this new one pristine. That was until he watched Runt's dejection, called him back and opened the back door. Runt raced across the yard and took a flying leap into the back seat. Nothing like a happy dog, Chip said to himself.

***

In the two years Chip that had been a resident of Turners Bend, the main street of town had begun to come back to life. **Out of Business** signs were slowly being replaced with **Open for Business** signs. It had started with last year's renovation of the Bijou Theater. Since then, and much to Chip's pleasure, a tiny new and used book store opened. It was run by the same owner as The Book Shoppe in Boone. The Cinnamon Bun Café continued to thrive and was Chip's favorite place for home cooked food served with a dollop of town gossip.

"Lord," said Bernice, as she looked up when the café's door chimes jingled. "You look like you tangled with a hay baler."

"Hi Bernice. Just a little mishap up in Minneapolis. I brought you some apples. Figured you could make a pie or two." He handed the grocery bag over the counter and sat on one of the red Naugahyde-covered stools.

"Thanks Chip. I've got a new donut for you to try. A Maple Bacon Bismarck." She entered the kitchen and returned with a huge donut loaded with maple frosting and topped with two strips of crisp bacon.

Chip took a bite, then another. "Bernice, I thought your cinnamon and caramel rolls couldn't be beat, but this is nirvana."

"I don't know what nirvana is, but I can tell you these little porkers have been selling like hot cakes. I'm getting ideas for new treats from the folks at the Dutch Oven Bakery over in Boone."

Chip turned as he heard the door open and Turners Bend's police chief, Walter Fredrickson, sauntered in and looked around. The chief spotted Chip and sat down at the counter next to him. He looked at Chip's donut and said, "Bernice, give me one of those things and a cup of coffee, please."

He turned to Chip. "Well, I hear you had an eventful trip to the Twin Cities. I got a call from some detective named Franco. He spun me quite a tale and asked me to keep an eye on you. Seemed like a decent guy."

"Yes, he is. He reminds me a lot of one of my characters, Mike Frisco. Patrick Finnegan's murder is a puzzler, but I'm confident Franco will find the perp."

"You think someone's gunning for you, too?" said Fredrickson as he pulled the bacon off his Bismarck and munched on it.

"Nah, I was just in the wrong place at the wrong time," answered Chip. That's the story I'm sticking with for now, Chip said to himself, wanting to believe it was truly the case.

"I don't know about that. I think there's more to it than a drive-by shooting." The chief unsnapped his shirt pocket, removed a folded piece of paper and opened it. He showed it to Chip. "This is a printout from a security camera at the National Car Rental counter at the airport in Minneapolis. He's the dude who returned a black Escalade, about 45 minutes after your parking ramp encounter. I just got it from Franco. Name on the rental was Gomez. He used an international driver's license. You know him?"

Chip looked at the grainy photo of a man with a mustache wearing a baseball cap and wrap-around sunglasses. "Doesn't look familiar to me. Guess I don't have to keep an eye out for an Escalade anymore, do I?"

"Nonetheless Chip, be cautious and call me if you notice anything unusual. I'll send out an APB to local law enforcement and the Iowa State Patrol."

The chief returned the printout to his pocket. "Right now I've got a couple of cows missing…that's about as much excitement as I want in this town. Or ever again, to be honest."

Being vigilant in Turners Bend seemed unnecessary to Chip. He knew almost everyone and a stranger in town would stick out like a corn stalk in a melon patch. He lulled himself into a cocoon of small-community safety topped with a generous portion of denial that anyone could really be gunning for him.

***

Runt was asleep on the sidewalk outside the café where Chip had tied him to a lamp post. Chip thought Runt might enjoy a swim in Beaver Creek. And, maybe some time musing by the water would alleviate the nagging itch in his own head…the one that wondered if he truly was in some kind of danger.

The dog woke, jumped into the car and stuck his head out the opened window.

When Chip hit a long stretch of two-lane highway with no one ahead of him, he said, "Let's open this baby up, Runt, and see what

51

she'll do." He increased his speed, watching the digital readout rise past eighty miles per hour. He looked off in the distance at an approaching semi-truck. When the semi was close enough that he could hear the roar of its diesel engine, he slowed and edged over to the right to give it plenty of room. He hated the feeling of being sucked toward a semi as it passed.

He saw a flash of color on his right. He glanced over to the shoulder and saw a red Suburban alongside his car. He hadn't been paying attention to his rearview mirrors and hadn't noticed the vehicle behind him. It rammed into him; he fought to gain control of the car and reduce his speed further.

The large SUV rammed him again, this time the force sent him across the road and into the path of the oncoming semi. He tromped down on the accelerator and cleared the semi by just feet, the blast of the truck's horn reverberating through his head, adrenaline pumping through his body. Struggling with the wheel and unable to stop his vehicle, he flew through a guardrail and into a ditch, missing a utility pole by inches.

He was shaken and dazed; his heart was racing but his seatbelt kept him in place and the airbag exploded. The front of his car was caved in and smoke was rising from under the hood.

He turned to check on Runt, feeling a searing pain in his neck. He cried out in anguish, "Runt." The dog turned his head toward Chip and whimpered. Chip heard the semi's airbrakes bring the truck to a stop and a man's voice yelling. His vision dimmed, then darkness.

***

Two days after the highway accident Chip sat in the kitchen. He did not want to think about the crash or about Jane at the animal hospital in Ames where she was still attempting to mend Runt's broken body. He did not want to think about the driver of the red SUV who sped off or about his own foolishness at refusing to face reality.

That was no accident; someone wants to harm me, someone wants me dead. It must have been the same Suburban that followed me down 35W. Is it the mysterious Gomez, and if so, why is he after me?

Chapter Ten

Head Shot
St. Paul, MN
Late October

JOHN GOODMAN WOKE up to an empty bed several hours after he had returned home from performing surgery on Rick Wilson. The sunlight curled around the edges of their room-darkening shades. He snatched his cell phone off the nightstand to see the time…1:12 p.m. He blinked a few times and rubbed the sleep out his eyes.

He reached over and switched on the lamp on his side of the bed. Propped against his stack of medical journals and publications, he found her note, written on the back side of the one he had written the previous evening. It said,

> **John**
> **Looks like your head trauma case just became**
> **my case with Frisco. Sorry to screw up what's**
> **left of our Sunday…I will try to be home in**
> **time for a late dinner.**
> **Love, Jo**
> **P. S. And thanks for asking!**

Disappointment was replaced with happiness as he read the last line. He lay back on the bed, and allowed himself a moment to enjoy the thought of spending the rest of their crazy, busy lives together.

John realized he hadn't made the most romantic of proposals to Jo. There wasn't a ring – yet – and he hadn't gotten down on one knee, but the excitement he had seen in her eyes when she had said yes told him none of that mattered.

After years of being a confirmed bachelor at the ripe old age of thirty-six, he never thought he'd get married. His grandmother had never given up, though. He made a mental note to call her tonight and pass on their news. He knew she'd be over the moon, probably pushing next for great-grandchildren.

He sighed, and pushed back any more thoughts of his future with Jo. It was time to follow up on his patient's progress. Reaching for his phone, he padded down to the kitchen and started the coffee maker. Caddy followed behind him, nails clicking on the tile floor. He reached down to give her a quick, absent-minded ear scratch. While he waited for the coffee to brew, he dialed the number for the intensive care unit at the hospital.

When one of the intensive care nurses he worked with frequently answered, he said, "Hey, Cindy. Looking for an update on Rick Wilson."

He could hear the click of her keyboard as she pulled up his patient's file. "Well, Dr. Goodman, all I can say is that you must have done a hell of a job last night. Can't believe that kid made it. I just checked his stats myself. His BP is down to 135, heart rate is at 90, temp is slightly elevated to 100.1, and respiratory rate is 20."

John felt he had been holding his breath as she rattled off Rick Wilson's stats. He blew out a puff of air. "And how about the ICP?"

"I saved the best for last. The intracranial pressure is down to 14. Way to go, Doc."

The last vestiges of fatigue melted away and he let out a small whoop. "Now that's a step in the right direction. I'll be heading down soon to check on him. Thanks, Cindy."

He poured himself a cup of coffee, humming a few notes from "The LocoMotion". He pictured Jo singing on the ladder last night and couldn't suppress a grin.

***

After Jo and Frisco left Mazlo's house, they sat in the detective's car. Jo held up the injunction they had received from the adjunct professor. "This is great, but a copy of the documentary would be more helpful."

The detective nodded. "Agreed. Why don't I call Caroline Wilson and see if she knows if Rick was working with another student on his movie."

The detective pulled out his cell phone and dialed. After a moment, he said, "Mrs. Wilson. This is detective Mike Frisco. Look, sorry to bother you again, but do you happen to know if Rick was working with anyone else on his fracking documentary?"

Jo could hear snatches of the woman's voice come through Frisco's cell phone. "…would be Billy…address. Hang on…"

Frisco pulled out his notebook, and scribbled down a name and address. Into the phone, he said, "Thanks for the info. We'll be in touch."

As soon as he disconnected the call, he handed the paper to Jo. She pulled up the GPS system in Frisco's car and punched in the address for Billy MacGregor.

Frisco summarized his discussion. "The mother said Billy and Rick grew up together. He's not a student at the U, just helping him out with the project. Probably why Mazlo didn't know about him."

The detective put the car in drive. As Frisco wound through the streets, he glanced at Jo. "So, are you buying that Mazlo doesn't have a copy of Rick Wilson's project? Seems like he would have demanded to see it the minute that lawsuit from Wellborne Industries hit their desks."

Jo shrugged her shoulders. "You could be right, but why would Mazlo lie about it? Maybe the kid was a perfectionist and didn't want his advisor to see it until the final edits. Some people are just that way."

"Maybe, maybe not. I sure as hell wish we could get our hands on a copy of that video, though."

"Let's hope MacGregor has one."

The female voice on the GPS system directed Frisco to turn east on University Avenue, as they headed toward the area known as Frogtown. The avenue was dotted with restaurants serving various Asian and Mexican cuisines.

Jo realized she was suddenly famished. "What do you say we stop for a bite to eat after we're done talking to MacGregor?"

Frisco smiled. "Thought you'd never ask."

The GPS directed them to make one last turn. Jo knew this part of town had a rough reputation and she saw many houses with boarded windows, faded foreclosure signs flapping in the breeze.

They stopped in front of a hunter green clapboard house. Several of the shutters were missing and two more hung askew. Frisco said, "Looks like a crack house. Think he really lives here?"

As Jo opened the car door, she said, "Well, this is the address Rick's mother gave us. Let's give it a go."

Frisco followed her up the cracked sidewalk. Walking carefully onto steps that didn't look like they would hold her weight, she crossed the small porch area and rang the doorbell.

After a few moments of silence, Jo knocked and called out, "Mr. MacGregor. I'm Special FBI Agent Jo Schwann. I'm here with Detective Mike Frisco of the St. Paul police department. Could we have a word with you?"

When there was still no answer, Frisco said, "Let me go check around back. I'll see if there is another door."

Jo peeked into windows that were surprisingly clean given the shabbiness of the house, but couldn't detect any movement in the room. Frisco came back a moment later. "Place looks deserted."

"I'll try his cell."

Jo punched in the phone number they had acquired from Rick Wilson's mother. As she waited for the call to connect, she looked around the porch of the house. An old sofa moldered next to the front door. On the floor in front of the sofa was an old rusty coffee can, full of cigarette butts.

As she ended the call, she looked across the way to the adjacent house and saw a frail, elderly woman with faded denim jeans and an oversized man's coat shake out a rug over the railing of the porch.

Before the woman could re-enter her house, Jo called out, "Excuse me ma'am. Do you know the people who live here?"

The woman shrugged. "Maybe, maybe not. Who's asking?"

Jo stepped off the porch of Billy's house and began walking toward the woman. "My name is Special Agent Jo Schwann. I'm with the FBI." She fished out her badge and held it out for the woman to see. "This is Detective Mike Frisco. We're looking for Billy MacGregor. Do you know where we might find him?"

The old woman's eyes narrowed. "Billy's a good kid, unlike most of the scum that lives around here these days. Always willing to give me a hand. Whatcha want him for?"

Frisco spoke up. "We just want to ask him some questions about a friend of his. He's not in any trouble."

She seemed to consider this for a moment. Finally, she said, "Well, I ain't seen him around for the last day or two." She paused, as if trying to recall the last time she had seen him. "He carried up some boxes from my basement a couple of days ago. Seemed kinda jumpy and distracted, now that I think about it. I asked him if anything was the matter, but he told me he was fine. Didn't really believe him, but he clammed up after that."

The old woman frowned, and the lines around her mouth deepened. "You sure he's okay?"

"I'm sure he's fine," Jo assured her. "Does he have any roommates we could talk to? Seems like a big place, just for one kid."

"Yeah, but they're in some kinda alternative rock band. Billy says they're on the road a lot of the time, so I doubt you'd catch them."

Jo pulled out one of her business cards, and handed it to the woman. "Would you please call us if you see Billy?"

The old woman stared down at Jo's card and then looked up into her face. "Will do. If you find him first, tell him Sue was worried about him, will you?"

Sue turned and entered her house, the rug forgotten on the porch.

Frisco watched her retreating figure. "Hope we didn't just lie to that little old lady about MacGregor being okay. Guess you didn't catch him on his cell?"

Jo shook her head. "He didn't even have a voice mailbox set up, so I couldn't leave a message. I'll send a text message, but I'm not holding my breath that we'll hear back from him. Got any bright ideas?"

Frisco smiled. "Well, you did mention something about grabbing a bite to eat. I always think better on a full stomach."

***

John arrived at the hospital and went down the hall to Rick Wilson's room. Caroline Wilson was slumped in the chair pulled up alongside the bed. Her right hand rested on top of her son's and her head lolled back. John studied her sleeping form for a moment, and then gently shook her shoulder. "Ms. Wilson?"

She jerked up in her seat and stared up at him, as if she wasn't sure where she was or why she was there. John saw recognition in her eyes as she pushed back the grogginess. Her voice was hoarse when she said, "Doctor Goodman." She turned her gaze to her son. "How is he? He made it through the night."

John smiled. "It's an excellent sign. His vitals have improved, particularly the intracranial pressure. I'm very encouraged." He studied her face as he explained her son's current situation in greater detail. There were dark purple smudges beneath her reddened eyes. It looked as if she hadn't slept more than a few minutes the whole night.

When he had finished describing his patient's progress, John said, "How are you holding up? Why don't you head home for a bit and try to catch up on some rest. We'll call you if there is any change in his condition."

She yawned. "No, I'm ok. I want to be here when he wakes up."

John said, "It may be quite some time before that happens. He's going to need you at your best. I know this is hard, but you need to take good care of yourself, as well."

John could see the struggle on her face. She looked back at her son again. "Well, if you are sure...they'll call me right away? I'll be quick. Just long enough to grab some clean clothes and maybe a short nap."

He patted her arm. "I promise. You will hear from us if anything changes."

Caroline Wilson leaned over her son's bed and kissed him gently on the forehead. When she passed by John, he could see the tears threatening to spill over. "He's a good boy. Please, take care of him."

"Will do. Get some rest."

After she had gone, John double-checked Rick's vitals and scribbled down some adjustments to the dosage of medications. Just as he was finishing, he heard shouting coming from down the hall.

"Get outta my way. I'm telling you, I've got to see Rick."

John poked his head out the door and looked toward the commotion at the nurses' station. A young man in low-riding jeans and a hooded sweatshirt pounded his fist onto the counter top in front of the nurse. "Damn it! Just need to see for myself that he's okay."

Cindy, the ICU nurse whom John had spoken to earlier, was on her feet. She said in a calm, but firm voice, "Sir, you can't go that way. I will call security if you don't leave. Only family is allowed in the room."

The young man paced back and forth in front of the station. "Oh, man. Oh, man. I am so royally fucked here. You've got to let me see Rick. I've got to know. We didn't think they'd do it! Why won't you people let me see him? Is he gonna make it?"

Cindy's voice was less patient now. "Sir, don't make me call security."

John quickly walked to the nurses' station. "Can I be of some assistance?"

The man stopped pacing and grabbed John's arm. "Tell her I can see him."

John could see the young man's eyes were clear and his gut told him the kid wasn't dangerous, just desperate for news of his friend. John felt sorry for the guy; he'd probably do the same thing, if it were his close friend in there. John turned toward the ICU nurse. "Cindy. I got this. Let me have a word with him."

Her face was still flushed with anger, but she nodded curtly. "He's all yours."

John grabbed the young man's arm and gently steered him down the hall. "I am Doctor Goodman, Rick Wilson's surgeon. I am afraid I can't let you see him right now, but why don't we go down to the café and I'll see if I can answer some of your questions. I don't know about you, but I could use a shot of caffeine."

John felt the kid relax a fraction. "Uh, yeah. Guess we can do that. I didn't mean to cause trouble. Just wanted to make sure he's ok. Jesus, shot in the fucking head."

The young man followed John down to the café. He absently thanked John for the cup of coffee, but just fidgeted with the handle when they sat down at a table in the nearly deserted room.

John studied him for a moment. "Why don't you tell me a little bit about yourself. Can I ask your name and how you know Rick?"

The young man looked up and mumbled, "Name's Billy MacGregor. Rick and me go way back. I've been helping him lately."

Billy's eyes darted around the room and his leg jiggled up and down. When he didn't say anything more, John said, "What have you been helping him with?"

"Look, what's with all the questions, huh? I just want to know how Rick is."

John could see the kid was winding up again and he needed to defuse the situation. In a calm voice, he said, "Of course you do. Look, your friend isn't out of danger yet, but his body is working hard to heal right now. He's in an induced coma to help him get better."

Billy shouted, "A coma? A fucking coma? This is bad, this is really bad." He jumped to his feet, knocking over his chair. He began to pace once more.

John quickly stood up and gently pulled Billy's arms down. "Billy, it's ok. Come on; let's go sit back down, where we can talk."

John righted Rick's chair and they both sat down. John said, "Billy, I know you are worried about Rick, but he's getting excellent care. Is there something else going on? You seem pretty worried. Maybe I can help?"

"Nobody can help me with this. It was just some dumb college assignment, you know? Rick needed an A in the class and he knew the prof would be jazzed about the topic."

John prompted, "The topic…."

"Yeah, you know. Fracking. The topic du jour. About how those fuckers are getting away with raping the land, yadda, yadda. I was just the camera guy." His leg resumed shaking and he looked into John's eyes. "Do you think I'll be next?"

John wanted to tell this kid everything would be okay, that he was just being paranoid. But after what had happened to his friend, who could blame him?

Clearing his throat, John said, "Billy, I don't know anything about why your friend was shot. Maybe he was at the wrong place, at the wrong...."

Billy interrupted him. "No, that's not it! Those fuckers were after *him!* They knew he was getting close. And they knew I was there, right next to him the whole time. Oh, shit."

He folded his arms, laying them on the table in front of him. He bumped the cup and coffee sloshed over the sides. Billy rested his forehead on his arms and his shoulders shook.

John was surprised to see the young man cry. He was just a kid, really. He was obviously scared, but of what exactly? John thought about Rick Wilson lying in the hospital bed in a room above their heads and thought, *Maybe he has a right to be scared.*

"Billy, look. I have a friend who is working on Rick's case. You could tell her what you know and she'd protect you. I'm sure of it."

Billy looked up with red-rimmed eyes. "Nobody can do anything to protect me, don't you get it? They have all the power."

"No, they don't. My friend works with the FBI. She needs to know what you know, so she can protect you and find whoever did this to Rick."

Billy continued as if John hadn't spoken. "Rick was worried. I told him he was paying too much attention to all those conspiracy websites he'd been reading lately. Guess there was something to it after all." He scrubbed his face with his hands. "Shit, man. I'm just a glorified gofer."

John gripped Billy's forearm. "Please, just talk to my friend, she...."

"No, I shouldn't even be talking to you. Look, can I see Rick or not? 'Cause I've got to go, man. It isn't safe for me anymore. Didn't even feel safe coming here. It's just that I owe Rick a lot. We go way back, you know? He convinced me to get clean. Wasn't easy, but Rick was always right there, telling me I could do it."

John realized the young man needed to talk to someone. He would rather it be Jo, but maybe if he listened to what Billy had to say, he could convince him to talk to her. He sat still, letting Billy continue without interruption.

Billy ran his index finger through the coffee puddle around his mug as he spoke. "When he asked me to do this fracking project, I was like fuck yeah, road trip across the states. But then we started seeing some heavy shit. Like what those suits were doing to the environment, just to fill their pockets."

He absently pushed up his sleeves. John saw a tattoo of some phrase running up the inside of his left arm, but he couldn't make out the words. He also noticed some small white scarring from needle marks. They all looked old and well-healed. John was glad to see the kid was apparently telling the truth about getting clean.

Billy must have seen John's glance at his scars. He rubbed his thumb across a few of them. "Yeah, I shot up. A lot. But I swear I'm clean now. Rick got me there. I thought about using again when I heard what happened to him. Then I realized he'd be ashamed of me if I went back to being an addict now. It would be like giving up on Rick if I gave up on myself now, you know?"

John nodded. "I'm sure Rick is proud of you."

Billy took a sip of his coffee, and then started talking again, "I saw what was going on in Williston, North Dakota. Like the fucking old Wild West there, you know? Couldn't even get a hotel room. We had to sleep in the car. Not that I haven't done that before, but Jesus, we had the money. Just nothing was available. Rick called it crazy town."

He stopped speaking abruptly and closed his eyes for a moment. "Jesus. Here I am, just talking away and he's lying in that fucking bed up there."

John prompted, "Maybe you know something that can help find who did this to your friend."

Billy sat back in the chair for a moment, thinking. Finally, he spoke, "We got to know a guy who worked for the head honcho out there. We first met him when we filmed the documentary, but after a while, he met us on the sly. Said he was sick of covering things up and he wanted it to stop. He worked in a department with a name like conformance, um, something like that."

John said, "You mean compliance?"

Billy snapped his fingers. "Yeah. That's it. Anyway, the guy said they made him shred a shitload of papers about water quality and replaced them with bogus ones to send to the Feds."

John heart beat faster. He wondered if Rick and Billy had uncovered something that had put Rick in the hospital.

He quickly said, "Look, Rick would want you to be safe. Please, talk to my friend and let her help you."

For the first time, John saw Billy hesitate. "Well...maybe. Are you sure I can trust her?"

John smiled, thinking about how many times his own life had been in Jo's hands. "She's protected me a time or two. She's the best. I can call her now, if you'd like."

Billy bit his lip. "All right. But only if I can pick the time and place to meet her. Tell her I'll meet her tomorrow morning at ten. At Nina's café, on Cathedral Hill in St. Paul. But she's gotta come alone. Tell her I have a copy."

John had pulled out his cell phone by the time Billy had said the last phrase. The way the kid said it sounded important. *A copy of what, exactly?* John wondered.

He nodded and quickly punched in Jo's number. He offered up a small prayer of thanks that this scared kid had agreed to let her help him.

Chapter Eleven

Turners Bend
Early October

Chip STRETCHED, ROTATED HIS shoulders and flexed his fingers. Long hours at his computer made him stiff. He put on a pot of coffee and began to hunt for the chocolate chip cookies Ingrid made the evening before. A little jolt of sugar would take him through the morning.

Then he heard it, an easily recognizable sound. The rumble in the driveway could only mean one vehicle. Chip peered out the kitchen window to see Iver's road maintenance truck. Out stepped his best friend, the guy who always had his back, his partner in adventures and mishaps, the first person he always called in an emergency. Circumstances had forged their relationship and brought together the two most unlikely friends one could imagine...a ne'er-do-well crime writer from a prominent Baltimore family and a plain-folks road maintenance worker. Big, burly, unassuming, with a heart as big as the state of Iowa was how he would describe his friend.

Chip met Iver at the door and welcomed him with a cup of coffee. Iver sat in one of the kitchen chairs and removed his seed cap, revealing a deep tan line across his forehead. He wore a blue plaid Western-style shirt with snaps and jeans held up by a pair of red suspenders.

"I pulled that fancy car of yours out of the ditch and towed it to the insurance claims center in Ames. My guess is it will be a total loss. That car sure isn't your lucky charm, is it? I never knew a guy to have as many accidents as you, buddy. Who do you reckon forced you off the road?"

Chip grimaced as he took the chair opposite Iver. Every muscle in his body ached. Doc Schultz warned him about what to expect a few days after his accident and had given him Flexeril to relax his muscles, Percocet for pain and a cervical collar for his whiplash.

He felt like crap.

"Damned if I know, Iver. It wasn't the same vehicle from the parking ramp in Minneapolis, that was a black Escalade, but it was no accident. The guy purposely ran me off the road."

"What's the word on Runt? He gonna make it?"

Still disturbed by the news from Jane that morning, Chip hesitated and sighed deeply before answering. A lump formed at the back of his throat. "Jane is going to assist in surgery today over at the Hixson-Lied Small Animal Hospital. One of his front legs has to be amputated. They can't save it. The other broken leg is going to be okay. They used an external tibial fixator, a metal rod, which Jane said will stabilize the break and aid in rapid healing of the bone. I can barely think about him without breaking down, Iver. I love that pup like he was my own flesh and blood."

Iver leaned across the table and put his hand on Chip's shoulder. "I remember the day he was born and how you resuscitated him. He'll be a rascal again in no time, you just see."

"Jane tried to tell me that three-legged dogs learn to cope just fine. She sent me videos of three-legged dogs running and playing Frisbee, but I just feel so sorry for him. If I only had made him stay home that day, as I intended."

Iver pushed back his chair, crossed an ankle over his knee and started to chuckle. "Hell, this reminds me of Gus, a three-legged goat Knute and I had when we were kids. There wasn't anything that Billy goat couldn't do. Plus, you know Jane wouldn't sugar-coat it; she tells it like it is when it comes to animals. Your boy is going to be just fine."

The strains of Beethoven's "Ode to Joy" sounded, and Iver unsnapped his shirt pocket and pulled out a cell phone. "I never thought I'd get one of these stupid things, but Mabel insisted. Look here, it says Chief Fredrickson's calling," Iver said as he showed the screen to Chip, then pressed a button and put the phone to his ear, "What's up, Chief?"

Chip listened as Iver nodded, shook his head and said, "Sure thing; I'll be right on it."

"Trouble?" asked Chip, after Iver had disconnected.

"Two steer reported out on County Road 17. Bet they're the two that Tom Schmitt thought were rustled. Want to take a ride and check it out with me?"

On previous occasions Chip had ridden shotgun in one of Iver's vehicles…snowplow, road grater or maintenance truck. Every ride had been eventful. "Sure. I want to get out of this house. Let's ride, partner." He smiled for the first time since his accident.

***

Chip winced with each bump in the road. He wished he had taken another Percocet before leaving the house. The hot dust that billowed into the cab did not seem to faze Iver, but Chip was feeling more than a little queasy and was beginning to regret his decision to ride along with his friend.

Iver looked over at Chip. "You okay?"

"I was just thinking about how smooth riding that Ford was before the accident. This thing got any shocks?"

Iver laughed. "Little hard on your body, huh? Speaking of the accident, I was wondering if any of this has to do with that Finnegan guy who was murdered up in Minneapolis. Is someone gunning for crime writers? You and he nosing around in dangerous stuff?"

"Maybe he was, but I'm writing about fracking. It's a hot topic, but hardly something someone would kill over. Except in a crime novel, that is."

Iver pointed to two steer grazing in a pasture. "There they are," said Iver. "There'll be hell to pay. That's Rod Mueller's place, and they've broken through his fence."

Iver used his cell phone to report the sighting and location to Chief Fredrickson. "The chief is calling Tom to come and get them, and he's coming out to make sure there isn't any trouble. We'll wait here until the two of them arrive, just in case the steer wander off on us."

"What kind of trouble?" asked Chip.

"You never know with Mueller. He's a lunatic."

The heat began to rise in the cab and Chip felt light-headed and nauseated. He feared he was going to vomit. The cervical collar felt like a bull constrictor around his neck. Sweat began to roll down his face. "I've got to get out of here, Iver, get some fresh air, move a little."

He stepped down onto the roadside just in time to spew his breakfast into the tall weeds. Iver jumped down and handed him a bottle of water, looking away. "Ah Chip, you know I can't handle sick people. Lord, you look like hell."

They heard a rifle fire and a bullet ping off the side of the truck. "Get on the other side of the truck and keep low," yelled Iver. "This is the kind of trouble I was talking about."

Chip did as told, crouched down with his hands over his head and his forehead resting against the truck door. *This is insane. I lived in Baltimore for more than forty years and never got shot at. I come to the Midwest and bullets fly at me every time I turn around. I write a couple of lousy crime novels and all of a sudden I'm a target. What the...*

Iver placed another call to the chief, who was in route. "Walter, we got a situation here. Mueller's shooting at us."

The Turners Bend police cruiser came speeding down the road, sirens blaring, lights flashing, dust flying. It stopped, and with the motor still running, Chief Fredrickson jumped out and laid an assault rifle over the top of the car. "Rod, it's Walter. Put that damn gun down. Schmitt's cattle wandered onto your property. We'll remove them and leave you alone. Just back off...you hear me?"

"Can't you read?" yelled the man. "The sign says 'No Trespassing.' This is the Republic of Iowa and you've got no jurisdiction here."

"We can read, Rod, but the cows can't. Calm down. We'll get them out of here and no one is going to get hurt."

"I'll give you half an hour. If them cows ain't off my property, I'll shoot the buggers and have myself a fine barbecue."

The chief kept his rifle on top of the cruiser until Tom Schmitt arrived, loaded up his cattle and drove off. Iver helped Chip into the police vehicle and the chief took him home, sirens sounding and lights flashing, just for the fun of it.

***

Chip took two muscle relaxants, went to bed and slept for twelve hours straight. His dreams were full of danger. He was being followed and Agent Schwann was urging him to run, but he couldn't seem to move; frac sand was clogging his throat and stinging his eyes, and Dr. Goodman threatened to amputate his leg if he didn't finish the next chapter of *Head Shot.*

Chapter Twelve

Head Shot

St. Paul & Minneapolis, MN
Late October

Jo AND FRISCO SAT AT A table in a Thai restaurant in the area known St. Paul's Little Mekong. The food was authentic and Jo's mouth watered at all the exotic aromas wafting by her nose as they waited to order.

As if reading her mind, Frisco said, "God, it smells great in here. Nice and spicy, just the way I like it. Have you eaten here before?"

"Yes, I usually get their Pad Thai, but I've been meaning to try the whole steamed tilapia. It got rave reviews online."

After they had put in their orders, Jo said, "So, I've got some big news to share."

Frisco raised his eyebrow. "Do tell."

"John asked me to marry him last night, and I said yes."

Frisco let out a whoop, which caused the woman next to them to give him a sidelong glance. "It's about damned time. So, when's the big date?"

Jo smiled, "We haven't had any time to discuss it. He asked me right before the call came in about Rick Wilson. I swear, between our two careers, it may take a couple of years to be able to plan anything."

Jo was surprised to find herself getting excited, the more she talked to Frisco. He was right; it *was* time to make her life with John more permanent. She resolved to not let their crazy schedules get in the way of planning a wedding.

She brainstormed out loud, as if she were working a case with Frisco. "It'll be something small. I have no close relatives and John lost his parents in a car accident several years ago. His grandmother is still around, so of course, we'll fly her here. Or, maybe a destination wedding."

Her thoughts were interrupted by the ringtone of her cell phone. She smiled when she saw John's name on the caller ID. "Hey, I was just telling Frisco about our engagement. What do you think about....?"

John interjected. "That's great, love. But, listen. I have a young man here at the hospital by the name of Billy MacGregor. He wants to meet with you and says he's a friend...."

Jo sat up straight in her chair. "Wait, I'm confused. *You're* talking to MacGregor? We were just at his house, but there was no sign of him."

Frisco gasped across the table from her. She ignored the question in his eyes and gripped the phone tighter.

She listened as John said, "Yes, Billy came in to see Rick Wilson. Since he's not family, we couldn't allow him in the room, but I managed to talk him into speaking with you. I think he's got a lot to say, but he's scared. Sounds like he met with a whistleblower and I think he's got a copy of whatever they were working on."

Her heart sped up. "Really?"

"I think so, but hear him out and see what you think. Look, Jo, he'll only meet with you. Otherwise, the deal is off."

"Of course. Where and when does he want to meet?"

Jo dug through her purse and pulled out a small pad of paper, jotting down: *Nina's at 10:00 a.m.* When he had finished, she said, "Can you get him to meet sooner, like tonight? I can meet him in an hour."

"Hang on. Let me ask."

When she waited for John to come back on the line, she couldn't hear his conversation with Billy, as if John had covered the phone with his hand. Finally, he returned. "Sorry, Jo. He said he's got some important things to take care of tonight." His voice was firm when he continued, "Tomorrow morning at ten or the deal is off."

Jo was disappointed at the delay, but she didn't feel like she could push Billy harder for an earlier meeting. She didn't want to spook him. "I'll be there. Great work, Doctor. May have to put you on the FBI payroll."

Jo could hear the humor in his voice when he responded, "Oh, I think I have enough on my plate as is." He paused for a moment, and then continued, "Look, Jo, I gotta run. Let's talk later."

"Oh, John. One more thing. Tell Billy to be careful tonight. If we are on the right track, he may be in danger."

"Trust me; the thought has already crossed his mind."

She clicked off the call and turned to Frisco. "Well, that was an interesting turn of events."

"Yeah, you could say that. How did John end up talking to the guy we were looking for?"

Jo shrugged. "The kid was trying to see Rick Wilson. John couldn't let him in the hospital room, but got him talking. Sounds like MacGregor has some news for us. I'll meet with him tomorrow morning. One thing, though. John said the kid will only talk to me."

"No problemo. I've got enough other stuff to follow up on and I need to check to see how much progress my co-worker Riley has made on the other two vics. Gotta tell you, it feels more and more like this case is about Wilson, not the others."

"I'm with you on that."

The waitress arrived with their order and neither spoke for some time as they both tucked in to the steaming plates in front of them.

***

John Goodman ended his phone call with Jo and looked at the young man sitting across from him. "She'll meet you tomorrow at Nina's. You won't regret this."

Billy shrugged his shoulders. "Shit, I already do. But I owe it to Rick."

He stood up. "Look, I've got to go. Thanks for the coffee and, well, you know. Thanks for helping Rick."

John stood up and grasped the young man's hand. "Good luck, Billy and take care of yourself."

Billy MacGregor's eyes were watery when he quietly responded, "I 'preciate that, Doc."

As he watched Billy walk away, John couldn't help worry about the kid. He put their mugs of now cold coffee in the dish bins and headed to his locker in the doctor's lounge.

He slipped on his running clothes and headed out the door. *Might as well get in a lap or two around Lake Calhoun before I head home.*

***

In spite of the cooler temperatures, the path around the lake was as busy as ever, crowded with people trying to get into - or stay in - shape. All looked to be enjoying the beautiful late fall day.

John began running on the three-mile asphalt trail, and passed by an elderly couple walking their yellow Labrador. His body fell into the rhythm of his stride and his mind soon tuned out the people around him. He thought more about Jo and their life together.

About half way around the lake, he glanced across the street at the house he and Jo had always admired. It was a classic Tudor, set atop a small, well-manicured hill, with a paver stairway that wound gracefully down toward the lake. They had often wondered who might live in the house. Today, he noticed a for-sale sign in the yard.

As he continued on his run, he pictured himself living there with Jo. Quickly, his thoughts morphed into raising kids there with her.

He almost came to a dead stop when he realized he wanted kids for the first time in his life. Admittedly, he didn't have a clue about how Jo felt about having children. The topic had never come up, which, he reflected, might be an indicator of how she felt about motherhood.

John rounded the corner by Thomas beach, and made up his mind to bring up the subject soon. *But how do I approach it?*

As he began a second lap around the lake, he concluded he'd rather have a happy Jo with no kids, than an unhappy Jo with kids and no career.

John's thoughts bounced back to the house he had noticed earlier. *Jo loves her house and she just painted the office. It would be too much change to expect her to think about getting married and moving to a new home, all at once.*

Frustrated, he lengthened his stride. Passing the house once again, he thought, *It is a beautiful house.* He made a mental note to look up the listing, just out of curiosity. *We could paint the office in a new house the same shade of green....*

The funny part was that John *could* picture them as parents, there in that house. A part of him noted there was room for a playground in the back yard.

Jo may not want kids, most likely not. He realized he shouldn't get his hopes up and pushed himself hard for the final yards of his run.

Chapter Thirteen

Turners Bend
October

Chip was feeling better. Jane had returned from Ames, leaving Runt behind for physical therapy and the eventual removal of the exterior fixator on his broken leg.

"Really, Chip, he's making amazing progress. He's eager to please his therapist and working hard on his balance. By the time we bring him home, he'll be walking, maybe even running. There's an online support group for owners of tripawds. You should check it out," suggested Jane.

Chip goggled tripawds and was encouraged to see how many dogs survive with three legs. He did groan, however, when the site referred to owners as "pawents." Nevertheless, the advice on exercise and massage made him feel less apprehensive about caring for Runt.

"Let's go for breakfast at the Bun," said Chip. "I'm beginning to feel disconnected from our friends and want to catch up on what's happening."

Jane laughed and shook her head. "Well, there is never a lack of gossip at the Bun, that's for sure. Plus, I want to see what Bernice has baked today."

***

The Bun was full of regulars, folks who frequented the café almost every weekday. Jane and Chip stopped at each table and were greeted with questions about the accident and Runt's welfare. Chip marveled at the friendliness of a small community. Two years ago he had arrived not knowing a soul, a stranger in a strange place, and now he was one of them, married to a hometown woman.

They finally settled at a table with Chief Fredrickson and his wife Flora, the City Clerk. Chip took a quick visual scan of the café…no strangers with mustaches in sight.

"Lordy, lordy, Chip, aren't you a sight?" said Flora. "Have one of Bernice's new creations. First it was those Maple Bacon things and now it's Apple Cranberry Fritters. I don't know how I am going to keep my girlish waistline." Chip guessed Flora hadn't had a waistline in many years, but he knew it was best to keep that supposition to himself. He ordered fritters and coffee for himself and Jane.

"Chief, what's the story on that Mueller guy? Is he a nutcase or what?" asked Chip.

Ignoring that the question was posed to her husband, Flora answered. "He is the only son of Hans and Greta Mueller; they once owned the butcher shop in town. He joined the army during Desert Storm and came back a mess, probably had PTSD. After his parents died, he bought that place out on County Road 17 and got real weird. He joined one of those anti-government patriot groups and calls his place the Republic of Iowa."

"He's relatively harmless," added the chief. "The two of us have an agreement; he stays out of Turners Bend and I leave him alone."

"But he took a shot at us," said Chip. "I wouldn't call that harmless."

"That was just a warning shot. Believe me, if he had wanted to shoot you, you'd be dead. The guy was a sharp-shooter in the war."

"Oh dear, look at the time, Walter," said Flora. "We have a city and a police department to run. We're glad to see you up and around, Chip. Take care."

As the two exited the café, they passed Lance Williams, the husband of Chip's literary agent, as he was entering. As always, Lance looked like he walked off the pages of *GQ*. Tall, slim, always impeccably dressed. He was an architect turned organic vegetable farmer and a transplant from Chicago. Lance was wearing designer jeans and a pink Polo shirt. Not too many men could pull off wearing a pink shirt, especially in Turners Bend, but Lance could, thought Chip.

Lance joined Jane and Chip at their table. "Just the two people I wanted to talk with," said Lance. "Lucinda's got me worried and I need your advice."

"Baby fever getting out of hand?" asked Jane.

"It's entirely my fault, you know, low sperm count and slow swimmers," Lance said, his face flushing as he averted his eyes from Jane. "Lucinda's now hunting for a baby online and madly putting together a nursery and researching baby names and signing us up for parenting classes, you name it. But..." Lance hesitated.

"But what, Lance? You don't want a baby, is that it?" guessed Chip.

"Oh no, I want a baby as much as Lucinda does. It's just that I'm uneasy about searching for a baby online. When I brought it up with Lucinda, we had a row and it ended badly."

Bernice came by with refills and Lance ordered bacon and eggs and black coffee.

Jane ventured forth with advice. "There are lots of adoption scams out there, Lance. It's best to adopt through a legitimate agency. There are several safer options. The internet is just too risky."

"Maybe if you would talk to her, Jane, she would listen. She won't accept anything I say right now."

"Sure, I'll give it a try. She'll see reason soon."

***

Jane dropped Chip off back at home and went on to make several farm visits. Getting back to work, Chip placed a call to Special Agent Angela Masterson at her office in Omaha. Agent Masterson had been involved in several local cases, and Chip and she had become friends. Or at least as close as he suspected anyone got to the formidable FBI agent. She was not available, and he was transferred to another agent, Josh Klein, whom Chip had also met.

"Agent Klein, this is Chip Collingsworth from Turners Bend, Iowa. I don't know if you remember me or not."

"Actually, Mr. Collingsworth, you are quite unforgettable. What can I do for you?"

"I'd like to talk with Agent Masterson about a plot point I need to clarify for a book I'm writing. I understand she's not in the office. Could you have her call me?"

"Agent Masterson has been transferred to our Chicago office, but I can get a message to her. Your saucy FBI agent having troubles?"

"Nothing I can't write her out of, Klein. I've got Agent Masterson's cell number. I'll contact her myself. Thanks." He placed a call to her cell and left a message.

Chip was trying to distract himself with work, but his thoughts kept returning to the events in Minneapolis and his car accident. They were always there nagging at the back of his mind like a toothache. Instead of working on his book, he placed a call to Chief Fredrickson about something he had forgotten to ask him at the Bun.

"Walter, Chip here. Just wondering if you have heard anything more from Franco lately."

"Funny you should ask. I just got an update from him. Nothing definite on Finnegan's murder. The bullet they removed from your car did not match the bullet that killed Finnegan. Not a big surprise, though. Most criminals these days have a whole arsenal of weapons."

"Did he have any information about the parking ramp shooter?"

"Said he has both the FBI and immigration people looking into Gomez. Seems he might be an illegal from South America. I told Franco about your road incident down here. Although there's no obvious connection with Finnegan's murder, Franco and I agreed not to dismiss it and to keep each other posted."

"I'm worried, Chief. Not only for myself but for Jane and Ingrid, too."

"Can't say as I blame you. I'm going to assign Deputy Anderson to keep a watch on you, so if you see him nosing around you'll know why. I'll give the county sheriff a call and see if he can provide some back-up for us.

The news from Franco further disturbed Chip. He had experienced a wide range of emotions in his life ranging from euphoria to deep depression, but his recent experiences with fear were new to him. He outwardly tried to downplay his brushes with death, but in the pit of his stomach was an ever-growing ball of terror.

Someone is trying to kill me, hunting me down. Right now I could be in the cross-hairs of some deranged killer.

Chip had written about psychopathic killers. Jo Schwann had been stalked by one, but Jo was an FBI agent trained to control fear. Plus, she carried a gun. He thought about getting a gun, recalling Franco's question about packing a firearm. He wondered if Jane had a gun. It was something he had never thought to ask his wife.

Chapter Fourteen

Head Shot

Minneapolis, MN
Late October

JOHN GOODMAN UNLOADED groceries, while Cleo wound her way in and out of his legs. Caddy barked twice and John chuckled. "Okay, okay. I get it. You guys are hungry. Jeez, a little patience here."

He served their dinner, and then started on his own. After the chicken went into the oven, he turned on the stereo and poured himself a glass of red wine.

John decided he had enough time to begin organizing his new home office. He uncovered his desk and pushed it into place. Once he was satisfied with its placement, he climbed the stairs to the attic, and pulled out the boxes stored there since his move to Minneapolis. Dust motes flew around the unused space and John sneezed several times.

He dug through a box of medical textbooks and smiled when he found a faded snapshot that fell from between the pages of one of them. It was of Mark Tinsdale, his college roommate. Mark was now an FBI agent and was the reason John occasionally helped the bureau on cases related to brain injuries. If it for weren't for his old buddy, John would never would have met Jo. He made a mental note to give Mark a call tomorrow and thank him for sending him to Minnesota in the first place.

John carried down a few of the boxes and put some of the books on the shelves. When he realized he was missing his desk lamp, he climbed the stairs once more, Caddy in tow. "Finished with dinner and decided to explore with me, huh? Nice to have the company."

He knelt down to dig through a few more boxes, but still didn't find the lamp. He stood up, brushing the dust off his knees and looked around the room. In a far corner, he could see an object covered in a sheet. Curious, he stepped over a beat-up trunk and stood in front of the object. It was flat and rectangular in shape, about three feet tall by two feet wide. Caddy gingerly sniffed at the sheet and looked at him as if to say, "Well, don't you want to know what it is?"

"Guess we'll have to investigate." When he carefully pulled the sheet away, he saw it was a portrait of a gray-haired man dressed in a dark suit. The man had struck a solemn pose, but John detected a twinkle in his green eyes.

While he had never met the man, John knew immediately this was Jo's father. He had died years ago, when Jo was still in high school. There was no mistaken those green eyes; they held the same hint of mischief he saw in Jo's face every day.

"I'll be damned." John knew Jo still struggled with her father's death, all these years later. The first time he and Jo had been intimate, Jo told him the sad tale about her father. He had been well-loved by everyone in the community, until he had been falsely accused of making sexual advances toward a patient. He was eventually cleared of all charges, but his reputation had been destroyed and he took his own life, leaving Jo an orphan.

John searched the painting for the artist's signature, for the image was incredibly lifelike. He was astonished to see Jo's autograph in the lower right corner.

"Wow. I never knew she could paint like this. She couldn't have been more than seventeen when she created this. I wonder why she stopped painting."

Caddy studied John with her soft brown eyes, but provided no answers. John suspected losing her father in such an awful way probably had a great deal to do with Jo giving up on her talent.

John held the painting in his hands, trying to decide what to do with it. Jo obviously kept it in the attic for a reason, and he wanted to respect her privacy. However, he hated to see her talent go to waste. Maybe she'd even decide to pick up a paint brush again.

In the end, he carried it into his office and leaned it against the wall, facing outward. He wanted to talk to her about it. Approaching the topic wasn't going to be easy.

***

Jo arrived home several hours later. She kicked off her shoes at the door and sniffed appreciatively at the savory aromas lingering in the kitchen. Caddy greeted her with a gentle nudge. Bending down to rub her golden ears, Jo said, "Mmm, I smell John's famous chicken. Did you guys leave any for me?" Jo was surprised to realize she was hungry. Again.

She hung her jacket on the back of a kitchen chair and then stepped into the darkened den, searching for John. Caddy followed closely behind. "Hey, Sweetie, where are you?"

Jo heard his voice call out from upstairs. "Up here, in the office."

She stepped into the room, just as he was adjusting his medical license on the wall. Walking into his outstretched arms, she gave him a long, lingering kiss. Even after months of living together, her stomach still did a little happy flip when she came home to him. "I've missed you."

John smiled down at her with that sexy grin of his. "Maybe not as much as I've missed you." He set her apart from him a bit. "I'll bet you're hungry and tired. Why don't I warm up some leftovers and you can tell me about your case."

Jo took a minute to look around the room. "Looks like you've been busy. The office looks great, I...." She cut off her sentence when she spied a familiar set of eyes.

Her shock felt like a physical blow. She hadn't seen the portrait of her dad in quite some time and seeing it again brought back a flood of emotions. Her father had missed out on so much, including meeting his future son-in-law. Jo blamed him for that. If he hadn't taken his own life....

She ruthlessly cut off the thought. Her voice sounded flat when she said, "John, why is the painting of my dad down here?"

John stepped over to the portrait. "I found this in the attic. It's remarkable. I knew you could paint, but I thought that was only walls, not works of art. Why didn't you tell me?"

Jo could hear the slight hurt in John's voice that she had kept that part of her hidden from him, but she didn't care. She felt slightly dizzy and she could feel tears creeping into her eyes. *Dammit! Why did he have to meddle, to remind her of what she had lost?*

She angrily swiped away a tear that threatened to fall. She could only stare at the painting, and waves of sadness and anger rolled over her like a brewing storm.

"Jo? Talk to me. What's going on?"

Finally, Jo spun to face him and shouted, "What the hell, John? What gives you the right to bring this down here? Is this what it's going to be like when we're married? I have a right to my privacy."

John's face turned white and she could see she had wounded him deeply with her outburst. She could feel the heat creep up her neck and was embarrassed that tears now fell unchecked down her face.

His expression softened and he thumbed at the wetness on her face. "Jo, I'm sorry. I didn't mean to interfere. I just...I just wanted to talk about your incredible talent. I didn't realize it would cause so much pain." He reached down for the painting and lifted it up. "I'll take it back up to the attic. Let's forget about this. You're right, it wasn't my place."

Jo was ashamed at her outburst. She realized she had overreacted and knew John hadn't meant any harm. Why was she feeling so edgy? It didn't seem like it had to do with the stress of her case.

After a moment, she reached out to grab his arm and pull him back. "No, it's me who should apologize. I know you would never do anything to knowingly upset me. I don't know why it bothered me so much." She shrugged. "It was just a shock, that's all."

She looked down at the painting in John's hands and smiled. "It is pretty good, isn't it? My dad loved that picture. He used to say it made him feel important that such a talented artist had bothered painting an old coot like him."

John studied the portrait. "You look a lot like him, you know. Especially around the eyes."

They both studied it for a moment, each lost in separate thoughts. Finally, John said quietly, "Why did you stop painting, Jo? You have a real gift."

Jo sniffled at the remnants of her tears. "I don't really know. This was the last thing I painted. After my dad died, I couldn't seem to pick up a brush without thinking of him. I eventually sold the easel and other supplies when I went to college."

Jo was surprised to find her fingers itched to hold a brush again, to create again. She looked at John. "Do you think we can find a spot in the den to hang this?"

John's grin was infectious when he said, "I know just the spot."

***

John read in bed while Jo clicked away at the keyboard of her laptop next to him. He set aside his medical journal. "Find anything that might help you with your case?"

Jo rubbed her eyes and John thought she looked more tired than usual when she responded, "I've been doing some research on Wellborne Industries, a company that may be at the center of this case. Seems the founder of the company, Jonathon Wellborne, is a self-made billionaire. He grew up in the Iron Range of northern Minnesota, received a full-ride football scholarship at Texas A & M and became a petroleum engineer. He began his career with Halliburton and then left to start his own company, which last year had revenues of four-and-one-half billion dollars. Here's the kicker: he's only fifty-five years old."

John whistled. "Amazing. Think he cut any corners to get to that level?"

"Funny you should mention that. There've been several lawsuits filed against his company, but they've all settled out of court. All had to do with fracking and most of them to do with ground water contamination. The federal government fined them a few years ago for failing to properly report contaminate levels, but the penalty was minimal."

"Think Rick Wilson stumbled upon something he shouldn't have?"

Jo shrugged. "It's looking more and more like that all the time. I'm hoping Billy MacGregor has some answers for me tomorrow. You said he had a copy, right?"

"He didn't specifically say a copy of what, but maybe it was the documentary. I didn't want to push too hard, for fear of spooking him. I knew you would rather talk to him yourself."

Jo closed up her laptop. "You did great. This could be the break we're looking for." She reached over and pushed aside John's journal. "Enough work. You know, we haven't had a chance to properly celebrate our recent engagement."

John's pulse sped up when he saw her frisky grin. Gathering her to his chest, he bent down and kissed her neck. In a low voice, he said, "Now, just what did you have in mind?"

"Oh, I think you're well on your way to figuring it out."

Chapter Fifteen

Turners Bend
Late October

THE LOVELY INDIAN SUMMER had made way for a gloriously gem-colored fall in mid-October, but by late in the month most of the leaves were down, the result of a couple of windy days. The air had turned from crisp to chilly. Chip sat on the back porch huddled in a wool shirt and looked at his watch, as he had been doing every five minutes or so. Jane was due to arrive soon, and he didn't want to miss it...Runt's homecoming. His feelings vacillated between joy and heartbreak. Jane had assured him Runt could not only walk, but he could climb stairs and run in a rocking fashion. Yet, the prospect of seeing him for the first time since the accident caused a resurgence of Chip's guilt and sadness.

Jane was also bringing home a veterinary student who would be completing a two-month practicum with her. She had offered him Sven's room, since Turners Bend lacked lodging for him. Jane described him as an international student who was brilliant and charming, but Chip knew little else.

Chip had mixed feeling about having a stranger in the house. It would change the fragile family dynamics they were trying to forge during their first year of marriage. Jane, however, had a soft spot for anyone who needed a home or a job. She argued the student would ease her workload and give her more free time to spend with him and Ingrid. For that reason, Chip reluctantly approved of the plan.

Chip heard Jane's pick-up before he saw it turn down their road. He rose and walked quickly to meet the truck. It came to a halt a few yards from him. Jane hopped out and ran to release the tailgate. Chip knelt as he watched Runt bound out of the truck and fly into his arms. Chip laughed when the dog gave his face a washing with his slobbery tongue, while wagging his tail like a metronome set for a scherzo's tempo.

Then Runt ran to the house, climbed the steps up to the backdoor and barked three times. Perched on the sill of the kitchen window was Callie, making the strange chirping sound cats make when excited.

Chip returned to the truck to give Jane a hug and kiss. A figure unfolded himself and stepped out of the passenger's side of the truck. He was about six feet ten inches tall, very slender with long arms and legs. He wore white cotton pants, like scrubs, and a white dashiki shirt topped with an orange nylon ski jacket. On his feet were Nike's that Chip guessed were at least size fourteen.

"Chip, this is Tolla Dibaba. Tolla, this is my husband Chip," said Jane.

Tolla shook Chip's hand and bowed formally. "It is a pleasure to make your acquaintance, Sir," said the young man in very precise English. "My friends in Ames call me Baba, and you may do so, too, Sir."

Chip was momentarily speechless. Surely he must be Ethiopian, he thought. Somehow when Jane had said international student, Baba was not what he had imagined.

"Welcome," stammered Chip. "No need to call me Sir; Chip is just fine. Your name is Dibaba? Are you related to the famous Olympic runner?"

"He is one of my many cousins," said Baba. "But I have too many cousins to name them all for you, Sir."

"In many languages doesn't baba usually mean father?" asked Chip.

"You are correct, Sir. I think if my American friends knew that, maybe they would call me Dude instead. I would like that."

***

During the course of a protracted dinner, the household peppered Baba with questions. They learned his mother had died in childbirth when his younger brother Hakim was born. His father was a village leader in the Afra region of Ethiopia and a prosperous goat and cattle herder. He sent Baba and Hakim to a Christian boarding school in Addis Ababa.

"How did you end up in Iowa?" asked Ingrid, who Chip noticed was entranced by their guest.

"I won a scholarship to Stanford University to study biology, and my brother won a scholarship to study chemical engineering at Cambridge University in England, Miss Ingrid. Now I study veterinary

84

medicine at Iowa State, so I can return to my homeland and attend to the herds of my village. I desire to learn how to breed drought-resistant animals."

"What about your brother, Baba? Where is Hakim now?" asked Jane, as she started to clear the dishes from the table.

Chip observed Baba's disarming smile fade and his body stiffen. "Hakim has returned to our country. My father tells me he has become what you call radicalized. I fear he has allied himself with some very bad people, Wahhabi Muslims who want to turn Ethiopia into an Islamic state."

"Are you Muslim, Baba?" asked Ingrid.

"No, we are Christians. I do not understand my brother and what he is doing, and I fear for his life."

During their meal, Runt sat next to Chip with his head on his lap. Although fascinated by Baba's story, Chip's divided his attention between the young man and the dog, stroking Runt's head and feeding him scraps from the table when Jane wasn't looking.

***

Later than evening Chip sat on their bed watching Jane change clothes. The turn in weather had ended her season of sleeping in sheer nightgowns. She donned a pair of light blue flannel pajamas dotted with penguins and turned around, modeling them for him.

"Sexy, huh?" she said laughing. "My mother gave these to me for Christmas last year."

"Maybe she will give me a matching pair this year," he replied. "Are you taking Baba to the Bun tomorrow? I'd love to see the locals' reactions to him."

Jane put her hand on her hips and gave him a harsh, scowling frown. "We may live in a small town, but we're not hayseeds or provincial. You of all people should know this town is open and accepting of all kinds of people. Anyway, when they see him with animals, he will win their hearts. He's really quite extraordinary and knows more about goats then I ever will."

Chip stood and took Jane into his arms. "Hey Red, I love it when you get hot tempered. I thoroughly like Baba, and he has certainly won Ingrid over already."

"Aren't you going to get ready for bed, Sir?" Jane asked with a little bow, Baba-style.

"I think I'll work in the kitchen for a while, keep Runt company on his first night home. You won't reconsider and let him in here, will you?"

"Absolutely not. I know you; next he would be sleeping in bed between us with his head on a pillow."

***

Chip found Runt in the dog's bed in the kitchen. He sat on the floor and Runt edged over and laid his head in Chip's lap. "I'm sorry about the leg, boy. You've been so brave, such a good dog. I bought you a Frisbee. Tomorrow we'll play in the back yard, okay?"

Runt thumped his tail on the floor.

Chapter Sixteen

Head Shot

Minneapolis & St. Paul, MN
Late October

JO WOKE UP EARLY, FEELING exhausted and sick to her stomach. She had felt better most of the day before, and assumed she was finally getting over the flu, but she had to admit she still felt awful. A wave of nausea came over her and she staggered into the bathroom, just in time.

John rushed in behind her. "Jo, are you alright?" He handed her a damp washcloth.

A suspicion crept into her head that something else was going on, but she quickly quashed the thought before replying to John's question. "I…I think I picked up another bug. I was feeling a little off yesterday, but then it passed. Ugh, I feel like crap."

Her brought her a glass of water and as she rinsed out her mouth, he said, "Jo, I know you are supposed to be meeting with Billy MacGregor this morning, but you can't go anywhere like this. Why don't I meet with him and convince him to talk to Frisco?"

The idea was tempting, but she shook her head. "You had a hard enough time getting him to trust me in the first place. I'm feeling a little better now. It'll be fine…."

There was a deep frown line between John's brows. "Really? The paleness of your face would suggest otherwise." He put his hand to her forehead. "You don't seem to have a fever. Any other symptoms? Headaches, body aches...anything like that?"

She walked to the sink and rinsed the washcloth in cold water. When she replaced the washcloth on her forehead, the coolness made her feel a bit more in control. "No. Seriously, I'm already feeling better. Look, I'll meet with MacGregor and come straight home again if I'm still feeling bad afterwards."

John didn't look convinced. "Well, I know how important this is to your case, but you need to take care of yourself. You're not going to be able to solve anything if you are laid up in a hospital."

Jo forced a smile on her lips. "It would take a lot more than a stomach bug to put me in the hospital. I'm a tough FBI agent, remember?"

He didn't return her smile and looked only a little less worried when he said, "Can I get you something?"

"Just my dignity. Not cool to get sick in front of my fiancée."

Jo got ready for work and only felt dizzy once, which she managed to hide from John. She was shoving the notes she had taken on Wellborne from the previous evening into her briefcase when her phone buzzed.

She nabbed her keys from the hook. Tucking her cell phone between her chin and shoulder, she said, "Hey, Frisco. What's up?"

The detective's voice was grave. "We got a call this morning from a bakery over off of University. One of their people went out back for a smoke and found Billy MacGregor's body in the alley."

Jo put the keys back on the hook and closed her eyes. "Any idea what happened to him?"

Frisco's voice sounded as weary as she felt when he responded. "An apparent heroin overdose. The ME is on her way over, so we'll know more soon. Looks like you can forget your meeting with him."

Jo watched as John came into the kitchen. At his raised eyebrows, she whispered, "Frisco" and he nodded.

Into the phone, she said, "Are you heading over to the scene? Do you want me to join you?"

"Nah. I got this. I'll call you if anything comes up."

"Thanks for the heads up, Frisco. I'll talk to John again and see if he has any additional details. Call me when you get back from the scene and we'll head over to Billy MacGregor's house again. I'd like to look around and see if we can find whatever it is he said he was going to show me. Guess we're back to square one."

She could hear his sigh through the phone. "Yeah, I was thinking the same thing. Feels like we've gone down a rabbit hole with this case."

Ending the call, Jo turned to John. She felt so tired. Tired of human lives being wasted. She said, "Billy MacGregor's body was found in an alley in St. Paul early this morning."

John's mouth fell open. He said, "Jesus. What happened?"

"It looks like a drug overdose, probably heroin."

Jo was shocked to see the transformation in John's features. His face was white, but his voice was firm, "I don't believe it. I know he used in the past, but he told me if he started using again, he'd be giving up on not only himself, but Rick Wilson, too. And I believed him."

Jo reached out and touched his arm. "John, I know you want to believe that, but I've seen it happen before. The addiction is too tempting, especially when someone's under that much pressure...."

John ran his hand through his hair. "Look. I saw plenty of relapse cases when I was a medical intern and I know all the depressing stats on recidivism rates.

"However, I don't believe this guy would fall back into his old drug habits. You didn't see the fear in his eyes. The kid was in survival mode; he wouldn't have wanted to give up any self-control to drugs. Don't you think it's a bit convenient this kid dies of an overdose, just before he meets with you?"

Jo caught her lower lip between her teeth. *Good point.* She said, "Let's go through everything you remember about what he told you. Maybe we can figure this out."

They sat down at the kitchen table and John went through what he remembered of the conversation at the hospital. Jo listened carefully, without interruption.

When he finished, she said, "And he was convinced they were after him next?"

He nodded. "I'm telling you Jo, the kid was scared out of his mind. I don't think he was just being paranoid. I think he was murdered."

Jo stood up, feeling restless and frustrated. "You said they talked to some guy in the compliance department, about doctored water quality reports. Did he mention the name of the company or the name of the guy they spoke to?"

John looked down at his hands. "No, and I didn't push him. Now I wish I had. At the time, I thought it was best if you talked to him."

She rested her hand on his shoulder. Jo could tell John was taking this kid's death hard. "John, this isn't your fault. You did the best you could to convince him to come forward with what he knew so we could protect him."

He looked up at her, his eyes tired. "But it wasn't enough, was it?"

***

Jo met Frisco at Billy MacGregor's house later that morning. The outside of the house looked even more depressing than when they had visited it the previous day, so she wasn't at all surprised at the mess inside. The furnishings were mismatched and screamed early-modern college student. Clothes were strewn around the floors, and there were piles of books, DVDs and stuff everywhere.

Frisco said, "Some things never change, do they? Like how single guys don't pick up their shit."

Jo picked up one of the books jutting out from a plastic shopping bag on the battered coffee table and read the title, *Complete Poems and Songs*, by Robert Burns. She pulled out another, entitled, *Ordinary Grace*, by William Kent Krueger. "He certainly had an eclectic taste in books."

Jo slid the books back in the bag. "Let's see if we can find a laptop or computer somewhere."

A quick sweep of the house showed there wasn't a laptop or computer to be found.

Frisco said, "Maybe he took it with him."

"Did anyone find his vehicle at the scene?"

"Yeah, but the windows were smashed and the tires were lifted before the cops found it." He shook his head, "Not exactly the safest neighborhood to leave your car unattended, for even a short period of time."

"So, his laptop could have been swiped."

"Could be. If it was even there, in the first place."

While Frisco rummaged around the bathroom and kitchen, Jo searched the family room. At the very least, she hoped they would find some connection to the companies Billy and Rick had been researching. However, she was also on the hunt for anything that might prove or disprove that Billy's death was an accident.

She picked up a paystub from the coffee table. Judging from the year-to-date earnings, it appeared Billy had been a part-time employee of Subtext, a bookstore in St. Paul.

Jo carefully pushed aside a row of DVDs and music CDs. As she read through the titles, she was surprised by Billy MacGregor's taste in music and movies. Horror flicks like *Saw III* were mixed in with *Singing in the Rain*. As she dug through novels on a sagging bookcase, she realized something felt off about the mess in the room. It was frustrating she couldn't quite put her finger on it.

Jo continued her search in the bedroom, kicking aside a pile of discarded clothing. At once, she realized what was wrong. She went out into the family room to verify her suspicions.

Once she was satisfied, she called out, "Frisco, can you come in here a minute?"

Frisco walked into the room. "Find something?"

"It's more like what I didn't find. Have you noticed something strange about the mess in this house?"

Frisco smirked, "You mean like the fact that the scattered dishes in the kitchen are clean and the bathroom is spotless?"

Jo said, "So you noticed it, too? There is no dust anywhere, and the clothes strewn around the floor still have fold marks."

She thumbed at the shelves behind her. "Take a look at those DVDs. They are arranged in alphabetical order. Doesn't quite fit with the mess in this room, does it?"

Frisco looked at the shelving above her shoulder and whistled. "Wow, you're good. I wouldn't have caught the alpha-order thing. So, someone searched the place and then made it look like this kid was a slob to cover their tracks."

"Billy MacGregor's death is looking more like murder all the time."

Jo filled Frisco in on her conversation with John and how he vehemently disagreed with the preliminary assumption that the young man had died of an accidental drug overdose. She concluded by saying, "We need to make damn sure this kid's death wasn't an accident. What did the ME say?"

"She sent off the tox screens, so we'll know more after those come back. There were plenty of old needle marks on his arms, but they were healed over. It wasn't until she looked at his legs that she found a fresh mark on his upper thigh."

Jo shrugged. "Not unusual...hard core users do it all the time."

"But there were no signs of other marks on his legs. Why change methods now?"

"Did you find any drug paraphernalia?"

He shook his head. "I found half a joint in the medicine cabinet, but that was it. You?"

"Nothing."

Frisco frowned. "Let's get a hold of that tox screen ASAP. I'm betting my next paycheck this kid was murdered."

"Let's keep looking for a copy of that documentary. Maybe the person who tossed the place missed something."

The detective smirked. "Not betting my paycheck on that."

Chapter Seventeen

Turners Bend
Late November

A MONTH HAD PASSED and Chip's writing had suffered. The household had been busy with their house guest and with hosting a big Thanksgiving dinner. And if he was being honest with himself, a good dose of procrastination had stalled the progress of his book. He resolved to get back on the saddle and pound out a new chapter.

He was alone in the quiet house. Runt was sleeping at his feet and Callie was sprawled across his keyboard, writing a cat tale with random letters. Instead of concentrating on his writing, his thoughts turned to Finnegan. A search of online news did not produce any recent information on the author's murder. He called Detective Franco at the MPD and the duty officer put him on hold. He put his phone on speaker, rose and began to make himself a pot of coffee using the Free Trade Ethiopian blend he had become addicted to since Baba's arrival. It was dark and rich and packed a powerful dose of caffeine.

Jane had been right. Turners Bend had fallen in love with Baba in the past month. He quickly ascended to rock star status. He taught Bernice how to make injera, a spongy Ethiopian flatbread, and the Sunday school kids at First Lutheran how to sing "Jesus Loves Me" in Amharic. He was an animal whisperer, according to many of the local farmers. He was drawing Ingrid out of her shell. And, Runt who never left Chip's side during the day, slept with Baba every night, head on the pillow next to the young man's closely-shorn head. *I'd be jealous, if I didn't like the guy so darn much. There's something very special, magical about him.*

A voice from the speaker phone drew Chip away from his musings. "Franco here."

"Hi, this is Chip Collingsworth," Chip responded, as he poured himself a cup of steaming black coffee, the rich aroma curling up his nose. "I wondered if you could give me an update on Finnegan's murder. How's the investigation coming along?"

"Hello there, Chip. I'm not at liberty to say too much, but I'm sure it has something to do with the research he was doing. His back-up files have proven to be very interesting. The investigation has now crossed state lines and I'm working closely with an FBI agent."

"Is the agent a good-looking woman?" asked Chip, envisioning Agent Jo Schwann.

"About as far from it as possible. That only happens on TV or in your books. This agent is about fifty and he looks like an ex-prizefighter."

"What about *Shanghaied*, the book on Finnegan's chest and the Asian gang connection?"

"I think that was what you would call a 'red herring'. The Gang Task Force has an undercover guy among the Asian gangs. He claims none of them is taking credit for the kill. I think the book was a deliberate move to throw us off track and pin it on the Purple Brothers or Crazy Bloods or one of the other Asian gangs."

Chip began to make a sandwich with left-over Thanksgiving turkey, Swiss cheese and lettuce. "Well, what about Gomez, the guy who rented that black Escalade, the one who did a number on my car in the parking ramp? Any news about him?"

"That's out of my hands and real hush-hush. A raft of federal agencies are involved…DEA, FBI, NSA, HSA and just about every other three-letter group you can name. Did you know those guys do not play well together? Seems they are squabbling over jurisdiction and not sharing intel with each other. Weird. Any more incidents since you were run off the road?"

"Nope, all's quiet on this end. Hope you'll keep me posted if you have anything you can share about either case. I feel pretty intimately involved."

"You betcha," said Franco, as he ended the call.

Chip took a big bite of his sandwich and realized he forgot to add mayo. He grabbed a jar from the refrigerator, but it was empty. *Who in this household would put an empty jar back in the fridge? Huh, most likely me.*

He took his sandwich to the back porch and sat in a spot of noonday sun. Runt padded along and sat by his chair, accepting the piece of turkey Chip took out of his sandwich. "Jane doesn't approve of table scraps for dogs, but I suppose you know that, don't you?" Runt cocked his head, as if trying to understand Chip's words.

Chip thought about Franco's question. It had been quiet for weeks. No more mishaps. He had stopped searching for unfamiliar faces and cars, no longer jumped at unexpected sounds. His jitters were gone for the most part. He could possibly dismiss the parking ramp shooting as a random drive-by, but not the red Suburban forcing him off the road. There was no explanation for that, except someone wanted to do him harm. A nagging feeling about that accident surfaced every once in a while.

Their law enforcement protection had slackened, but Deputy Anderson still did a safety check every day and patrolled the area looking for suspicious characters. The Turners Bend post office tacked up a picture of Gomez and the State Patrol was on the lookout for the red Suburban, but no sighting or tips from the public were called in.

An unfamiliar mini-van came barreling down the driveway. It was a new-looking, seven-passenger mini-van, white and sparkling. It came to an abrupt halt, immediately alarming Chip. He felt a surge of panic and his skin began to prickle, his mind racing to try to think of a weapon to protect himself. *Damn, why didn't I follow-up on getting a gun? There isn't even a baseball bat in the house.*

He ducked down and waddled to the utensil drawer, opened it and pulled out a knife. He crawled to the window and stood by sliding his back up the wall. He drew back the curtain just enough for a peephole and saw Lucinda Patterson-Williams, his literary agent, step out of the van. His tension deflated like a tire's slow leak. He wiped his hand across the sweat on his forehead and blew out a puff of air.

Lucinda was dressed in pencil-legged jeans, tall leather boots, and a puffy vest. A voluminous scarf was artfully draped around her neck. Urban mommy look, thought Chip. This impression was further enforced when Lucinda slid back the side panel door with the remote control and withdrew what seemed to be a large diaper bag. He had heard about her baby craziness and this was solid proof.

He opened the back door for her. "Jeez, Lucinda, you scared the crap out of me."

She entered and looked at the chef knife still in Chip's hand. "What were you planning to do? Slice and dice an intruder?"

"Sorry, guess I get paranoid when I see an unfamiliar car approaching the house. Still on edge about that drive-by shooting in Minneapolis." He returned the knife to the drawer and poured a cup of coffee.

As he held out the cup to her, Chip could see Lucinda was on the verge of tears, biting her lower lip and rapidly blinking her eyes.

"Is Jane here?" she said in a shaky voice.

"No, she's out on a farm call. You look upset Lucinda. What's up?" Lucinda plunked down her heavy bag, sat in a chair and began to weep, first a few tears and then sobs.

Chip had never had to deal with a vulnerable Lucinda. He was clueless as to what to do, so he retrieved a box of Kleenex from the bathroom and waited. He thought about touching her arm or patting her shoulder but realized he had never, in all the years he had worked with her, touched her. They did not have that kind of relationship, so he continued to wait. When her tears subsided, he said, "Okay, want to tell me what this is all about?"

She blew her nose and wiped the running mascara from under her eyes. "Jane was right to warn Lance about the online adoption scams. We checked and a lot of people have shelled out money without getting a baby. So we took her advice and contacted a couple of adoption agencies. They said it could take years to get a baby and that maybe we would age out, get too old for a baby to be placed with us. Poor Lance, he's beating himself up because of his lousy sperm. This all just sucks."

She blew her nose again and continued, "Oh Chip, I did the nursery all in Ralph Lauren. We picked out names. I bought that friggin' mini-van with a custom built-in infant seat and a rear video entertainment system for the baby." She pointed to the vehicle in the driveway. "I even started wearing my hair in a ponytail, just like all the celebrity moms in *People* magazine. I bought yoga pants for chrissake. Now I just feel ridiculous."

"Hey, Lucinda, go back to the fertility clinic and explore other options, in vitro fertilization or artificial insemination. It's not like you to give up. Pull yourself together. It will happen for you two and you're going to be great parents."

"Thanks Chip. I needed that. I know there are other options, but I was set on adoption rather than subjecting myself to medical procedures."

She shook herself and straightened up. "Okay, that's about enough drama for today. Now let's get down to business. When will you have the manuscript of *Head Shot* done? No more lame excuses. Oh, and by the way, get back on the book tour. Sell, sell, sell is the name of the game."

I don't know who that other woman was in my kitchen just now, but this is the Lucinda I know…my kick-ass literary agent.

Chapter Eighteen

Head Shot

Minneapolis, MN
Late October

SPECIAL AGENT JO SCHWANN and Detective Mike Frisco spent the better part of two hours searching the home of Billy MacGregor, looking for any sign of the fracking documentary he was working on with Rick Wilson.

They were working side-by-side in the family room when Frisco wiped his brow. "You find anything else?"

Jo stood up from her search of the decrepit built-in cabinet beneath the TV. "I don't know. I was just looking at this photo of Billy with Rick." In the picture, Rick stood with his arm draped across his friend's shoulder. They both looked carefree and full of the devil. It made her sad to think one of the boys was now dead and the other was lying in a coma.

She looked closer at the photo. They stood next to a pick-up truck, their bodies obscuring most of the writing on the side of the door. "Hey, Frisco, does that look like some kind of logo to you?"

Frisco pulled out a pair of reading glasses and perched them on his nose. When he saw Jo's smirk, he said, "Don't laugh. You'll be wearing them one day soon, you know."

He took the picture in his hands and examined it. "Yeah, I think you're right." He pointed to the logo. "Looks like a 'v' to me."

"Or maybe a 'w'. I'm pretty sure it's the logo of Wellborne Industries. I did some research on them last night. Hang on a minute, I'll check."

She pulled out her tablet and brought up the website for Jonathon Wellborne's company. Immediately, a large 'W' dominated the screen. Looking over her shoulder, Frisco compared the photo to the logo on the website. "I'll be damned. It's a match. Funny how Wellborne keeps popping up."

"I was thinking the same thing. Mazlo said they were the ones who filed an injunction to halt the documentary. That's why I was doing research on the company last night. Billy told John they were talking to some compliance guy, but didn't mention the name of the company. Could be Wellborne Industries."

Frisco nodded. "So, where do we go from here?"

Jo said, "Time for me to head to the oil fields of North Dakota. I'd like to find this potential whistle-blower and see if we can get some answers."

"Damn, wish I could go with you, but it's out of my jurisdiction. I'll follow-up on the tox screens for MacGregor and see if anything else shakes out here."

***

Jo managed to grab the last seat available on the evening flight to Williston, North Dakota. The plane was overcrowded, mostly with men who appeared to be commuting to work in the Bakken oil fields. She had seen many tearful goodbyes as they hugged their wives and children before stepping into the security lines in the Minneapolis/St. Paul International Airport.

Jo took her seat after she was finally able to find a spot for her overnight bag in the bin above her head. When she smelled the vestiges of the plane's jet fumes seeping through the air vents, she had to fight back the bile that arose in the back of her throat.

A young woman with light brown hair swept up into a messy ponytail sat in the seat next to her. Jo was surprised to see her breastfeeding a small baby. The woman looked up and smiled warmly, although she looked tired. Jo offered a polite nod and then busied herself, clicking her seat belt into place and arranging her work files in the seat pocket in front of her.

Once the plane was in the air and settled into the cruising altitude, Jo's stomach felt a little bit better. She pulled out her case notes, but read through one section several times before she gave up. Jo stole a glance at the small, round head of the child next to her. She thought about the child she was all but certain she carried, and absently touched her midsection.

She spoke out loud before she even knew what she was going to say. "Does it hurt?"

The woman looked up, startled by the question. Her smile was wry when she said, "Breastfeeding or raising children in general?"

Jo hesitated, and then answered. "Both, I guess."

The young mother lightly caressed the cheek of the infant, who had apparently fallen asleep. Jo was surprised to see the baby's lips curl up into a faint smile. "Truthfully, sometimes they both hurt. I have two more at home, so I know what I'm talking about." She sighed. "I wouldn't trade it for anything."

Jo was silent for a moment, trying to form her next question. She knew she had no right to ask a total stranger such personal questions, but she needed to know so much and had no one to ask. "How did you know what to do?"

"Before my first one came along, I read all the books and talked to every parent I knew, so I would be ready. But nothing prepares you, until you hold that child in your heart the first time. Don't get me wrong; sometimes you screw up. But most of the time, you figure it out."

The young mother slipped her arm out from beneath the sleeping child and held her hand out to Jo. "My name's Kristin."

Jo blushed and gripped it. "I'm so sorry. My name's Jo. I'm not usually so blunt...well, that's not entirely true. I didn't mean to embarrass you with such personal questions."

The young mother's smile was bright. "Not at all. I'm pretty hard to embarrass. You kind of get over that when you have kids."

Jo looked at the child nestled in its mother's arms. "Your baby is beautiful. I didn't ask, boy or girl?"

The mother looked down at the baby and smiled tenderly. "It's a girl. Her name is Emily." She glanced back at Jo. "So, when are you due?"

Jo was startled. "How...?" and followed Kristin's glance at the hand that rested on her still-flat stomach. Jo could feel the heat rise in her face again when she replied. "I'm not sure. I haven't been to the doctor yet. You're the first person I've told."

She lowered her eyes and quietly said, "I've not been around kids and never really thought about having any."

Kristin reached out and squeezed Jo's hand. "I obviously don't know you. But I do know this: sometimes life just hands you what you need, whether you ask for it or not."

After that, the conversation changed course. Jo suspected Kristin was giving her time to digest her words, so she moved onto safer topics. Kristin mentioned she was flying out to surprise her husband for his birthday. He hadn't been able to come home for the last four weeks and sounded homesick the last time he called.

Kristin bit her lower lip. "Truthfully, I'm not sure if he's going to be happy I'm coming. He's always going on and on about how it's not a great place for women. The living arrangements are god-awful and expensive, and there's no privacy. Worse, he said that while most of the guys he works with are great, some of them are pretty obnoxious around women. Guess it gets pretty lonely there."

She tilted her head. "What brings you out to the oil fields? Your husband out there, too?"

Jo smiled. "Not married...yet. I'm going to Williston for business."

"Oh, what do you do?"

Jo said the first thing that came to mind. "I'm...uh, in compliance." She felt a twinge of guilt for lying to the kind young mother, but she didn't want to get into the real reason for her trip. *Besides, I didn't totally lie about what I do. I do make sure people comply with the law.*

Their conversation came to an abrupt halt when the baby woke up and demanded her mother's full attention. Jo pulled out her tablet and was finally able to focus on a few news reports on ground water contamination from fracking.

***

As the plane neared the airport, Jo could see the juxtaposition of farmhouses, barns and fracking wells. The oil machinery dotted the snow-covered landscape like sentinels.

Before Jo hopped off the plane when it landed at Sloulin Field International Airport, she briefly hugged Kristin and the

101

baby. "I can't tell you how much I've appreciated talking to you. I'm sure your husband is going to be excited to see you both."

Kristin said, "Thanks, Jo. And good luck to you. I'll be thinking about you."

Jo was startled to feel a tear welling up in her eye. She quickly wiped it away and pulled her bag down from the overhead bin. *Time to get to work.*

Jo was eager to wrap up this case and get back to John as soon as she could. They had a lot to talk about.

Chapter Nineteen

Turners Bend
December

CHIP WAS ALONE AGAIN, this time with a baseball bat beside his desk. Jane and Baba were at a symposium on chronic wasting disease in Iowa City for two days, and Ingrid was on the annual senior class trip to Chicago. He had dropped her at the bus at 6:00 a.m. to send her off along with forty-two of her classmates, some dressed in flannel pajama pants and TBHS sweatshirts, clutching their pillows, others with cans of Mountain Dew or Red Bull in their hands.

The landline phone rang and he went to the kitchen to answer it, noting the caller ID indicated it was Chief Frederickson.

"Hello Chief."

"Chip, I've got a couple of your friends here in my office who want to talk with you and Jane. You better come over as soon as you can."

"Friends?"

"Yeah, Special FBI Agent Masterson and Detective Franco."

"Jane's in Iowa City with Baba, but I'll be right over. What's this all about, Walter?"

"Just get your butt over here, then we'll tell you."

***

When Chip arrived at the police station. Detective Franco and FBI Agent Masterson were both seated in the chief's office and the chief was behind his desk.

Agent Masterson stood and shook hands with Chip. "Good to see you again, Collingsworth."

On two previous occasions Chip had dealt with Angela Masterson. He knew she was not as hard-assed as she appeared at times. No mistaking that she was a tough, fearless and highly-trained agent, but underneath her precision and starch was a kind heart. He was no longer intimidated by her manner.

As usual she wore a trim black suit and bright-white shirt, no make-up on her ebony face and no jewelry. Chip checked for the slight bulge that indicated a shoulder holster and spotted it.

Chip then shook hands with the detective. "Franco, this is a surprise. What brings you to Turners Bend?"

"My oldest daughter, Maria, is touring Iowa State today. Since I was near, I thought I'd drop in and meet Chief Fredrickson, and share some new findings with him. I'm glad I did. I gained some very interesting information from Agent Masterson here."

Chip's curiosity was piqued. Three law enforcement officials in one meeting. *This might be even more serious than I had expected.* He took a deep breath, trying to control a nagging feeling of dread. "Okay. What's this all about?"

Chief Fredrickson took over. "Agent Masterson and I were chatting by phone last week, and I mentioned the shooting in Minneapolis and your road mishap here. She had a hunch and it paid off. She checked with several federal agencies and confirmed her suspicions. It was enough to bring her here. Agent," said the chief turning the floor over to Agent Masterson.

"We have unconfirmed intelligence that Hal Swanson may have returned to the states via a narco-sub."

"A what?" said Chip.

"Drugs from Colombia no longer enter the US in Miami. The Coast Guard became too adept at chasing down their fast boats. Now drugs are smuggled in along the coast of California, south of San Diego. The Russians designed a nifty little submarine for the cartels; the DEA calls them narco-subs."

"How do you know Hal might have been on one of these narco-subs?" asked Chip.

"Good question. It was a sting operation devised to get Swanson back in the country. He was supposed to arrive with an undercover Colombian drug agent, a guy trained by us at Quantico and part of what the Colombians call the Sensitive Intelligence Unit. We don't know what happened other than the plan failed and the DEA has lost track of Swanson."

Chief Fredrickson took over. "The FBI's profiler says if Hal is in the country, he may try to contact Jane or his kids. When I heard this, we put two and two together."

"You mean Hal may be gunning for me? But why would he want to harm me?" Chip had a sinking feeling he knew the answer to his own question.

"Chip, Hal knows you provided evidence about the various charges against him, but even more importantly you married his ex-wife, took his place with his children. He's got plenty of reasons to be hunting for you," said the chief.

"It all makes sense," said Franco. "Remember, the rental car was registered to a guy named Gomez with an international driver's license. It could have been your wife's ex-husband. We've spent hours looking at security camera tape from the airport car rental area. We singled out this guy. You saw a photo earlier. Here are some more pictures. What do you think? Could it be Swanson?" Franco handed Chip three grainy photos.

"Hard to tell, but it certainly could be Hal. What do you think, Chief, you know Hal Swanson much better than I do?"

"I agree with you, Chip. All the pieces are fitting together. I think we should go forward under the assumption it might be Hal, and he may be the guy we're looking for."

Agent Masterson took the photos and studied them for a few seconds. "Franco, please make all those security tapes available to the FBI in the Minneapolis office."

She turned to the chief. "Fredrickson, I request that you provide police protection for Chip and his family members until my own detail can arrive to take over. I'll be setting up a temporary office here. I assume the space above Harriet's House of Hair is still vacant. Looks like I'll be spending Christmas in Turners Bend."

"We're a small operation, but I'll call in the Boone County Sheriff to give us extra officers and back-up. To think I once played high school football with Hal. He must have a screw loose, gone off the deep end."

Still in her take-charge mode Agent Masterson continued. "Chip, I cannot stress enough how dangerous Hal Swanson might be. Extreme caution is needed. Do not go anyplace or do anything without informing the authorities."

The meeting broke up and Chip followed Franco out to his car and waylaid him. "Thanks for coming down, Franco. Looks like my troubles have no connection with Finnegan's murder. What's the status on his case?"

Franco hesitated, and then said in a low voice. "I'm close, so close I can smell it, and it smells rotten; stinks in more ways than one. You'll hear about it when the case breaks open."

***

Chip's emotions were jumbled and his mind kept switching between fear at possibly being stalked by Hal and dread at having to tell Jane and ruining their first Christmas together as a family.

He re-played the parking ramp scene, now picturing Hal behind the wheel. He put Hal in the red Suburban and wondered if Hal had followed him home from Minneapolis and later tried to run him into an oncoming semi. He envisioned a Christmas dinner scene with Hal showing up with guns blazing.

Before I was jittery, now I'm scared to death, not just for myself but for Jane and the kids, too.

Chapter Twenty

Head Shot

Williston, ND
Late October

Jo STOOD AT THE CURB outside the airport, waiting for her ride from the Williston Police Department. Several cars and trucks went by, picking up the passengers who waited with her, until she stood alone. At one point, a red shiny pickup truck cruised by, the men inside hooting catcalls at her. She ignored them, and the truck eventually sped off, tires squealing.

The wind was brisk and she wished she'd worn her hat. She stood under the street lamp in a puddle of light. Jo noticed a black SUV idling across the street from where she stood. She briefly wondered if it was her ride, but the driver made no move to contact her. Although the windows of the SUV were tinted, she had the distinct feeling she was being studied. Out of habit, she glanced at the license plate, but the number was obscured by mud.

A shiver went through her that had nothing to do with the cold air. She looked back at the terminal entrance and watched an airport security guard walk through the door, apparently taking a smoke break. A moment later, the SUV pulled away from the curb and she let out the breath she didn't know she'd been holding.

Pulling up the collar of her jacket, she glanced at her cell phone to check the time. 8:30 pm. She mumbled through gritted teeth, "Where the hell is the detective?"

Jo had hastily set up a meeting with the Williston PD before she left Minneapolis. She called them out of courtesy, to let them know she would be working a case in their jurisdiction. The police chief hadn't been terribly welcoming, she noted, but he gruffly agreed to assign Detective Fischer to assist her in any way possible.

When a gust of wind blew up again and a fresh load of passengers joined her at the curb, she began to think the detective had forgotten about her. Pulling out her cell phone, she thumbed through her recent calls until she found the police department number. Just as she was about press "call", a large, dark blue pick-up truck pulled up to the curb and a man rolled down his passenger window.

"You the FBI agent?"

Jo nodded. "I'm assuming you are Detective Ron Fischer." When he confirmed his identity, she pulled out her credentials and showed them to him.

The man jumped out of the truck and came around to take Jo's bag, tossing it into the back seat of his extended cab. He opened the passenger door for her and waved her in. "At your service. Hop in."

The truck was high enough off the ground that Jo had to boost herself into the cab using the footrest running along the side panel. As she clicked her seat belt, she took a moment to size up the detective as he slid into the driver's seat. Detective Ron Fischer filled his side of the cab. He wore a knit cap on his head. She couldn't see any hair peeking out from beneath the cap, so she assumed he was bald. His face was ruddy and he had a long, jagged scar that ran along his jaw line.

As the detective drove, he said, "Sorry to keep you waiting. I've been working a case since late last night. The owner of one of our fine drinking establishments didn't like the way some drunk dumb-ass was feeling up his waitress's backside and shot the guy in the chest. Guess he wasn't too worried about repeat business." The detective's chuckle was gravely and ended in a cough.

Jo was surprised. "Do you have that kind of street justice around here often?"

Fischer shrugged his beefy shoulders. "You'd be amazed. Half my business these days isn't too hard to figure out, since it usually involves a guy getting a little too randy with someone else's girl. Always ends up with some kinda weapon."

It felt as if she had stepped through some time portal into the Old West. She had observed some of the crazy behaviors herself, waiting for the detective at the curb of the airport. Jo could only imagine what happened in the rest of the area.

An oil tanker truck went by, the second she had seen in as many minutes. Recently she had read that the roads in and around Williston, which previously carried the occasional rancher's truck, now withstood up to 3,700 trucks a day. The road had a wash-board surface, a sure sign the infrastructure was overworked. Traffic ground to a halt whenever another tanker pulled out.

The detective turned to Jo after one of the stops. "So, I hear you want to have a word with one of the oil outfits around here. What can we do to help?"

Jo wasn't sure how much the chief of police had told him, so she filled him in on the pertinent details, without giving away too much information. "I'm working a case that involves three victims; two dead and one in critical condition. On top of that, we may have just picked up another murder, related to the others."

Her eyes caught the logo on the truck in front of them. It was the large "W" of Wellborne Industries. She continued, "We have reason to believe two of the victims were filming a documentary about fracking and had talked to several people in the oil business. I would like to talk to the same people to determine if there is a direct link."

The detective absently rubbed at the scar on his face. "Happy to help, but you're going to have to be a bit more specific."

She tilted her head in the direction of the truck with the logo in front of them. "I plan to start with Wellborne Industries."

The detective jerked the steering wheel and then swore under his breath as a tanker truck coming from the opposite direction swerved to miss them. The other driver let them know his displeasure by laying on his horn. Ron said, "Well, shit, lady. You don't mess around, do ya?"

He blew out a puff of air. "That's the biggest outfit we got out here. You're going to be pretty popular around these parts, if you ask enough questions. Got a person's name for me?"

Jo bit her lower lip and shook her head. "That's part of the problem. One of the victims is in a coma. The other victim gave us the briefest information before he was killed. He mentioned they were talking to a man in the compliance department."

Detective Fischer scratched under his knit hat. "Always did like a challenge. Let's get you settled for the night and then we'll get a fresh start tomorrow morning."

Jo looked out the passenger window and saw a network of flames rising from the pumpjacks and drilling rigs. In the waning hours of the day, it was an impressive sight.

Jo yawned and realized how wiped out she was. She said, "Sounds good. You can just drop me off at the nearest hotel and I'll see you in the morning."

The detective's laughter boomed in the enclosure of the truck. "Lady, this here is Williston and you are in the middle of the biggest oil boom this country has seen in a hundred years. Where in the hell did you think you'd find a place to stay?"

He pointed toward the lit-up parking lot of the Walmart store as they passed. "Until just a few months ago, you couldn't even get into that parking lot, because it was crammed full of RVs setting up house. Every hotel, motel, flop house and apartment building in the surrounding counties is filled up for the next couple of years, at least. They keep building new hotels all the time, but they fill up as fast as they open them. You are going to stay at my house, with my wife and me."

Jo opened her mouth to protest, but the detective cut her off. "Really, it's fine. Micki - that's my wife - is looking forward to meeting you. She has dinner waiting on us." He smiled and patted his rather large belly. "My Micki is a helluva cook, as you can probably tell by looking at me. Besides, you'll be doing me a favor. She gets pretty sick of all the testosterone around here these days. She'll be glad to have another woman to talk to."

***

By the time Jo settled in the spare bedroom in the Fischer's sprawling ranch house, it was well past eleven. Dinner with Ron, Micki and their three boys had been an entertaining, sometimes boisterous affair, punctuated by an amazing home-cooked meal. Micki had made a huge pot roast, with three side dishes, including mashed potatoes and gravy. Jo almost moaned out loud when Micki placed a large slice of flaky apple pie, topped by a generous scoop of vanilla ice cream in front of her. Jo hadn't eaten so much food in a very long time and the waistband of her pants was now uncomfortably snug.

It dawned on her that soon enough she would not be able to fit into her work pants at all. Which made her think about talking to John. She didn't want to talk to him about her news just yet, not until she was absolutely sure. This was not a conversation to have over the phone. However, she felt a need to hear his voice, just the same. She glanced at the clock beside the bed and was disappointed to realize it was too late to call him. Jo knew he had an early surgery scheduled the next morning and was probably already asleep.

Just as she was about to head into the bathroom, her cell phone buzzed on the nightstand. It was Frisco.

"Hey, Jo. Get into boomtown okay?"

"Not a problem. What a crazy place this is, though. I'm staying in the home of one of Williston's detectives, since they tell me it's impossible to find a hotel room around here."

"No kidding. Well, I won't keep you, but I thought you might like to hear about the tox results on Billy MacGregor."

Jo was surprised. "You got those back already?"

"Yeah, well somebody owed me a favor and you know..."

Jo sat down on the bed. "Thank God for favors owed. So, what did they find?"

"It was definitely heroin, but what surprised me is what they *didn't* find. I half-expected the heroin to be laced with fantanyl or some such crap. You know they usually cut the heroin with an opiate like that, or morphine. But it was pure, Jo. The lab tech said some of the cleanest they've seen. Close to 99.8 percent pure, if you can believe it. No wonder the kid died."

Jo shook her head in disgust. "Purity levels of heroin keep increasing while prices drop - a double-whammy. No wonder overdose rates are out of control." She thought for a moment. "Still, drugs that pure...do you think he had the cash to obtain it?"

She could hear Frisco's puff of air through the phone. "Yeah, I wondered about that myself. So I dug through his bank account. After looking at his finances, I can't believe he could make rent most of the time, let alone buy grade-A prime heroin. He had a part-time job working at a bookstore, but doesn't look like he made much more than minimum wage."

"He could have stolen the drugs or money to get them."

"Always a possibility, but there weren't any priors on his record." He paused and then continued, "I saved the tastiest tidbit of info for last."

Jo sat up straight. "Don't keep me in suspense."

"After MacGregor's body sat at the morgue for a few hours, a few bruises showed up on his upper thighs and arms, like someone sat on him or at least held him down shortly before time of death."

Jo could feel her heart pounding. "So John was right. Looks like Billy MacGregor was murdered."

"Yup. Right before he could tell you anything more and maybe give you a copy of that documentary."

Chapter Twenty-One

Turners Bend
Christmas Week

Jane was not prone to panic, much less hysterics. She was good in crisis situations. Whether it was her training or her innate temperament or her Nordic blood, Chip was not sure. He did not withhold anything from her, told her everything about the meeting with Franco, Masterson and Fredrickson. It did take some of the wind out her Christmas planning frenzy, but she immediately set into action. First she called the Chief Frederickson.

"Walter, check Hal's hunting shack; you know where it is. He may be there. If not, remove all the guns and ammo. I'll feel better if he doesn't have access to those weapons. Bring me one of the shotguns."

Next she called a local handyman. "Mark, Dr. Jane here. I wonder if you could come out today and put motion detector lights in around our house and yard and install deadbolt locks in the back and front door. I've been meaning to do that for some time." She paused. "Good, see you soon."

She rubbed her temples. "Chip, I refuse to let this ruin our holidays. We have the kids and guests to think about. We can't make the kids over-anxious, but you and I will have to be vigilant and double check doors and windows. I used to be able to predict Hal's behavior, but I don't know where his head is anymore. He's a loose cannon."

Garrison Keillor knew what he was talking about, thought Chip. Women in the Midwest were strong. He was also sure Ingrid and Sven were above average. As for the good-looking men, he thought Keillor may have missed the mark on that one.

***

The next day was bright and sunny. The temperatures remained below freezing. It had finally snowed and Turners Bend would have a white Christmas.

Behind her back, Chip began calling Jane the "Christmas Grand Poobah." She was in a take-charge mode and the whole household was at her mercy. At 5:00 a.m. she was up making lists and at breakfast she assigned duties for the day.

"Baba, stop eating the Christmas cookies," she said. "Start dividing them into those tins so Chip can deliver them today."

She thrust a list into Chip's hand. He read through it. "Why are we giving cookies to Mabel and Flora? Won't they be making cookies and giving them to us?"

"Yes, of course. We'll end up with as many or more cookies than we give away. It's just the way it's done. Although we will be getting fudge and divinity from Flora, not cookies."

"How do you know?"

Jane sighed in exasperation. "Chip, just trust me and go with the flow, please. Now, Ingrid you must practice your Christmas Eve cello piece, and then you can start washing all the good china and glassware by hand."

"But it was clean when we put it away. Why does it need to be washed again?" asked Ingrid.

"People, people, people, work with me here. I can't do all this by myself. Now where is the Christmas dinner guest list?" She shuffled through her lists. "Oh, here. Lucinda and Lance, Mable and Iver, the four of us and Sven. He sent me a text last night. He will only be home for a week, and then he has to return to Minneapolis…something about his fracking project."

With list in hand, she turned to Chip. "While you are in town stop into Agent Masterson's office and invite her to dinner. We don't want her to be alone on Christmas. You better invite Deputy Anderson, too, since he's always skulking around here and providing us police protection." She rolled her eyes. "Lord, help us. He's just so over-eager most of the time."

Consulting her list again, she added, "And don't forget the Tom and Jerry batter."

Chip had further reason to be in awe of his wife. Jane told Sven and Ingrid what was happening. She didn't sugar-coat it, but only told them what they needed to know for their own safety and well-being, reassuring them no harm would come to any of them.

"How did the kids react?" Chip asked her.

"Ingrid with denial and concern for you. She doesn't want to believe her father would hurt you."

"And Sven?"

"With an uncharacteristic outburst. He called Hal a bastard and said he hoped he would be caught and sent away for a long time. Then he cooled down and asked if I was okay."

"Are you, darling? You're so controlled it scares me a bit," said Chip as he drew her into his arms.

"I refuse to live in fear, Chip. I want the best possible Christmas ever. All of us, including Baba, together for the first time. I won't let Hal take that away from me, from us."

She lifted her head and planted a gentle kiss on his lips. She tasted like sugar cookies and smelled like vanilla.

Her positivity seemed to brush off on Chip. There were still too many unknowns and suppositions. Maybe Hal was still in Colombia, maybe California. He certainly hadn't been spotted in Turners Bend, and lots of law enforcement people were searching for him. He became wrapped up in Jane's Christmas planning and began to let his guard down for the holidays.

Chapter Twenty-Two

Head Shot

Williston, ND & Minneapolis, MN
Late October

JO WASN'T SURE WHERE she was when she woke up; she just knew the coffee down the hall smelled wonderful. It took her a moment to remember she was in Williston, North Dakota, in the home of Detective Ron Fischer and his family. For the first time in a while, she felt refreshed and not sick to her stomach. *I smell bacon.*

Peeking at the alarm clock on the nightstand, she was glad to see she hadn't overslept. She shoved back the heavy quilt that had kept her snug in bed and stepped into the guest bathroom to quickly freshen up.

When she walked into the kitchen, Ron's wife was helping their youngest son Jacob into his Halloween costume. Jo knew from their dinner discussions the previous evening that all three of the Fischer boys were excited to show off their costumes at school for the Fall Festival. Jo smiled. "Glad to know we'll all be a little safer today with Iron Man on the job."

Jacob turned to Jo and rewarded her with a big grin, showing the gaps in his smile where he had recently lost some teeth. "Hi, Jo!" He glanced at his mother, who shook her head in slight disapproval. "Um, I mean, good morning, Special Agent...um, Jo?"

Micki, his mother, covered up a snicker with her hand. "Special Agent Schwann, Jacob. Now, run along and get your brothers. You will be late for school if you don't get a move on." She lightly smacked him on his backside and watched as he tore through the hallway.

Jo said, "Great kids, Micki. It's been a pleasure staying here with all of you." She frowned. "I hate you are going to so much trouble on my behalf, though."

Micki walked over to where Jo stood by the refrigerator and briefly touched her shoulder. "Glad to have you. With all the guys in this house, I'm usually outnumbered. Having you here evens things out a bit." Her smile was warm and open. "Hey, can I grab you a cup of coffee? Breakfast will be ready in a sec. Hope you like bacon and pancakes."

Jo pushed away from the wall. "Coffee would be great, thanks. Can I help with anything? First dinner last night and now breakfast...."

Micki brought the coffee pot and a mug over to Jo. "Nah, you just sit at the table and relax. I've already fed the boys. Besides, Ron tells me you've got a busy day ahead of you."

"Yes, we do." As she took a sip of coffee, she reflected that while her investigation currently lacked some key details – such as the name of the compliance person who had spoken to Rick Wilson and Billy MacGregor – she hoped they would make great progress today.

Micki continued to bustle around the kitchen, and poured pancake batter onto a griddle. "If you don't mind me asking, how did you get into this business in the first place?"

"Well, that's a long, boring story. I can't imagine doing anything else."

Just then, all three boys burst into the kitchen. Michael, the oldest, whined, "Mom, my batman mask keeps falling off. Can you tape it on or something?"

As Jo listened to Micki and the boys, she couldn't help but think of how different her own life would be next Halloween. If she was right about being pregnant, maybe she'd be helping her child into a costume in another couple of years. She was surprised the idea didn't scare her as much as she thought it might. As a matter of fact, she found she was looking forward to it.

Ron walked into the room and admired his sons' costumes. "Wow. We've got Batman, Iron Man and Spider Man, all at our house. Now, where did those darn kids of mine run off to?"

The boys giggled and Jacob said, "Aw, Dad, you're so silly. It's just me, Michael and Connor."

"Oh, well. You sure had me fooled for a minute there." He looked up at the clock on the kitchen wall. "Better get going boys, the bus will be here any minute now. You've got lots of super-hero adventures waiting for you at school."

They grabbed their coats and backpacks and ran out the door.

Ron turned to Jo. "Morning, Jo. Sorry about the delay in getting out." He kissed his wife's cheek as she loaded up their breakfast plates. "Looks great, honey."

The three of them ate in companionable silence for a while, and then Jo said, "You've got a nice life here, with a wonderful family. But I'm curious, how did you get into law enforcement? This looks like a working ranch."

"You're right about that. Actually, this ranch belonged to my dad and his dad before him. I grew up in this house. But I joined the army, fell into a job as an MP and ended up as an investigator on base. I found I was pretty good at it, but didn't want to stay in the army. So, I headed back home and got a job with the Williston PD. We rent out most of the farm land now for grazing and crops."

"I noticed you don't have oil drills on your property."

Micki stood up from the table and began clearing away the empty plates. "We're about the only ones around here who don't get monthly royalty checks from Wellborne Industries. Everyone bitches and moans about the noise, the traffic, the crime, but I don't see anyone handing their checks back."

The detective briefly scowled at his wife. "Micki thinks I'm a damned fool for not renting out our land to the oil companies."

"Do the ranchers here still own their mineral rights?"

Micki stuck a hand on her hip. "Nah. Most mineral rights were sold off years ago. The royalty checks are to pay rent for the land under the drill pads and a few have scoria quarries."

At Jo's quizzical look, Ron explained. "Scoria is the red clay they use like gravel to build the new roads we need for the extra truck traffic."

He turned to his wife. "Micki, you would hate having those damned oil wells on our land as much as I would. Don't you wonder what pumping all that crap into the ground is doing to our water? No sir, I'd rather skip a Caribbean cruise or two to make sure we have safe drinking water coming out of our well."

Jo thought of the online video she had seen about contaminated fracking fluids getting into the water supply in Pennsylvania. She shivered slightly as she recalled watching a homeowner set his tap water on fire as it left the faucet. She said, "Have there been any problems with groundwater here?"

Ron glanced sidelong at his wife and then returned his attention to Jo. "Not that I've heard. Yet. But that doesn't mean I'm ready to wallow in the stuff. I like my body parts just the way they are, thank you very much."

As Micki put the last of the breakfast plates in the dishwasher, she mumbled, "Still would be nice to have some extra cash to put aside for the boys' college fund."

Ron compressed his lips and his face was more florid than usual, but he said nothing in reply.

Jo decided it was time to tactfully change the subject. "Ron, we should head over to Wellborne Industries, don't you think?" She turned to the detective's wife. "Thanks for another great meal."

Micki's lips curled into a smile, smoothing out the frown line that had appeared during the disagreement with her husband. "My pleasure, Jo." She smirked. "Try to keep my big guy out of trouble today, will you?" She reached up and gave her husband a light kiss on his cheek.

***

As he headed down the hospital corridor, Dr. John Goodman glanced at his watch to see if he had time before his next surgery to check on Rick Wilson. Satisfied that he had about an hour, he detoured toward the intensive care ward and entered Rick Wilson's room. The young man's mother was sitting at his bedside holding his hand and talking quietly to her son. At John's soft knock on the doorframe, she turned weary eyes to face him.

She stood up. "Doctor. Is there any news?"

John smiled. "That's what we're going to find out." Glancing at the patient chart, he noted Rick's intracranial pressure was down. John was pleased to see his patient had come a long way in a short time.

He turned to Caroline Wilson. "He's making great progress. I think it's time we see what happens when we wake him up."

Rick Wilson's mother bit her lower lip, but said nothing.

John called one of the nurses into the room and she reduced the dosage of the sedative. They waited without comment for Rick to respond. After a few minutes, his eyes fluttered open and he blinked a few times.

Caroline Wilson uttered a small cry when her son turned to her and offered a ghost of a smile. She grabbed at his hand. "Oh, honey, it's so good to see you." John could hear the catch in her voice.

John cleared his throat and was further encouraged when Rick followed him with his eyes as John moved to his bedside. "Hi there, Mr. Wilson. We've been waiting for you. I'm Doctor Goodman. I would like to ask you to a few questions. I know it's a little early to expect you to be able to speak, so I just want you to indicate that you understand me by raising one finger for 'no' and two fingers for 'yes.' Do you understand?"

He was rewarded with the slow, but definite movement of two fingers on Rick's right hand. John wanted to give Caroline a big fist bump in triumph. Rick was not paralyzed, and the part of his brain responsible for processing instructions was still intact. John ran through a few other simple tests.

Caroline's eyes were wide, and John could tell she was waiting for him to say something. "This is excellent news." He explained what the tests indicated.

After he finished, she dashed around to John's side of the bed and gave him a big hug, tears streaming down her face. "So, what happens next?"

"Initially, the brain swelling was Rick's most serious threat. Now, that we've got that mostly under control, our next step will be to replace his respirator with a tube that goes directly into his windpipe. This will involve another surgery, I'm afraid, but a minor one."

"Will he be able to talk soon?"

John shook his head. "The breathing tube will make speech difficult, but it won't be forever."

Aware that his patient was able to hear what was being said, he motioned for Caroline to follow him to the far side of the room. He frowned, and then continued. "Mrs. Wilson, as I've said, I'm very pleased with Rick's progress. It's nothing short of a miracle he even survived the trauma, let alone that he is awake so soon. However, I want you to be aware that Rick has a long road ahead of him.

"The biggest risk factor now is seizures. So far, we've been lucky in that regard, but I wanted to let you know that it is a distinct possibility."

Caroline Wilson nodded her head slowly. "But it's a good sign he's not had any yet, right?"

"Definitely."

"Then I'm going to celebrate the miracles where we find them and you worry about the what-ifs." She held out her hand.

John accepted her handshake. "It's a deal."

Just as John turned to leave the room, Rick's mother reached out for his arm to pull him back and whispered, "How should I tell him what happened to him? I don't...know how to begin."

He hesitated a moment, and then tilted his head in Rick's direction. "If it were me, I'd want to know. He's going to find out soon enough when the police come to question him. Now that he's awake, I have to notify them. It would be better coming from you, I think."

Caroline's face was pale, but she squared her shoulders. "That's what I think, too."

Chapter Twenty-Three

Turners Bend
Christmas

As JANE DRESSED FOR THE Christmas Eve service at First Lutheran, Chip looked at her lists. There were checkmarks by every item. When she appeared in her simple purple velveteen dress with a single strand of pearls around her neck, he whistled.

Behind her brief smile, he saw weariness in her eyes. She was putting up a good front, but Chip was learning to sense all the various nuances of his wife's body language. *God, I love this woman. How did I get so damn lucky?*

As they entered the church, Chip spied Chief Fredrickson and Deputy Anderson in separate corners, each surveying the crowd that filled the pews. Jane did the same. Chip replayed in his mind the many instances where gunmen entered churches, mosques and temples. *Would Hal be so brazen, so crazy?*

Sven and Baba had volunteered to usher. They sat Jane and Chip up front so they would have a good view of Ingrid. Her cello performance of "Lo, How a Rose E'er Blooming" was technically flawless and her dynamics stirring. Jane fumbled in her purse for a tissue. Chip wished he had a handkerchief to offer her but the days of men carrying them seemed to have passed. His father probably still used them, he thought.

Christmas Eve was family only, including Baba, who was now family in everyone's eyes and hearts. Jane introduced Chip and Baba to the traditional Swanson Christmas Eve supper: chicken wild rice soup, fresh-baked bread, orange Jello with pineapple and shredded carrots and rice pudding.

When the pudding was served Ingrid explained the tradition. "It called *julegröt*. There is one whole almond in the pudding. Whoever gets it will have a lucky year ahead of them, and they receive the almond present."

They all inspected their dishes of pudding, searching for the almond. Baba's voice rang out. "I found the nut. I found the nut." Jane presented him with the almond present, a marzipan pig, which he accepted with grace and total bewilderment.

After dinner they sat in the darkened living room with the warm glow from the fireplace and the twinkling lights on the Christmas tree. "Just one, Mom?" said Sven.

Jane laughed. "We open gifts on Christmas morning, but ever since Sven and Ingrid were beyond the Santa Claus stage, they have begged to open one gift on Christmas Eve. So, I don't see why not."

***

The next few days of the holiday season flew by and Chip did not find time to write. The house was full of young people and plans for New Year's celebrations kept everyone busy.

After the holidays he hit a slump, and Jane noticed. "Chip, you're not writing. Is it this thing with Hal? We all can't help but be edgy until he is caught, but if anyone can track him down it will be Angela. And, having that new agent, Sam Harden, hanging around is our safety net. I can't ignore my practice, and I think you'd feel better if you got back into your story."

"You're right, of course, Jane, but I'm out of my depth at this point in my story. Jo is pregnant."

Jane's face lit up. "How wonderful! Why is that a problem for you?"

"I obviously don't know a thing about pregnant women. What was it like for you Jane?"

Jane left the room and returned with a photo album. She turned to a picture of herself, nineteen years prior, very pregnant with Sven. "Here I am, eight months pregnant. One day I was thrilled and excited; the next day I was worried about being a good mother, and then the next day I lamented the interruption in my career. Hormones gone haywire. That's the way you should write it."

And he did.

Chapter Twenty-Four

Head Shot

Williston, ND
Late October

DETECTIVE RON FISCHER drove along rough roads, flanked by ditches filled with rusty-tinted snow from the scoria clay. Special Agent Jo Schwann regretted her big breakfast. Each bump caused her stomach to churn. She rolled down the window a few inches and breathed in the cool air, waiting for her nausea to subside.

To distract herself, Jo brought up the earlier conversation from the Fischer's breakfast table. "You know more about water contamination from the fracking process than you said, don't you?"

Ron looked away from the road for a moment. "Yeah. I do. I have a friend who hauls what the oil companies call 'produced water'. Only the haulers call it 'dirty water.'"

He turned his attention back to the road. "Old Griff said the first time he opened the hatch atop one of the tanks, he just about passed out from the fumes. Now he wears a hydrogen sulfide detector and carries a gas mask in the cab of his rig. You can't tell me some of that crap doesn't find its way into our water supply."

Ron slowed the truck to a crawl to let an oil tanker pull onto the highway. "I hate to talk about it too much in front of Micki, 'cause there's not a lot of independent research on the water around here. I know it's hard on her, seeing all her friends driving new cars and taking fancy vacations all the time. But, something about the whole thing makes me nervous. Like who's really in charge?"

Jo studied the detective's profile. "I take it you're against fracking?"

"Nah, I didn't say that. But I'd feel better if someone was watching the henhouse a little more closely."

He rubbed the scar on his chin. "The safety regulations – for the water and everything else - always seem to be about twenty steps behind the progress. So, I have to ask myself, who's keeping a lid on the regulations? Gotta be big oil, right? Everybody in the whole damned country is so thrilled we're becoming less dependent on foreign oil that they don't stop to think about the consequences of moving too fast."

"Plenty of people out there are trying to change that, like the fractivists."

"Yeah, I know." He shook his head, as if to clear it. "Maybe I'm crazy. We should probably rent out some of our land on the back forty acres and wait for the checks to roll in like everyone else. Micki's right. It would be great to put some money aside for the boys."

They drove along in silence for a few minutes, each lost in their own thoughts. Finally, the detective pointed through the windshield to a gray, prefabricated metal building on the right-hand side of the road. "There's Wellborne Industries."

Jo recognized the large "W" on the sign in front. Ron pulled the vehicle into the parking lot, passing a huge crane and a truck-wash bay. Several men working near the crane stopped what they were doing and watched them get out of Ron's truck. One of the men nudged the guy next to him and pointed in Jo's direction. He made a crude rocking gesture with his hips and the others laughed.

The detective followed her gaze. "Ignore those idiots. We've got a lot more men than women around here these days and it makes some of the guys forget their manners. You wouldn't believe some of the crap Micki has dealt with, just shopping in the grocery store." Jo thought about the driver in the SUV at the airport the previous night and felt a small tremor of apprehension.

Ron opened the door and followed Jo into the building's office space. A stern looking woman with rimless eyeglasses glanced up from her desk. "Morning, Ron. What brings you to our neck of the woods this morning? Finally decide to rent out some of your land?"

"Nah. Here on official business this morning, Marge." Marge turned to Jo and raised her eyebrow, as if noticing her for the first time. Jo pulled out her credentials. "I'm Special Agent Jo Schwann of the FBI. I'm here to see Jonathon Wellborne."

The woman tilted her head. "Must be pretty important to get an FBI agent all the way out here."

Ron said, "Is he in or not?"

"Yeah, he's in. Hang on a sec." The woman picked up the phone and placed a call. "Mr. Wellborne, Detective Ron Fischer and an FBI agent are here to see you. Should I send them in?"

After a moment, she spoke into the receiver, "They didn't say." Finally, she hung up the phone. "You can go in now. He's in the last office on the right."

When they entered the office, Jonathon Wellborne stood up to greet them. Although Jo had seen pictures of the founder of Wellborne Industries on the Internet, the photos hadn't done him justice.

Jonathon was a very attractive man. His casual dress shirt looked hand-tailored and he wore it with an ease that belied his humble beginnings in the Iron Range of Minnesota. He was fit and tall, almost the same height as the detective. There was only a hint of grey hair at his temples to suggest his fifty-five years.

He reached out a tanned hand to Jo. "Pleased to meet you. I'm Jonathon Wellborne."

Jo shook his hand. "Special Agent Jo Schwann. I believe you know Detective Ron Fischer?"

Wellborne turned his dazzling smile toward Ron. "Good to see you again, Detective." He shook his head, and chuckled a bit, as if a bit bewildered at their appearance in his office. "I have to say, this is a bit of a surprise. How may I be of service to you both?"

Jo spoke up. "I am looking into a couple of homicides and an attempted murder in St. Paul. We have reason to believe that one of your employees has some information that could help us in our investigation."

Jonathon raised an eyebrow. "What would a murder investigation in Minnesota have to do with our company?"

"The victim was filming a documentary about fracking. Do you recall meeting a young man by the name of Rick Wilson?"

The surprise on Jonathon Wellborne's face looked genuine, but he quickly straightened his features. Clearing his throat, he said, "Why, yes. I believe he was working on some project for a college class. I spoke with him briefly while his friend videotaped the interview. He asked several questions about the ethics of fracking and possible threats to the environment."

The detective said, "What did you tell him?"

"I told him the same thing I tell all our skeptics. We follow all state and federal regulations to the letter."

Jo said, "I understand your company filed an injunction against Mr. Wilson in an attempt to halt the documentary." She waited to see his reaction, hoping to shake him.

She was disappointed. Wellborne merely shrugged. "Our legal department sends those things out on a regular basis. I'm not usually involved unless the parties we're dealing with become more than just a nuisance. Most back off as soon as they hear from our legal team."

Jo tried again. "Speaking of federal and state regulations, we have a witness who indicated Mr. Wilson may have spoken with someone in your compliance department. May I assume we have your full cooperation in speaking to any of your employees?"

Jonathon Wellborne's smile did not reach his eyes. "Be my guest. We have nothing to hide. Marge will be happy to introduce you around."

He walked them to the door of his office. Just as they were about to leave, he said, "You know, fractivists never stop to wonder where the oil comes from that allows them to drive to protest rallies. The fact of the matter is, we live in a world that runs on oil, and until that changes, the world needs companies like ours. Just keep that in mind."

Jo noticed a muscle jumped in his jaw. She was satisfied to finally see a brief nick in the charming façade of the founder of Wellborne Industries.

***

The two woman working in the compliance department looked up as Marge entered the room with Jo and the detective. One of the women looked to be near retirement age, while the other couldn't have been older than her early twenties. Both of the women had been interrupted mid-stroke on their computer keyboards, and the younger one looked down at her hands, as if she had been caught doing something wrong.

Jo was disappointed there were only women in the department. Billy MacGregor had been clear he met with a man in the compliance area. However, she noticed a third, empty desk in the room and wondered about the previous occupant.

Marge indicated the older woman first. "This is Karen Rogers, our senior compliance officer." She then turned to the other woman. "And this is Kaitlin Weber, our compliance associate. Ladies, this is Detective Fischer and Special Agent Schwann. They have a few questions for you. Mr. Wellborne would like you to give them your full cooperation."

Jo almost missed the exchange of a brief, but meaningful, glance between Marge and Karen Rogers before the receptionist left the room. Kaitlin wiped her palms on her pants and Jo wondered what was making the young woman nervous.

Crossing her arms, Jo said, "We're here because we're investigating a couple of murders and an attempted murder. We have reason to believe one of the victims may have spoken with someone in your department recently."

Jo pulled out a picture of Rick Wilson. "Have you seen this person?"

Karen Rogers studied it carefully. "Yes, Mr. Wellborne asked me to share our reports with him. He glanced through our most recent state and federal reports."

She shrugged. "He asked me to explain some of the data to him, and seemed to be satisfied. I didn't meet with him after that first day, although I know he interviewed Mr. Wellborne a few more times." Karen looked at the photo of Rick Wilson again, and frowned. "He didn't have anything to do with the murders, did he?"

Jo said, "Rick Wilson is one of the victims."

Ms. Rogers said, "He seemed like such a nice kid. Is he...is he dead?"

Jo shook her head. "He's in critical condition, but he's holding his own so far."

The older woman said, "I'll add him to my prayers." Jo detected a note of insincerity in the woman's tone.

Detective Fisher turned to Kaitlin. "How about you, Miss? Did you meet with Rick Wilson?"

The young woman quickly looked away from the photo, but Jo thought she saw Kaitlin's eyes widen slightly. She shook her head and mumbled, "No. Karen said...um, she mentioned he was here; I think I had a doctor's appointment that day. Sorry."

Jo doubted the woman was telling everything she knew, and she would bet her next paycheck that Kaitlin recognized Rick Wilson. Jo walked over to Kaitlin's side of the desk and stood right next to her, hoping to rattle her further. Jo watched a flush creep up the woman's neck.

"I noticed there is an empty desk next to yours, Ms. Weber. Do you have an absent co-worker?"

Kaitlin Weber flinched and looked at Karen Rogers in desperation. The older woman responded. "It's only the two of us. All our reporting is computerized, so it's simple enough to handle on our own."

With the woman neatly side-stepping the question about the empty desk, Jo decided to drop the subject. She walked toward Karen Rogers. "I'd like to see the reports you shared with Mr. Wilson."

"Certainly."

They spent the next hour poring over the reports. Jo asked several questions, but in reality, she knew it was a fishing expedition. What she really wanted was more time to question Kaitlin Weber.

She was impressed with some of the questions Ron Fischer asked. He obviously had done his research, possibly because the data would impact the water quality in his back yard.

Finally, they packed up their notes and Jo thanked the women for their cooperation. They walked back toward the truck. Jo noticed a dark SUV parked next to Ron's truck. She could have sworn it was the same one she one she had seen at the airport, but black SUVs were ubiquitous, especially in northern states. She had been unable to see the license number the previous evening, so she couldn't be sure this was the same vehicle. There was no one in the SUV. This time, she made a mental note of the plate number.

Ron interrupted her thoughts. "Well, that was a bust. Could your informant have met with a compliance officer in another oil company?"

Shifting mental gears, Jo climbed back up into the truck cab and replied, "It's possible. But I'd like to know who used to sit at that extra desk."

The detective was silent for a moment. Finally, he said, "Did you notice Kaitlin Weber seemed a little squirrely?"

Jo smirked. "Oh, yes. She definitely knew more than she was saying." She dug through her bag and pulled out her cell phone to check for missed messages. When she did, a piece of paper fluttered to the floor by her boot.

She picked up the note and read it. Jo's heart sped up. "Looks like there may have been a good reason Kaitlin was acting squirrely. She must have slipped a note in my purse when we were looking over the data with Karen Rogers. Kaitlin wants to meet with us alone later today."

Chapter Twenty-Five

Turners Bend
Early January

CHIP WAS SO DEEP INTO his writer's zone that the ringtone on his cell barely registered. He finally realized the strains of "Call Me Maybe" were playing from his phone on the bedroom nightstand.

He raced to pick it up, saw it was from Jane and answered, "Hi, babe."

"Chip, come quickly. Two federal agents were just here and took Baba to the police station. They wouldn't tell me why. He was so frightened."

"Are they from immigration? Maybe he has a visa problem."

"No, they're from Homeland Security. He needs our help and I can't leave the clinic right now. Hurry."

Chip hung up, snatched his jacket off the hook by the back door and strode into the yard only to realize he had no vehicle. Ingrid had taken his new car and Jane the pick-up. "Crap."

He placed a call to Iver. "Iver, I need a ride to town. Are you busy?"

"No. With no snow I'm just sitting around here at the Bun eating beef stew with that strange Ethiopian bread Bernice is making for Baba. Is this about the government car I saw down by the clinic?"

"Yes, I'm afraid so."

"Be right there, buddy."

***

Hours later a shaken Baba sat on the living room couch, his walnut-colored face now ashen, ghost-like. Ingrid sat next to him clutching his hand, tears leaking from the corners of her eyes. Jane paced back and forth, trying to get the details from an almost hysterical Baba, as Chip observed. The scene was surreal to him, like something he would write in one of his novels. Surely this kind of thing didn't happen in real life, at least not real life in Turners Bend, Iowa.

"They asked me many questions about my brother and about my cellphone calls and emails with him," said Baba. "They asked me if I was ordering bomb-making materials and sending money to anti-American terrorists. They took my computer, my phone, even the clinic's computer. My life is over. I am a dead man."

Jane halted. "Look at me, Baba." The boy raised his head and stared intently at Jane. "You're over-reacting. You must remain calm. They are not going to find anything incriminating on your phone records or computer. There's nothing that will implicate you in wrong doing. I've overheard you begging Hakim to stop his political activities and use his education to help your people. I'll give evidence to that. They didn't take you into custody or arrest you. It was merely an interview about your brother."

Chip hesitated to speak. The Boston Marathon bombers came to mind. He could see how easily the feds would link the two brothers to terrorist activities, how Baba could find himself in deep trouble, even though he was innocent as a newborn puppy.

"No, Dr. Jane," Baba cried. "They will throw me in Guantanamo. I will be tortured. I will never see you or my family again. I must go, run away, hide. I will leave and try to cross into Canada."

In his third book Chip had written about the Boundary Waters, so he knew it would be almost impossible for Baba to navigate the lakes and sneak across the border. "Baba, you know the desert, but you know nothing of lakes and rivers and forests. You'll never make it. Plus, it'd be impossible for an almost seven-foot Ethiopian to hide anyplace. We have to come up with a better plan. Let us see what we can do to help. For now, just sit tight."

"How can I be tight, Sir, when I am falling apart?" said Baba.

***

Late that evening the Swanson-Collingsworth household was like the frayed end of a hot electrical wire. Ingrid and Baba sat whispering in the darkened living room, the muted HD TV flickering, casting an eerie aura on the scene. Jane and Chip were in the bathroom with the door shut, speaking in low voices.

Chip sat on the toilet seat watching Jane bathe. As she stepped out of the tub, his eyes ran over the petite, slender body of his wife. She had piled her red hair on top of her head and damp tendrils escaped and clung to her forehead and neck. A lovely Degas ballerina, he thought, as she began to dry herself.

Jane wrapped the towel around herself, tucking it in to secure it, and perched on the edge of the tub. "Chip, I'm scared for Baba. His fears may not be so farfetched after all. I can see how the government could assume he's guilty merely by association with his brother. If they only knew him; he's such a gentle sweet soul."

Jane put on her terrycloth robe. "Chip, you don't think he'll bolt, do you? And what about Ingrid? She's been to the Gunflint Trail twice with her church youth group. Would she be foolish enough to think she could get him out of the country? What are we going to do?"

Chip stood. "It's not what you know, it's who you know. You go to bed. I'll stay up tonight and keep a watch on Baba and Ingrid. First thing in the morning I'll call Agent Masterson. She doesn't work for Homeland Security, but I trust her. She'll get Baba out of this mess."

***

Chip managed to get everyone to go to their respective bedrooms to try to get some sleep. He brewed a pot of extra-strong coffee for himself and prepared to spend the night as a sentry. He booted up his laptop and read over the last couple of chapters he had written and began to make minor edits. After an hour he got up and put his ear to each of the bedroom doors.

He heard a soft whiffling sound from Jane, and he smiled because she repeatedly claimed she did not snore. He heard nothing at Ingrid's door and was relieved. Baba's room was not silent and Chip could hear mutterings in a language he did not recognize.

It was going to be a long night and Chip knew he would have to fight sleep. He drank another cup of coffee and ate a piece of cold pepperoni pizza he found in the refrigerator.

Hope for the best, but plan for the worst, he told himself. Not exactly the Boy Scout motto, but it seemed apropos for the situation.

Chapter Twenty-Six

Head Shot

Williston & Stanley, ND
Late October

Since they had some time before their scheduled meeting with Kaitlin Weber, the compliance associate from Wellborne Industries, Detective Ron Fischer drove Jo to the Williston police department. She noticed several things as soon as she entered the building. There was a constant buzz about the place, crowded with civilians and police officers. The other thing that was glaringly obvious was the majority of the officers looked to be younger than she.

When Jo pointed this out to the detective, he chuckled. "Yeah, I feel like the old man of the group. Most of the new hires aren't many days past their twenty-first birthday. If you hang around long enough, you'll find out most of them come from your home state."

"Really...why is that?"

"Looking to cash in on the oil patch money like everyone else. I hear the police department budgets are a lot tighter over in Minnesota. We can't hire them here fast enough."

"How do they do out in the field, when they're so young and inexperienced?"

The big man shrugged. "They don't stay green for long. One year here equals about five years everywhere else. I met a guy last week from International Falls, Minnesota, who is already the chief of police of Watford City at the ripe old age of twenty-eight. They take a lot of shit from the public about their age. You know, comments like 'What's this; take your kid to work day?' But I tell you, they have a lot thrown at them at once, so it doesn't take long to become a veteran. Drug busts, loaded weapon charges, domestic disputes, you name it, we've got it in spades."

Jo shook her head. "Crazy."

"You got that right."

While Ron went to his desk to catch up on work, Jo settled into the relatively quiet break room and checked her voice mail.

John had left her a message, and it gave her a warm feeling in the pit of her stomach, just to hear his voice again. It felt like she had been gone much longer than just a day. His recording said, "Hope you are making great progress in North Dakota and will be heading home soon. I've got some great news for you. Rick Wilson is out of his coma and is doing well."

Jo was excited to hear the news, but her enthusiasm was tempered by his next statement. "He isn't able to speak just yet, but can communicate in a rudimentary way for brief periods of time. I've already contacted Frisco, so I imagine he'll be on his way to the hospital by now." He had concluded the message by saying how much he missed her and hoped she was being careful.

The second voice mail was from Frisco. "Jo, you may have heard that Rick Wilson is out of his coma. I stopped by to see him, but he can't talk and falls asleep easily, so I'll try again in the next day or two. Haven't made much other progress on the case since you left, so hope you are having better luck."

Jo tried calling John, but received his voice mail. She left him a brief message and then listened to the rest of her voice mails. Just as she finished checking her emails, Detective Fischer returned to the break room and held out a cup of coffee to her. While she took a grateful sip, Ron said, "Any news out of the Cities on your case?"

Jo nodded. "The kid who was shot has come out of his coma. He isn't able to communicate well, but he seems to be aware of his surroundings."

"Well, maybe we'll get more information this afternoon after we meet with Ms. Weber."

He looked down at his watch. "Speaking of which, we should probably head out. Ms. Weber said to meet her at Joe's Pizza in Stanley, right? That's about seventy-five miles from here." He frowned. "She must have wanted to make sure no one saw her talking to us."

Jo stood up and grabbed her coat off the back of her chair. "That's what I was thinking."

***

The drive to Stanley was slow. The winds rushed across the plains and even Ron's heavy-duty truck was buffeted around when a particularly strong gust swept over the roads. The drizzle started about fifteen minutes into the drive, and Jo could see from the thermometer on the dash that the outside temperature had dropped into the lower thirties. The main highways weren't bad because the heat from the constant truck traffic kept them clear. However, the side roads were starting to get slick.

Ron grumbled, "Looks like it's gonna be a crappy night for trick-or-treating."

Several times during the drive, Jo glanced in the side view mirror, half expecting to see a black SUV following them. She eventually relaxed into the heated seat of the truck and kept her eyes on the traffic in front of them.

They drove past a large clump of buildings resembling long rows of trailers placed end to end. Jo asked, "Is that one of the man camps I keep hearing about?"

The detective's eyes briefly shifted from the road to where Jo was pointing. "Yeah. Hundreds of people live in them, mostly guys. I've been to several of them. They feel like a cross between an army barrack and a dormitory. They aren't too bad. They have cafeterias, pool tables and computer rooms. The oil companies provide them for their employees. Most have pretty strict rules about no booze, no guns and no visitors."

"Does it work?"

He looked at Jo out of the corner of his eye. "Pretty much, although there's always some jerk who likes to test the rules. Besides, there are plenty of other places where lonely, bored people can get into trouble, if you know what I mean."

They drove on in silence until the detective pulled into the parking lot of Joe's Pizza. The restaurant was crowded for lunch and the room smelled of pizza, beer and damp bodies. The majority of customers were male, and it seemed to Jo about half the heads in the room swiveled in their direction when she followed the hostess to their table.

Ron handed her a menu, and they were discussing which type of pizza to order, when the hostess brought Kaitlin Weber to their table.

Drops of rain shimmered on her coat and knit hat in which she had tucked up her pretty brunette hair. Jo could see she still wore her work clothes beneath her coat. Kaitlin was a very attractive young woman, but her brown eyes were sunken, as if she hadn't been sleeping well.

Kaitlin bit her lower lip and her eyes darted around the room. She quickly slid into the booth when Ron made room for her on his side of the table. Removing her coat, she tucked it into the space between them, but left the hat on her head.

Jo could tell by watching Kaitlin's nervous demeanor she was probably taking a huge risk in seeing them. Hence, the meeting in a neighboring town. She was grateful the young woman had screwed up the courage to reach out to them.

Kaitlin quietly studied the menu for a long time, and it seemed to Jo she was using the menu as a prop to put off their discussion. Jo reminded herself to be patient and wait for the young woman to start the conversation.

They ordered an extra-large pizza to split between them. While they waited for their order, Kaitlin was silent and picked at the napkin underneath her glass of soda. Finally, she took a deep breath and leaned forward. In a voice clearly not meant to be overheard, she said, "Sorry I was late. I told my boss Karen I was feeling bad, like I was coming down with the flu. She's a germaphobe, so it wasn't too hard to convince her, but I had to make it look good, you know?"

Jo said, "Thank you for agreeing to meet with us."

Kaitlin nodded. "I had to. You see, the empty desk next to mine belonged to Trevor. Trevor Wallace. He and Karen were the original employees of the compliance department. They hired me when they had more work than the two of them could handle alone."

The young woman's hand shook slightly as she paused and took a sip from her glass. "Trevor and I started dating about a year ago. We kept our relationship secret, because it's against company policy, you know?"

Jo nodded for her to continue. She noticed Kaitlin kept referring to Trevor in the past tense, but had learned a long time ago that sometimes it was best to let witnesses unspool their story at their own pace.

"We moved in together a couple of months ago, to save rent money. We both liked our jobs, until the first time Trevor noticed the amounts of arsenic in the local water supply were at levels above the EPA's maximum limits."

Jo leaned forward to make sure she didn't miss a word.

Kaitlin took another sip, and then continued. "He immediately went to Mr. Wellborne and told him. At first Mr. Wellborne seemed concerned, but asked Trevor not say anything to anyone else until he could review the data himself and he asked for copies of the reports."

Jo spoke up, "Did Mr. Wellborne do anything about the reports?"

Kaitlin shook her head. "No. Trevor waited and waited, but he was afraid to push it. Then the next month, the arsenic levels were even higher. I told him he should go talk to Mr. Wellborne again, and he did. At that point, Mr. Wellborne told Trevor he needed a favor from him." She abruptly stopped talking when the waitress came by with their pizza.

Jo thanked the waitress, but no one moved to grab a slice of pizza, as if they had forgotten why they had ordered it.

Jo prompted Kaitlin to continue, "What kind of favor?"

"He asked Trevor to falsify the data until he had time to correct the problem. He said he knew it was a lot to ask of Trevor, but it was a glitch he was working on. If they reported the correct findings, the government would put a stop to their drilling and they would lose a ton of money. Trevor reluctantly agreed. He thought Mr. Wellborne seemed truly concerned."

Ron spoke for the first time. "Why do I hear a 'but' coming?"

Kaitlin turned her attention to the detective. "But the arsenic levels continued to climb and Trevor had a hard time sleeping.

He began drinking heavily and we fought. Trevor felt he couldn't just quit his job, because, well....we needed the money. We both hated living in Williston and talked about moving away, once we had enough money put aside. Besides, if he quit, who would hire him? He knew Mr. Wellborne would have him blacklisted."

Jo guessed the next part, "So, when Rick Wilson and his camera guy came into town, it seemed like the perfect solution, right?"

Kaitlin's nodded. "How did you know?"

"Because a friend of mine met the camera man. He said that he and Rick talked to a whistleblower in the compliance department of a major oil company. That's why we came to your office in the first place. Do you know where they met and what Trevor shared with them?"

"Trevor told me they always met out of town." She gave them a small smile. "Sometimes they met here, as a matter of fact. That's why I thought of this place to meet you. Trevor smuggled out copies of the actual and falsified reports and passed them along to Rick Wilson."

"Did Trevor keep any copies of those reports at home?"

"No, he said it made him nervous to keep the copies around our apartment, like they were live snakes or something."

Ron spoke up. "Do you have access to the data at the office?"

She shook her head. "No. Only Karen and Trevor dealt with that detail. As an associate, my responsibility is data entry and sending the reports to the various state and federal agencies. I worked from the data they gave me. I never saw the original info."

They were silent for a moment, and then Jo gently asked, "Ms.Weber, where is Trevor now?"

Kaitlin's eyes filled, but her voice was flat. "He's dead."

Not surprised by the young woman's news, Jo nodded grimly. "I'm so sorry for your loss. What happened?"

Kaitlin sniffled and Ron handed her his napkin, which she used to dab her nose. "They say it was an accident. He pulled in front of a tanker truck, out on eighty-five. He was killed instantly. Trevor's truck caught fire before anyone could get him out."

Ron rubbed his chin. "I remember that case. I knew his name sounded familiar." He tilted his head, considering. "You don't believe it was an accident."

The young woman's jaw jutted out. "The investigators found a broken whiskey bottle in the wreckage and concluded Trevor was at fault. So many people had seen him drinking in the bars lately, so they said he must've been drunk at the time of the accident."

"But you don't believe it." Jo said this as a statement, not a question.

Kaitlin looked Jo in the eyes. "No. I know he was drinking heavily for a while, but that was before he met up with Rick Wilson. Once he could tell someone else about what was happening, it was as if a weight had been lifted off his shoulders. He was obviously nervous about being caught, but he believed the documentary would make a difference."

Kaitlin fidgeted with her mug for a bit, and Jo could tell there was more she had to say. After a moment, Jo prompted, "Any other reason you don't believe it was an accident?"

"Yeah. Something else weird happened the day of the accident."

Ron said, "What was that?

"When I got home from work, it looked like someone had carefully searched our apartment. Nothing too obvious, just a few things out of place, here and there, you know?" Kaitlin wiped her nose on the napkin again.

Jo said, "Anything missing?"

"No, not that I could see."

Kaitlin was silent for a moment and stared down at her glass. Finally, she raised her eyes to Jo and said, almost as an afterthought, "One more thing, though. A few days later, Karen and I got very big bonuses. Mr. Wellborne said it was because they decided not to replace Trevor and so we would be taking on additional duties."

She frowned. "It felt like hush money."

Chapter Twenty-Seven

Turners Bend
January

CHIP HAD NOT BEEN ABLE to keep awake on his sentry post the night Baba was questioned by Homeland Security. He laid his head on the kitchen table to rest at about 4:00 a.m. and woke with a start almost two hours later. When his head came up, he was looking directly into the face of an animal sensing his predator...Baba.

Chip stretched his stiff neck and wiped drool from his mouth with the back of his hand. "Baba, how long have you been sitting there?"

"A long time, Sir. I did not want to wake you. I do not sleep."

Baba was a pitiful sight and Chip couldn't help but share in the Ethiopian's anxiety. "Listen, Agent Masterson is back in Chicago. I have her phone numbers," he said, showing Baba the business card lying on the table. "We can trust her. She's one of the good guys, Baba."

"If you say so, Sir. I will put my life in your hands."

The onus of that remark came down on Chip like a mantle of heavy metal. It was a responsibility unlike anything he had ever experienced...a man's fate placed in his hands. He gulped. "Okay, I'll put my phone on speaker so you can hear."

Chip punched in Agent Masterson's cell number and she answered immediately. "Collingsworth, what's up?"

Caller ID always threw Chip. No greeting. No announcing who's calling. He stumbled through the beginning of the call. "This is...well, I guess you know who this is. I, I mean, we were wondering if you could give us some help. I have Baba here; you met him here at Christmas."

Masterson interrupted, "Cut to the chase, Chip. I haven't got all day. I assume Baba is in trouble. What's his nationality again?"

"I am Ethiopian," said Baba in an overly-loud voice.

"Okay, shoot," she said.

Between the two of them Chip and Baba told the agent the story of yesterday's visit from Homeland Security, adding that Baba was totally innocent of any wrongdoing.

"Homeland Security goes off half-cocked sometimes, but in this case I can understand why they are questioning Baba. I know some of the Homeland Security guys. Let me get as much intel as I can, then I'll pull rank and take the lead in this investigation. I'll be in Turners Bend at seventeen hundred hours. Keep a low profile until I arrive. If any of the Homeland guys come snooping around, Chip, tell them to contact me."

***

Jane went to the clinic. She had year-end reports to finish for the Iowa Agriculture Department and also wanted to file a glowing evaluation of Baba's performance with the Iowa State Veterinary School. "I'm hoping my report will strengthen his case," she said. "I can't think of anything else to do while we wait for Agent Masterson."

At Jane's insistence Ingrid went to school. "You can skip your afterschool cello lesson, but you have to go to classes today, Ingrid. Semester mid-terms are next week." Ingrid put up an argument, but lost out in the end. Both Jane and Ingrid agreed to act as normally as possible and to keep mum about Baba.

It was a long day for Baba and Chip. They kept their ears attuned to sounds of vehicles, anxious to talk with Agent Masterson and fearful the Homeland Security guys might seek Baba out for more questioning. Chip worked a little, but couldn't keep his mind on Jo and John. He finally joined Baba in the living room, and they watched daytime TV for hours…game shows, soaps, judge shows, talk shows. They took a break for a lunch of grilled cheese sandwiches.

In the afternoon, Chip challenged Baba to a game of Mancala, the African stone game. "In my country, we call it *Bao la Kiswahili*. As a child we just dug pits in the earth and used stones or seeds. We did not have a fine wooden set like this one," he told Chip.

Over the past two months various family members and friends had played the game with Baba. It was a relatively simple game, but somehow no one had beaten the young Ethiopian.

After losing three games, Chip asked, "Why is it that none of us can beat you at this game? What's your secret?"

"You must plan your moves ahead. That is my strategy."

"How far ahead do you plan them?"

A shy smile crept onto Baba's serious face. "From the first move to the last."

Ingrid returned from school and replaced Chip at the game. Of all his opponents, she had become his most competitive challenger.

Chip returned to his computer and to Jo and John. He was attempting to escape to another time and place…a place of his own making, where he could control the outcomes. Writing was becoming a refuge for him; it was no longer a chore. It was what he wanted to do with his life. Lately he entertained thoughts of writing a piece of literary fiction, his great American novel. For now, however, he was a crime writer with half a book done.

Chip was deep into his writing when he heard Ingrid's voice. "Hey look, Dad. It's snowing again."

It wasn't the snow that got Chip's attention; it was being called "Dad" for the first time in his life. He didn't know what to make of it. Was it an unconscious slip of the tongue or did it have a more significant meaning for his relationship with his step-daughter? Whichever, it caused a lump to form in his throat and left him momentarily speechless. He joined Ingrid at the living room window and put his arm causally around her shoulders as they gazed at the fat clumps of flakes floating down like fairies. Within seconds the downfall increased and the wind picked up; a layer of snow covered the grass and the roof of the pole barn.

"This reminds me of the day Runt's mother came to my door," Chip said. "It started out with a few flakes and turned into a blizzard."

"I miss Honey, don't you?" asked Ingrid. "She was a special dog."

"Yes, champ, I miss her very much. If it wasn't for her, maybe I would never have met your mother and you and Sven."

The phone chimed, breaking their reverie. It was Jane telling them she was on her way home and that Iver had reported the roads were already slippery and a heavy snow was on the way.

"Drive carefully, love. The three of us will make an attempt at fixing dinner and have it waiting for you."

Chip had no sooner disconnected from Jane, when his phone rang again. This time it was Agent Masterson reporting that she was delayed by weather and would not be in Turners Bend until the next morning.

Chip turned to Ingrid. "Tell Baba he has a reprieve until the morning and then the two of you can join me in the kitchen. We'll make something hearty for dinner and have a cozy evening by the fire."

Chip phone chirped, indicating he had a text message. It was from Detective Franco in Minneapolis. It read: *Planning to visit TB next week.*

Chip was curious about Franco's reason for coming to Turners Bend again. If it was something about his drive-by shooting or Finnegan's murder, Franco surely wouldn't have to make a trip to Turners Bend. He texted back to the detective: *What's up?*

The reply was simply: *More later.*

***

By the time Jane got home, Chip had a pot of chili simmering and Ingrid was taking corn bread muffins out of the oven. Baba had produced a roaring fire in the fireplace, and Runt and Callie were hogging the warmth emanating from the blaze.

"Boy, am I glad to be home. The roads are treacherous. We may be snowed in tomorrow morning. I can't believe how much snow has fallen in the past hour," reported Jane. "What smells so good?"

"Chili and corn bread with honey. And I found all the ingredients for making S'Mores for dessert," said Ingrid. "Can you believe Baba has never had S'Mores?"

Despite having Baba's predicament hanging over their heads, the household had a quiet, relaxing evening, snug in their home, while the first winter storm of the season howled outside and the snow piled up. Baba and Ingrid went to bed, and Jane and Chip snuggled on the couch with snifters of hot brandy in their hands.

"Jane, something happened today and I don't know what to think about it. Ingrid called me Dad."

Jane put her head on his shoulder, but said nothing.

"I know it's probably not some big breakthrough, but it did make me feel good. I never wanted to have kids and now, well, I sort of do. And someday, I want to be a grandfather. What do you say, Granny?"

Jane laughed, but then become very pensive. "I'm missing Sven, probably much more than he's missing us." She sighed.

"Let's call him and see what he's up to. I want to hear more about his trip to Williston."

They placed the call, but got Sven's voice mail box. "He's been sending me some text messages with observations for my story," said Chip. "He told me the oil fields are not a good place to meet girls. Well, those weren't exactly his words, but I got the picture," Chip said with a chuckle.

Jane's mood seemed to darken. "This conversation is making me think about Hal and thinking about him is still so frightening and painful. He is Ingrid and Sven's father. He must miss them and want to be part of their lives, and yet he has messed up big time and in doing so has caused his children so much heartache. Imagine not knowing where your father is and wondering if he is safe or in danger or possibly even dead. Or worse, that he is trying to harm you."

As rocky as his relationship had been at times with his own father, Chip could not imagine a life without him. Now that his Old Man was an old man, he loved him more than ever.

"Do you still love him, Jane?" This thought had suddenly occurred to Chip and the question popped out without forethought.

"Heavens, no. I stopped loving him a decade ago. Right now I'm just glad my children have you in their lives." Jane took Chip's face into her hands and smiling sweetly, kissed him. "I know I have kept you out of their parenting, but I now see how much my children need you. And as for me, my dear one, I feel pretty darn lucky to be married to a guy who can make a mean pot of chili."

Chapter Twenty-Eight

Head Shot

Williston, ND & Minneapolis, MN
Late October

As Jo Schwann and Detective Ron Fischer drove back to Williston, the earlier drizzle shifted to light snow. Jo was mesmerized by eddies of snow that waltzed across the highway in front of them. She was deep in thought about their conversation with Kaitlin Weber, the compliance associate at Wellborne industries.

She was startled out of her musings when the detective sighed. "Damn. Guess I'll be opening the Trevor Wallace accidental death file again."

Jo nodded. "After what Kaitlin Weber told us about Trevor passing the compliance documents from Wellborne Industries over to Rick Wilson, it sounds a little too coincidental he died in a traffic accident."

"Think she's in danger?"

Jo looked at the detective for a moment. He had just given voice to her thoughts. "Maybe. She said they tried to keep their relationship a secret at work, but they were living together. Kaitlin thought someone had searched their apartment, so obviously someone knew about their relationship."

The detective nodded. "I'll keep an eye on her."

"Think you can investigate Trevor Wallace's death without a lot of people knowing? If it wasn't an accident, then it would look suspicious if the case is re-opened just after I came to town, asking questions. Which in turn...."

Ron finished her statement, "Would draw attention to who might have told us to look in that direction, meaning someone in the compliance department."

"Exactly."

"I'll figure something out." He was silent for a moment. "So, where do you go from here?"

"I think I've done about all I can do here, for now." She glanced at the dashboard clock. "Maybe I can still grab a flight back to the Cities tonight. I hate to take advantage of your hospitality any more than I already have, but would you mind taking me to the airport after we pick up my things from your house?"

Ron smirked. "Not a problem. I'm not itching to get back to the stack of files on my desk."

They were both quiet for the remainder of the drive back to the detective's ranch. As they neared the driveway, Jo noticed a black SUV parked near the mailbox. Jo couldn't tell if it was the same vehicle she had seen previously, but her gut told her it was. The SUV drove off, tires spitting gravel behind it. She squinted, getting a look at the license plate.

"Ron, I've seen that vehicle before." She quickly told him about having seen the same SUV at the airport and at Wellborne Industries.

The detective's eyes narrowed. "The airport, huh? There were only a few people in my office who even knew you were coming. The captain, me and a few others….Shit, my family!"

Without saying another word, he put the truck in gear and sped down the driveway. The vehicle had barely jerked to a stop in front of the garage when he jumped out and ran through the open front door.

Yanking her gun out of her holster, Jo followed him into the living room. Before reaching him, she heard the big man roar, "No!" He fell to his knees in front of the prone bodies of his wife and sons. They were laid out neatly, side-by-side on the cheerful rug in front of the fireplace hearth. A plastic witch's caldron full of candy sat undisturbed next to Micki.

Jo rushed over and knelt alongside the detective. Ron had both hands wrapped around his bald head, as if trying to keep it from coming apart. His cries of despair yanked at Jo's heart.

Glancing around to make sure there was no threat, she set her gun on the floor by her knees and frantically searched Micki's neck for a pulse. Relief crashed through her body as she felt the faint, but rhythmic heartbeat of the detective's wife. Grabbing his arm, she said, "She's alive, Ron. She's alive. Here, check for yourself." Jo guided his hand to Micki's neck.

He released a choking sob and pulled his wife into his arms. Jo rushed over to check on the boys. A part of her brain registered that all three wore their super hero costumes and there was a smear of chocolate on the cheek of the youngest boy, Jacob. When she was satisfied they were all breathing, she looked at Ron. "They're alive, too. Thank God."

Jo noticed a white cloth sticking out from beneath Michael's shoulder. Bringing it up to her nose, she detected a slightly sweet, antiseptic smell. Instantly, she felt woozy and threw the cloth away from her. Just then, she saw a typed note propped up on the coffee table. A shiver went down her spine as she read, "Leave it alone, or next time they'll die."

Pulling out her cell phone, she dialed 911.

***

As the paramedics checked the vital signs of Ron Fischer's family, he turned haunted eyes to Jo. "Someone used chloroform on them. Who would do that? They're just little boys...."

The detective had aged ten years in the last hour. She felt responsible for the threat against his family. If she hadn't come to town, maybe none of this would have happened. She replied, "It was a warning for us to back off."

Ron nodded and his voice was gravelly when he spoke, "I think it's time for you to head back to the Cities."

Jo shook her head. "No way. These guys win if I leave now, I can't..."

His grip on her arm was like a vice. "And we're all at risk if you stay. If Wellborne is behind this, he has resources you've never dreamed of."

Ron released her arm. "It looks like someone in my department may be involved. Let me handle this my way. I'll trace the license plate number from the SUV, although I'm sure the guy has long since ditched it."

Jo bit her lower lip. "But what about you and your family, Ron? It's too dangerous for them here."

His response was steely. "I'll be fine. I'll send Micki and the boys to her mother's house in South Dakota. I'm going to find the son-of-a-bitch who did this."

He left her standing in the living room to follow his family in the ambulance. Jo thought about what was unspoken between them. What if the guy in the black SUV had not stopped with the chloroform...what if he had killed them instead?

Her thoughts turned toward her future with John. She couldn't imagine coming home to the scene Ron had just witnessed. Is this what it would be like for her...always wondering if her own family would be safe from the criminals she dealt with on a daily basis?

She hadn't even told John about the baby yet. She wondered how John would take the news. Would he be excited or scared, or both like she was?

Jo pulled out her phone and called for a taxi.

***

It had been a long day for Dr. John Goodman and he rubbed the aching muscles in his neck. He had checked on Rick Wilson one last time for the day. He decided he would stop on the way home and get a few laps of swimming in at the pool at the University of Minnesota in Minneapolis. He hadn't been in the water for over a week and could tell his body had missed the workout. Running was great, but it didn't work out the kinks in his neck like the rhythmic strides of swimming.

The drive to the "U" - as the locals called it - was short in terms of actual miles, but with all the road construction on campus for the new light-rail extension, John found it frustrating to wind his way through all the detours. He finally snagged a parking place and hopped out of his SUV. Just as he reached in to pull out his workout bag, he heard someone calling out to him.

"Doctor Goodman?"

John straightened and turned to the source of the voice. He saw a heavyset man with a full head of dark hair raise his hand in greeting. John was surprised to see Glenn Oates, a friend from his med school days.

"Glenn? What the hell are you doing here, buddy?"

His old friend's face lit up and he wrapped John in a bear hug. They clapped each other on the back and then each took a small step backwards.

Glenn said, "I'm Associate Professor of Neurosurgery here at the U. We moved here a couple of years ago. I'd heard you were in town and I've been meaning to look you up. Jeez, how long has it been?"

"Too long, I'd say. How are Sheri and the kids?"

"The same. Keeping me out of trouble."

John chuckled, "Now that's a full-time job, if I remember correctly."

Glenn smiled. "Hey, do you have some time? Why don't we grab a cup of coffee? I'm between classes."

"Lead the way." John returned his workout bag to the back seat, locked the car and fell in step beside Glenn.

After they settled into a booth in a local cafe with two steaming mugs of coffee in front of them, Glenn said, "So, whatcha been up to and how the heck did you end up in Minnesota? Last I heard, you were giving speeches all over the world and saving lives."

John smiled. "It's a long story, but the short version is that I met a wonderful woman and we're engaged." He thought about how great it was to share his news with an old friend.

Glenn whistled. "I never thought I'd see the day John Goodman would fall in love. You were the guy that never took relationships too seriously, breaking all the women's hearts." He shook his head, "And she managed to convince you to give up your practice in Baltimore and settle in flyover country? Must be quite a woman."

"She is. Truthfully I never thought I'd ever have someone in my life like you have Sheri. But I've never been happier."

Glenn tilted his head, as if considering something. "You know....I was just in a staff meeting. The U is looking for a new medical school dean and vice president for health services. You'd be perfect, you know."

John frowned. "Oh, I don't know...."

His friend interrupted, "They're looking for someone who's a leader in his field and you certainly fit that bill. You've not only taught at Johns Hopkins, but you've lectured around the world. That kind of presence brings in big research dollars."

He leaned forward, and John felt a hard sell coming. "Besides, I read in the paper yesterday about how you saved that college kid's life. It's how I knew you were back in town, as a matter of fact. That surgery was nothing short of brilliant. It made the national news."

John felt a flush creep up his neck. "Look, I'm flattered. However, I'm just getting settled here and I'm not cut out to be a dean."

"Well, tell me you'll at least consider it. I'd love to float your name past the board. They'll be very impressed, trust me."

John nodded. "Okay, I'll think about it. But I'm not promising anything. There's a lot to be considered. My current career for starters."

His old friend's face beamed. "Excellent."

.Chapter Twenty-Nine

Turners Bend
January

ON THE MORNING AFTER the snowstorm, the clock radio came on at 6:00 a.m. The announcer was reading school closings. "Ames public and private two hours late, Boone closed, Ogden closed, Perry closed, Roland-Story Community on plowed roads only…"

Jane stirred beside Chip. "It looks like none of us are going anywhere this morning," she said. "Let's make pancakes and bacon and hunker down until Iver gets the roads plowed."

"Sounds good to me, but this storm is only prolonging the agony for Baba. I don't suppose Agent Masterson made it to Turners Bend. Did you hear it howling last night? I wonder how much snow we got."

Jane and Chip got out of bed and put on their robes and slippers. Jane peeked into Ingrid's room. "No school today, honey. I'm making pancakes. You can stay in bed until they are ready."

"Yahoo, no biology test today." Ingrid rolled over and pulled the covers over her head.

Chip knocked on Baba's door, and when he received no answer, he opened it a crack and stuck his head into the room. In the dim light he could see the bed was made. He opened the door wider and surveyed the room. No Baba. His heart sunk.

"Jane, Baba's gone," he whispered. They searched the whole house and did not find him. Returning to Ingrid's room to question her about Baba's whereabouts, they found her at her window looking out into the early morning light. She turned and smiled when she heard them enter.

"Look," she said. "Baba's outside making a snowman. It's the tallest one I've ever seen."

***

An hour later, after they had consumed buckwheat pancakes with maple syrup, bacon and hot chocolate, Chip's phone sang out with his new ringtone, Bruno Mars this time. It was Agent Masterson and Chip spoke with her briefly.

"That was Agent Masterson," he announced. "She is stuck in Des Moines but hopes to make it to Turners Bend this afternoon. Homeland Security is pissed with her and they want Baba in custody. As soon as we can, we'll have to take him to the police station to wait until she arrives and can sort out this mess."

The call broke the snug, cozy atmosphere of a snow day at home. Gloom returned and the four of them dressed and sat around, their ears straining for the sound of Iver's snowplow. It came too soon, and they all headed for town, Chip riding with Iver to keep him company and Jane driving Baba and Ingrid, who insisted on going along.

The Turners Bend City Hall was an old stone edifice built by the Works Progress Administration in the 1930s. The front entrance led to the administration offices run with pride and efficiency by City Clerk Flora Fredrickson. The back entrance led to the police department, staffed by the chief, his deputy and a dispatcher.

With the addition of Chip, Jane, Baba and Ingrid, the front office area was crowded. With not enough chairs to go around, Baba and Chip stood, while Jane took the seat vacated by Deputy Anderson. They waited silently.

"Anyone want a cup of the swill we call coffee around here?" asked the chief.

They all passed. "Just as well," he said. "Just heard that Agent Masterson is on her way, she should be here soon."

A few moments later, in strode Agent Masterson and within seconds there was no mistaking who was in charge. She looked up at Baba from her five-foot two height to his six-foot ten, and addressed him in her professional persona, "Mr. Dibaba, I understand you have a problem."

Stark terror emanated from Baba's face. "*Ow...*I mean yes."

"Please be advised I speak Amharic plus several other African dialects. Now, Chief, please take this young man into your office. I suggest the rest of you wait at the Bun or some other suitable location."

"Wait," said Chip. "We have not had time to get legal counsel for Baba. I request to be his advocate during this questioning."

The agent gave Chip a stern look and shook her head. "Chip, you try me at times. It is highly irregular, but under the circumstances and knowing what I have to say to him, you may stay. The chief will be in attendance also. The rest of you, out."

Masterson took the chair behind the chief's desk and indicated to the other three to take the chairs in front of her. She removed a thick file folder from her briefcase and opened it. She started with a series of questions about Baba's name, birth place and date, and student visa status. These questions seem to ease Baba's tension, that is, until she asked about his family.

"I see your mother is deceased and your father resides in Afra. You have one brother named Hakim, who is associated with the Wabbabi Muslim movement, correct?" At this question Baba dropped his eyes and murmured his assent. His body stiffened, as if preparing for an assault.

Agent Masterson consulted her notes again. "While delayed in transit, I went over all the data from the file Homeland Security has amassed on you. There is nothing to connect you to your brother Hakim's activities. It is clear you are exactly who you say you are and you are concerned about your brother but you deplore his current actions in your homeland. I am not going to take you to the FBI office in Omaha for detainment, as I had originally planned."

Chip realized he had been holding his breath and released a puff of air. Likewise Baba's body seemed to deflate and shrivel, the tension oozing out.

She paused. "However, you will be on Homeland Security's watch list from now on. I'm sorry there is nothing I can do to stop that. When your student visa expires, you must return to Ethiopia, and I doubt you will ever be able to enter this country again. I know it seems unfair, and I couldn't agree with you more. Do you understand?"

Tears began to creep down Baba's face. He nodded and turned to Chip. Chip put his arm around the young man's shoulders. The chief cleared his throat, belying his emotional reactions to the situation.

"There is one more thing, Baba, if I may call you that," said the agent. "Things may be more favorable for you if you agree to pass along information about your brother's activities to federal agencies. We know that he has communicated with someone in central Iowa. We don't know who or why and that information would be very helpful. And, by the way you two," pointing to the chief and Chip, "that is privileged information."

"Baba, do you understand what Agent Masterson is asking you to do? It's called being an informant," said Chip.

"Yes, I understand, but I swear on my mother's grave I don't know anything. And, above all else, he is my brother. Right or wrong, I could never do anything that would cause him harm."

The agent softened her voice. "I understand, Baba, but I had to ask. Now go home and get some rest, you look exhausted."

She stood. "Chief, I need to get down to the bottom of this connection between Hakim Dibaba and someone in Iowa. Looks like I'll be extending my stay in Turners Bend."

Agent Masterson closed Baba's file, then turned her attention to Chip. "Detective Franco is due here soon, although this weather may be delaying him. When he arrives we have a proposition for you, a plan to verify if Hal Swanson is in the area and attempting to do you harm."

"With all this turmoil about Baba, Hal has been off my radar. There have been no signs of him, no trouble at all. I seriously doubt he's in the area."

Masterson looked as if she was going to say something, but hesitated and seemed to reconsider. "I'll call you when Franco arrives."

***

Chip knew he was in for another sleepless night. The parting conversation with Agent Masterson was playing over and over again in this mind. It was obvious to him that she was not sharing some information about Hal's whereabouts.

Does this mean Hal really is in the area? Why is Franco involved? None of this is making any sense to me.

Chapter Thirty

Head Shot

Minneapolis & St. Paul, MN
Late October/Early November

Jo SLOWLY DROVE DOWN THE winding streets to her house in the Tangletown area of South Minneapolis. Most of the houses had jack-o-lanterns on their front steps, as well as cobwebs, tombstones and even a ghost or two, in the form of bed sheets hanging from the trees.

She had been able to catch a late afternoon flight and stopped at a twenty-four hour pharmacy before heading to the house. Unable to wait another minute, she ducked into the store's restroom to use the pregnancy test.

Now on the way home, she wondered how she would tell John they were going to have a baby. Jo was excited, but nervous, too. *What if he isn't happy about our news?*

She took one hand off the steering wheel and placed it lightly on her stomach. *How on earth can I be a mother and an FBI agent, and be good at both?* Jo had no illusions about the safety of her chosen profession. She had certainly been in some dangerous spots. They *both* had been, for that matter. *Is it fair to bring this child into the world when I take risks on a regular basis?*

Thoughts swirled around her head like the discarded Halloween candy wrappers that tumbled in the wind across the neighborhood lawns.

***

A few hours later, she and John sat at the table in the kitchen. Several Chinese take-out containers were open in front of them. Jo was quiet, picking at the Szechuan Spicy Beef and rice on her plate.

John leaned back in his chair and swirled the wine in his glass. "Don't you like the food...too spicy?"

"No, I guess I ate too much earlier in the day."

She sensed he was still studying her. After a moment, he said, "Jo, what's going on? You've been a million miles away since you got home." His brows came together. "Is it this case?"

Jo looked at John and took a deep breath. She released it slowly, silently counting to ten before she said, "I'm pregnant."

John jumped up from the chair. His wineglass clinked against his plate and the red wine spilled out of the overturned glass. She looked up. In his eyes she saw shock and something else she couldn't identify.

"Of all the things I thought you might say that was not one of them. I...I was afraid you were having second thoughts about getting married." He fumbled with his napkin and quickly sopped up the spill. Jo stood up to help, glad to have something to occupy her for a moment while she processed his reaction.

She tried to catch his eye as he wiped down the table, but he was looking downward, focusing on his task. What had she seen in his face? Was he excited or upset? She wished he would say something more, anything that would let her know how he was feeling. She couldn't seem to push any more words past her suddenly dry throat, and so she waited for him.

When he spoke again, his voice was hoarse. He dropped the red-stained napkin onto his plate and smacked the heel of his palm against his forehead. "What the hell am I doing?" He reached for Jo and pulled her against him.

Jo felt his breath stir her hair as he spoke. "My God, Jo. I don't think I could ever feel...I mean, are you sure?"

He pulled slightly away from her, and she looked up into his face. Jo finally saw what she had hoped to see...excitement.

Jo felt a grin form itself on her lips and nodded. "Pretty sure. I picked up one of those home-pregnancy kits. It was positive, but I haven't seen my doctor yet."

John said, "I've heard those home tests are surprisingly accurate. Well, our first order of business is to get you in to see a doctor as soon as possible. I know you already have an OB/GYN, but let me check around. We need the best."

As he pulled her close once more, Jo buried a contented smile in his sweater. Having experienced his fiercely protective nature before, she knew he would be doubly so now that she carried their child. At some point, she'd probably chafe at his precautions, but for now, she snuggled closer to him. She could feel the pounding of his heart against her cheek. It seemed like the rhythm of his heart matched hers.

He said, "Any idea how far along you are?"

She blushed slightly, embarrassed that she didn't know her own body better. "I'm not quite sure...two, three months, maybe? I've never been particularly, uh, regular." Even though John was her fiancé and a doctor, it felt odd having this personal discussion with him. She continued, "I'm thinking the flu I had earlier in the fall wasn't the flu after all."

His arms wrapped tightly around her. After they were silent for a few moments, she felt a slight tension in his body. He stepped back and reached out to hold both of her hands in his. His touch was warm and reassuring. "Jo, how do *you* feel about having a baby? This isn't something we've discussed...or planned, for that matter."

As his blue eyes bored into hers, Jo took a minute to respond, knowing her answer to his question would be a turning point in their relationship. However, she felt he deserved an honest answer.

Would she ever stop having just a bit of doubt? She still wasn't sure what a baby would mean for her career; it was something she would need to check into at work. She dreaded telling her boss.

Having a baby would change so much about her relationship with John. Would it make it stronger or tug them in too many directions, something they already had problems with in their respective jobs?

And what about the real dangers inherent in her job? The image of Ron Fisher sobbing over the prone bodies of his family came to mind and she shook her head, to rid herself of the memory.

Jo wished for the twentieth time since she had first seen the plus sign on the home pregnancy test kit that her mother was still alive. Caroline Schwann had succumbed to cancer when Jo was in elementary school. Her father had done a great job acting as both mother and father to her before he had passed, but she had no idea how to be a parent.

John squeezed her hand lightly. She could see the concern etched in his features. "Jo, say something."

She reached up and stroked his cheek. "I've never been more excited *and* scared in my life."

Jo felt tears coming, and glanced away. In a quiet voice, she continued, "I can't wait to be the mother of your child. But I...I don't have a clue how to do this."

John's bark of laughter shocked her into looking up. "Do you think anyone does? We've got seven months or so to figure this out. Together."

He pulled her close once more. "You are going to be a wonderful mom. And I'm going to do my best to keep up."

***

On the first day of November, Jo made it a point to visit Rick Wilson before heading into work. She thought it was about time she met the young man who was at the center of their investigation.

When she entered his hospital room, she saw an older woman sitting in the chair next to the bed. Rick Wilson's eyes were closed and she saw the light rise and fall of his chest as he slumbered. Jo offered her hand to the woman and spoke in a quiet voice. "Hello. My name is Special Agent Jo Schwann. You must be Caroline Wilson. I'm involved in the investigation into the shooting of your son."

The woman's brown eyes widened, probably surprised Jo knew who she was. Jo quickly explained, "I'm a...friend of Doctor Goodman. He's told me a lot about you."

Jo pulled up a chair, wincing when it scraped the floor. "I'd like to talk with your son when he wakes up, if that's okay with you. How is he doing?"

Caroline replied, "He slept through the night. I find myself wanting to wake him up to make sure he's alright." Her smile was wry. "I haven't done that since he was an infant."

At that moment, Rick Wilson's eyes fluttered opened. He looked at his mother and offered a weary smile. He turned his head toward Jo and blinked a few times at her. She stood up. "Good to see you, Mr. Wilson. I'm with the FBI and I've been assigned to your case. I'd like to ask you a few questions, if you feel up to it."

The young man glanced at his mother before he nodded.

Jo said, "I understand you've been talking to Detective Mike Frisco, my colleague. I know he's asked you some of these questions before, but I thought maybe some of the details might be coming back to you. Do you remember anything at all about the night of the shooting?"

Rick Wilson slowly shook his head, his eyes showing his frustration. She continued, "Anything at all about the days leading up to the shooting?"

Again, the young man shook his head, more vigorously this time. Jo went through a few more questions, disappointed he didn't remember anything more that would help with the investigation.

Finally, Jo took a deep breath and stole a quick look at Rick's mother. Jo knew her final order of business was going to be hard on them both, but especially Rick.

Turning her attention back to Rick, she said, "I have some news for you that will be hard to hear. I'm afraid your friend Billy MacGregor is dead. I'm so sorry for your loss."

Rick's mouth formed an "o" of horror. His eyes filled with tears and his hand folded into a fist, and he hit the side rail of his bed. Caroline Wilson hopped out of her seat and grabbed at her son's arm, trying to keep him from ripping out his intravenous lines.

Jo felt sick to her stomach. She hadn't wanted to break the news of Billy's death to his friend, but felt that he had a right to know. Once Caroline had calmed her son down, he rasped, "Murdered?"

Jo simply nodded.

Rick closed his eyes and tears rolled down his cheeks.

***

A few hours later, Jo sat at her desk at the FBI headquarters building in Brooklyn Center, Minnesota. She caught up on all the mail and emails that had piled up in the short time she had been in North Dakota.

Just as she was about to step out to grab a Greek yogurt out of the refrigerator down the hall, her phone buzzed on her desk.

"Special Agent Schwann."

She immediately recognized the voice on the other end of the phone. "It's Detective Fischer. Did you make it back to the Cities in one piece?"

Jo sat back in her chair. "No problem at all. How's your family?"

His gravelly response sounded in her ear. "Fine. My mother-in-law is spoiling the boys and my wife is ready to strangle her, but other than that, they're safe. Thank God."

Jo let out a puff of air. "Glad to hear it. Did Micki remember anything about their attacker?"

"She said a short guy came to the door, wearing a Batman costume. He rang the doorbell and yelled 'Trick or Treat', so she opened the door, thinking it was a teen-ager getting an early start on the candy run. The last thing she remembered was opening the door."

Jo whistled. "Gutsy move. Any luck tracing the plates of the SUV?"

"Yes. I tracked it to a mom-and-pop hotel about forty miles out of town. Found a guy inside one of the rooms, dead from an apparent drug overdose."

"Damn. Are you sure it was the same guy who went after your family?"

The detective's voice was flat. "Yeah, I found the Batman costume shoved under the bed. His name was James Carson, a low-level thug with a mile-long rap sheet for domestic assault, petty theft, you name it."

Jo thought about seeing the SUV in the parking lot when they went to interview Jonathon Wellborne. "Any connection between him and Wellborne Industries?"

"Funny you should mention that. I checked into the accident report of our dead compliance officer, Trevor Wallace. Guess who was driving the tanker truck that hit him?"

"James Carson."

"Oh, yeah. In the report Carson said Trevor Wallace pulled out in front of him, but he couldn't slam on the brakes in time, so it was recorded as an accident."

Jo's mind jumped ahead. "Let me guess, he was driving a Wellborne Industries tanker."

Ron's voice rumbled through the phone. "Winner, winner, chicken dinner. However, there is no proof that Trevor Wallace's death wasn't accidental. People saw him drinking in a bar an hour before the crash."

Jo sighed. "Pretty convenient Carson died just as we were getting close to him. Damn, what is it with this case? Every time we get close to someone who knows something, they end up dead. We need to make sure Trevor's girlfriend Kaitlin is safe. If we were watched, she could be in serious danger."

"Way ahead of you. I had my cousin Tommy pick her up. She's staying with his family until this blows over. He's ex-Navy Seal. He'll keep her safe."

She was surprised. "Is there a reason you don't have someone from your department watching her?"

The silence on the line lasted so long Jo wondered if they had lost the connection. Finally Ron said, "I'm, uh, not sure she'd be safe. I looked at the call history on Carson's phone. There was a call received from my chief the night you arrived, and several between the two of them the whole time you were here."

Jo felt her shoulders slump. "Oh, Ron. What are you going to do?"

The detective's voice sounded ancient when he replied. "I haven't figured that out yet. Jesus, the Chief has been to my house more times than I can count."

They were both silent for a moment. There was very little she could say that would help Ron deal with his situation. Any reassurance would sound hollow, given the circumstances.

Jo felt a tension headache coming. She rubbed her forehead. "I still need a solid connection between my case and Wellborne. Any chance Carson was in St. Paul when my first victims were shot or the other one was drugged?"

"Maybe I can trace it on the SUV's GPS system. Give me some dates, times and addresses and I'll see what I can figure out."

After she gave him the information, she said, "Ron, be careful."

His tone was dry. "Will do. Micki will never forgive me if I get myself killed."

After they wrapped up the phone call a few minutes later, Jo leaned back into her chair, her fingers forming a steeple. *Why does it feel like every time we take a step forward in this case, we take four steps backward?*

Chapter Thirty-One

THE FBI'S TEMPORARY OFFICE was located above Harriet's House of Hair. Access to the upper level was by a wooden staircase at the back of the building. As Chip climbed the stairs, he was thinking that meetings with law enforcement were becoming all too frequent. His simple rural life in a small Iowa farm community was as complicated as his former life. However, his past was full of divorce courts, where the only ones gunning for him were his ex-wives.

The treads were icy and the handrail, when he grabbed it, was wobbly. When he reached the door, it was locked. There was no doorbell or knocker, but he noticed a new door lock, one with push buttons requiring a code. He rapped on the door and yelled, "Agent Masterson, it's Chip."

"I can see you, Chip. Look up."

He did and saw the security camera mounted under the eaves. He heard a series of mechanical clicks, followed by Masterson's permission to enter.

The office was one big room. It was sparsely furnished with a scarred wooden desk and mismatched wooden chairs. Detective Franco and Chief Frederickson were seated with to-go cups of coffee in their hands, and Agent Masterson was behind the desk working on a laptop. A bakery box from the Bun was on the corner of the desk.

The men greeted him as he took the only remaining chair. "Help yourself to Bernice's latest treat. She calls them Banana Bonanzas," said the chief.

Chip selected one of the puff pastries and took a bite. A glob of banana cream filling oozed out on his hand, causing both Franco and Fredrickson to burst into laughter. "Both of us did exactly the same thing," said Franco. "We were just saying that Bernice should put a warning label on those babies."

Agent Masterson looked up from her monitor, frowned and shook her head. "Enough of this pastry party, let's get down to business. Franco you start."

Franco straightened up in his chair and began. "Chip, do you remember me mentioning Margaret Murphy?"

"Sure, the true crime writer who committed suicide, right?"

Franco raised his bushy eyebrows. "Well, maybe not suicide. I had the case re-classified as a possible homicide and had the ME and the Bureau of Criminal Apprehension revisit the autopsy and evidence. There was enough doubt to look into it further."

"What led you to be suspicious?" asked Chip.

Franco smiled. "Good question, Mr. Crime Writer. I got a call from the director of the Minnesota Indian Women's Resource Center, Rita Running Bear. Seems she was interviewed last summer by Patrick Finnegan and Margaret Murphy. The two were apparently working together or researching the same topic. Rita knew about Finnegan's murder, but she hadn't heard about Murphy's death until recently."

"So you think they were both murdered for the same reason? What did they want to know about Indian women?"

"I'm keeping that under wraps for now until I can confirm a story I got from a lead Rita gave me. That lead was Winona Little Feather, a woman well known by the MPD. I traced her to the Hennepin County Detox Center, where she is drying out for the umpteenth time. If I can believe her, this case is going to blow a mile-high. The problem is Winona is not a very reliable informant."

Chip was fascinated by Franco's story, but bewildered. "What does this have to do with me?"

"I'll let Agent Masterson take it from here. Your turn," said Franco nodding to the agent.

"Change of topic, Chip. This has to do with you and Hal Swanson. We now have confirmation that Hal is in this country. The DEA heard from their counterpart in Colombia. Hal arrived in California as we suspected, but not on the day or at the place expected by the DEA. When the DEA finally found the narco-sub, they discovered the badly beaten undercover agent. He confirmed Hal had eluded them."

Chip's head was swimming with so much new information. He took a deep breath and let it out slowly. "So you think Hal is here? That he's the one who shot at me in Minneapolis and ran me off the road?"

"In a word yes, Chip, but not that he's here in Turners Bend," said Masterson. "If he were here, someone would have seen him. He can't hide here. Most of the residents know him and everyone seems to know we're looking for him and that you and your family are receiving police protection. But, I have to assume he is not far away and he will make another attempt on your life."

Chip put his elbows on his knees and his head between his hands. "Holy shit, I've got to get myself and Jane and the kids out of here. We've got to hide, maybe go to my parents' house in Baltimore, maybe leave the country for a while. This is just too damn freakin' scary."

"Settle down, Chip. Franco and I have a plan to flush out Hal and Finnegan's murderer, possibly both or at least one or the other of them. It involves some risk-taking on your part, but I can assure you we will keep you safe."

Chip could no longer stay in his chair. He paced the room, running his hands through his hair. "I don't think I want to hear this, but go on. What is the plan?"

Franco took over. "Just listen, Chip. We've worked out the details. We've weighed all the risks, planned for every possible outcome."

"I'm no James Bond, Franco. The only risks I've ever taken were at the roulette table. I'm your basic chicken, a 98-pound weakling. Whatever it is, I don't think I'm your man."

Franco ignored Chip's excuse-making and continued. "Next month there is going to be a benefit dinner for the Finnegan family. It will be held at the Saint Paul Hotel. You'll attend as the special guest. That's it."

"That's it? I attend a dinner in St. Paul, and I'm the sitting duck, out in public and somehow Hal is going to know where I am and come and try to kill me?"

"We'll do a media blitz so it's well known you will be attending. Hal will hopefully see this as the ideal time to get to you, and we'll nab him before he does," said Masterson.

"Hopefully, hopefully!" said Chip, his voice rising higher and louder. "Are you nuts, are you all nuts? And what in the hell does this have to do with Finnegan's murder? You guys have me totally confused. Chief, don't just sit there. Help me out."

"Chip, I know this is a lot to take in, but hear them out," said Fredrickson. "Lots of federal agents and St. Paul police officers will be involved in protecting you and nabbing these bad guys."

"Let me finish," said Franco. "There's one more crucial part we haven't told you yet. Prior to the event Maureen Finnegan is going to announce she is giving you Patrick's research and asking you to finish the novel he has outlined."

"Okay, now I get it. If Hal doesn't get me, Finnegan's killer will, and either way I'm dead. IS THAT IT? IS THAT YOUR PLAN?"

With an exasperated sigh Chip ceased his pacing and sat down. "Okay, lay it on me. How does the plan work so I come out of this mess alive?"

Chapter Thirty-Two

Head Shot

Minneapolis, MN
Early November

JO WORKED THROUGH THE MORNING, happy to be distracted by the files on her desk. After booking an appointment with the OB/GYN John had found, she got up to adjust the window blinds to cut the glare from the sun bouncing off the surface of her desk. When she sat back down, she saw she had received a text message from Ron Fisher, the detective in Williston, ND. The text read: *Can't talk now, but GPS showed no trips to Minnesota, only local. BTW, no tox panel run on compliance guy for alcohol...quashed by my chief.*

"Damnit." Jo tried calling Frisco. She received his voice mail, so she left a message and grabbed lunch from the deli in the lobby of her building.

She had just returned to her desk, and taken the first spoonful of soup, when the phone buzzed in her pocket. It was Frisco returning her call.

"Hey, world traveler. What's the good word?"

Jo wiped her mouth on her napkin. "Not a lot, to tell you the truth. Ron Fischer, the detective from Williston made a dotted-line link between the vehicular death of the compliance officer and Wellborne." She explained about the tanker truck accident with James Carson, the attack on Ron's family and the untimely death of Carson.

When she told him about the GPS system coming up empty to link Carson and their victims, she heard hear Frisco's puff of air through the phone. "Shit."

"You can say that again. I still have to make a direct link between Wellborne and our cases here. I know Wellborne is involved in some way, but with the GPS locations not matching and Carson's death, my latest lead has dried up. We'll have to find another connection, one that won't slip away." She paused, taking a sip of water. "This case is frustrating. Any progress on your end?"

Frisco snorted. "Nah. Our victim, Rick Wilson, is not much help so far. Says the last thing he remembers is driving over to North Dakota with Billy MacGregor. Must have been quite the road trip. I talked to John, and he said he's not surprised Wilson has some memory loss."

"Did John say if the amnesia is permanent?"

"He wasn't sure, 'cause every case is different. Especially with the amount of damage in that kid's head. Still amazes me he survived, let alone that he can talk. I'd say we're shit-out-of-luck at the moment."

Jo thought for a moment. "Why don't we get together late this afternoon and go over the files again. I have several meetings this afternoon, but would you be able to stop by the house later? I'll pick up some Pizza Luce on the way home from work."

Jo could hear Frisco's chuckle on the other end. "You are a lifesaver. The wife and kids are going to a friend's birthday party tonight at one of those indoor playground/arcade/crappy pizza joints. God, I hate those places. I'd rather spend the night in the Ramsey County Jail; it'd be a lot less dangerous."

She joined in his laughter. "Well, I wouldn't know about that, but glad to help out."

***

John had yet to return home from work, so Jo and the detective split the pizza. After they had finished eating, Jo cleared the dishes, while Frisco spread out their case files on the kitchen table. They spent the next hour pouring over the details, making notes for follow-up items.

Finally, Frisco pushed back from the table, his arms akimbo. "This case is driving me crazy. To recap, we have two dead kids who don't seem to have any connection to their killer, an almost-dead victim, who can't remember anything from the last several months, let alone his would-be killer. Then we have another kid who probably had the answers we're looking for, but he was bumped off before we could question him. Oh, and to top it all off, there is no solid link between our lead suspect and our victims." He blew out a breath of frustration. "Am I missing anything?"

Jo sighed. "No, you covered it rather nicely."

Frisco pointed to the to-do list they had compiled. "All of this is well and good, but it doesn't get us anywhere."

Jo stood up and stretched. "It feels like there is something here. Something we're missing. I just don't know what it is yet."

She pointed to the empty beer bottle at his elbow. "Want another?"

"Yeah, thanks." He glanced up at her. "Not joining me?"

As Jo handed him a bottle, she smiled shyly. "Ah, not a good idea right now. I, that is, we have some news. John and I are going to have a baby."

Frisco simultaneously let out a whoop and jumped up from his chair, which tipped over and clattered to the floor. He gave her a brief hug. "First, you tell me you're getting married to the doc and now you've got a bun in the oven. Best damned news I've heard in a long time! Wow, I kinda wondered why you were so green at the crime scene. When are you due?"

It felt good to share their news with Frisco, the man who had become a close friend to both of them over the last year. "I'm not sure. I haven't been to the doctor yet, so do me a favor and keep this under your hat for a while."

The detective mimed zipping his lips. "Won't tell a soul. Well, except maybe the missus and she's pretty great at keeping secrets. This is amazing news."

Jo's smile dimmed a bit as she thought more about telling others, especially her boss. Frisco must have seen her expression, because he said, "Feeling a little nervous about this baby?"

Leave it to Frisco to see right through me. Jo looked down at her hands and quietly said, "I never saw myself as mother material."

"How do you know what kind of mother material you'll be? You are pretty amazing at taking care of the people you love; I've seen it myself."

Jo thought about his comment before she responded. "Getting bad guys is what I know. What I was trained for. What do I know about raising a child? My mother passed away before I knew who she was. And God knows, my dad loved me, but he wasn't exactly around very much. I pretty much raised myself most of the time."

Frisco reached out and patted her hand. "So, there you go. You've already raised one terrific kid – you – and look how good that turned out."

Jo felt some of the weight lift off her shoulders. Tears formed at the corners of her eyes and she swiped at them. Looking at Frisco, she said, "How do you always know what to say to make me feel better?"

The detective took a swallow of beer. "It's what I do."

***

Frisco and Jo looked up when they heard John's key in the door. A cold blast of air followed him into the cozy kitchen, and Jo could feel the chill on his coat when he reached down for a kiss.

He grinned at Frisco, who stood to greet him. They shook hands and the detective's face split into a wide smile. He nodded to Jo. "I hear you have quite a year planned. First, an engagement, and now a baby. You two don't waste any time. Congrats."

John's eyes widened and a grin lit up his face. He hugged Jo to his side. "Thanks, Frisco. I'm a lucky guy."

He took in the files scattered across the tabletop. Jo saw the smile on his face fade when his eyes rested on a photo. He pointed at the picture. "Isn't that the tattoo from Billy MacGregor's forearm?"

Frisco said, "I keep forgetting you met with him before he died." He studied John's expression. "Mean anything to you?"

John's eyebrows came together. "I'm not sure." He read the phrase on the tattoo out loud, 'Nae man can tether time or tide.' Isn't that a quote from Robert Burns, the Scottish poet?"

The detective rubbed his chin. "Beats me."

Jo spun the photo toward her. She could feel her heart speed up as she made a connection. Turning toward Frisco, she said, "Remember all those books stacked all over MacGregor's apartment?"

Frisco tilted his head. "Yeah, there were an awful lot of them, now that you mention it. Lots of high-brow literature and poetry. Why do you ask?"

Jo turned to John. "When you met with Billy, didn't you say he was adamant that I had to meet with him at Nina's café in St. Paul?"

John frowned. "Yes. He was quite clear about it. It was at Nina's or not at all."

Frisco said, "Jo, I can see the gears turning in your head. Whatcha thinking?"

Jo pointed at the tattoo in the photo. "This kid was really into poetry; I know because I checked out a lot of the titles at his house." She smiled and continued, "Did you know there is a bookstore called Subtext beneath Nina's café?"

The detective's expression was quizzical. "No. What's the connection?" He paused, and then suddenly his face brightened. "Wait, Subtext sounds familiar. Didn't we find some paystubs from there in his apartment?"

John turned to Jo. "You think someone at the bookstore may know something about your case?"

Jo nodded. "Looks like we need to add a trip to Subtext to the top of our to-do list."

Frisco's eyes cleared. "A plan of action. I like it." He glanced at his watch. "It's just past seven. Let's see if the bookstore is still open."

Chapter Thirty-Three

Turners Bend
Late January

THE MEETING WITH FRANCO, Fredrickson and Masterson went on for hours as the three explained the plan and tried to enlist Chip's cooperation. It was no easy task.

"The best possible outcome is we catch both Hal Swanson and Finnegan's killer," said Detective Franco. "If that doesn't happen, at least we honor Finnegan and raise a lot of money for his kids' education fund."

"Think about it, Chip," said Chief Fredrickson. "You'll rest a lot easier when this manhunt for Hal is over, and we have him in custody. Don't you and Jane want your normal life and privacy back?"

"We'll suit you up in our best quality Kevlar vest and give you a wire so we can be in constant communication. Plus FBI field agents from our Omaha, Minneapolis and Chicago offices will be swarming all over the place," explained Agent Masterson.

"The Saint Paul Hotel is accustomed to having visiting dignitaries, politicians, rock stars and Hollywood actors, people who require a high level of security. And, the St. Paul PD will provide additional security, not only in the hotel, but for the whole Rice Park area surrounding the hotel," added Franco.

Chip began to see the benefits of the plan, but new concerns arose. "I want fool-proof protection for Jane and the kids. Rather than come after me, what if Hal decides to seek them out while I'm in St. Paul? Have you thought about that possibility?"

Agent Masterson nodded her head. "As we have explained, we have considered all the possible scenarios. We have a secluded safe house on the island of Captiva, off the Florida coast. It's staffed by a Secret Service detail. Jane and the kids will be flown by Air Force

173

transport to Captiva before the benefit dinner. Not only is it a beautiful place, but the security is top-notch."

"Sounds good," said Chip. "Can I join them for a few days after the benefit?"

Masterson chuckled. "You drive a hard bargain, Collingsworth. I'll see if I can arrange a little R&R for you."

"Besides putting my life on the line, what else do I have to do?"

"We will ask you to get your literary agent to implement the media blitz and for you to following through with interviews," said Masterson "She, of course, cannot know the true intent of your appearance. That's it."

"What about Jane? Can she know?"

"Jane's cooperation will be necessary. I'll tell her as much as she needs to know to be convinced this is a safe operation. The same goes for Maureen Finnegan. Any other questions or requests?"

Chip closed his eyes and took a deep breath. "No, I guess that's it for now. My father and brother have nerves of steel. They bravely drill holes in people's heads and cut tumors out of their brains with no fear or trepidation. Me, I didn't inherit those genes. If I can make it through the benefit dinner without passing out or having a panic attack, you guys will be lucky."

Despite all his ranting and raving, all his misgivings, all his fears, three-hours into the meeting Chip had agreed to the plan. The triumvirate of Masterson, Fredrickson and Franco had prevailed.

***

"OMG Chip, this is marvelous PR for you," gushed Lucinda, when Chip told her about the benefit dinner for Finnegan and the offer from his wife to finish the deceased writer's novel. "The media loves this kind of thing. Remember when it was announced that Kyle Mills would be finishing Vince Flynn's last novel? It made national headlines."

"I know you've got other things on your mind right now, but do you think you could send out a few press releases and snag me a couple radio or TV interviews?" asked Chip.

"Are you kidding? Of course. This is huge."

Lucinda threw all her energy into the project. Chip had appearances on *Good Morning America* and *The View*. He did radio interviews in a dozen major markets, including New York and Los

Angeles. When he wasn't being interviewed, he was blogging and tweeting. His last gig would be an interview on WCCO-TV, the CBS affiliate in Minneapolis. At all times he had FBI Agent Sam Harden with him.

***

Getting Lucinda to do her part was easy; getting Jane on board was not.

Jane sat on their bed, fiercely brushing her hair, static causing the red strands to fan up after each stroke. "You can't tell me the kids and I need a safe house in Captiva and you'll be fine at a very public gathering. I don't buy this, Chip, and I don't like it."

Chip changed into a pair of sweat pants and an old Colts jersey and tossed his suit on the chair by the bed. He had just returned from an interview in Chicago, and he was weary from his travels and equally weary of this ongoing argument with Jane.

"And hang up your suit. I'm tired of picking up after you." She threw her brush across the room.

This was so unlike Jane. Chip could see the stress coming out of her in unexpected ways, stripping away the logical, sensible Jane and laying open a woman with fears and anxieties, some rational and some irrational.

He hung up his suit and sat next to her on the bed, putting his arm around her shoulders. She leaned against him and put her head on his chest. "Oh Chip. I'm afraid for all of us, including Hal. I can't eat, I can't sleep, I have a sick feeling in my stomach night and day."

Chip was puzzled. "You're afraid for Hal?"

"Yes, don't you realize he could be killed, shot down like a common criminal? I don't want that to happen to him."

During this whole ordeal, that thought hadn't occurred to Chip. Yet, Hal really was a common criminal.

As if reading his mind, Jane said, "He is not a common criminal, he is a very sick, mentally ill man. He needs help. I just want this to be over."

"Me too, Janey. Me too."

Chapter Thirty-Four

Head Shot

St. Paul, MN
Early November

SPECIAL AGENT JO SCHWANN PARKED at the curb beside Nina's Café in the Cathedral Hill area of St. Paul. As Detective Mike Frisco pulled into the spot behind her, Jo stepped out of her SUV, her eyes taking in the neighborhood F. Scott Fitzgerald once called home. Several of the buildings that had gone into decline in the nineties had reclaimed their Victorian charm in recent years. The area now bustled with restaurants and shops, with St. Paul's curling club just a few blocks down the street.

The day had grown chilly and Jo pulled her collar closer around her neck. The days were noticeably shorter and the street lights lit the way to the doorway of the café.

Once inside, some of the customers looked up at the new arrivals, but most kept their noses buried in books or laptops plugged in along the front window facing Selby Avenue. A few chatted on couches placed around the room, hands wrapped around mugs of coffee.

Jo could smell the slightly burnt odor of roasted coffee beans and her stomach protested for a moment. She swallowed hard a few times and breathed through her mouth until the queasiness passed. She and Frisco walked past the counter and followed the staircase down to the lower level. They entered the store, stepping through the arched doorway.

Both Nina's café and Subtext were located in the Blair Arcade building, a Victorian gem. The lower level of the building was charming, with white stone-arched doorways. Rather than feeling like a gloomy basement, the store was cozy and inviting, with comfy arm chairs scattered throughout. The floor was covered in black and white checkerboard tiles, and bookshelves filled the store to overflowing, reaching toward the soffits covered in literary quotes and references.

When they stepped up to the check-out counter, Jo introduced herself to the man behind the counter. His nametag identified him as Paul, and Jo placed him in his late sixties, with a full head of gray hair and a beard to match. Jo found herself smiling at his dapper clothing choice; he wore a buttoned up baby-blue dress shirt with a green-and-pink polka dot bow tie. Frisco handed him the photo of Billy MacGregor. "Do you know this man?"

"Yeah. That's Billy. He works here part-time." He frowned. "He's missed his shifts the last couple of days. Not like him at all, especially since he didn't call in. Is he okay?"

Frisco glanced quickly at Jo. "I'm afraid Billy MacGregor died this past week."

Paul's face paled. "Died? How...I mean, jeez, he was such a nice polite kid. What happened?"

Jo said, "We're hoping you might be able to help us figure that out. Did he meet with anyone here?"

The store clerk shook his head. "No. He pretty much kept to himself and the bookcases."

Jo couldn't help but be disappointed. She tried again. "Did he bring personal items with him into the store, like a laptop or notebook?" She knew it was a long shot, but she held her breath, waiting for the clerk's answer.

Paul scratched his head and took a moment to respond. "Now that you mention it, he often carried a rather worn-out looking notebook. One of those old-fashioned, black-and-white composition notebooks. Is that what you mean?"

Her heart sped up, but before she could reply, Frisco jumped in. "Yeah, that's exactly the kind of thing we're looking for. Any chance he kept it here?"

"Well, all employees have a little locker space in the back, to store our personal belongings while we work. I have no idea what he kept in there, but I guess it would be okay if you want to take a look, if you think it would help."

Paul summoned another clerk over to the counter to take his place and led them to the back room. They wound their way through stacks of boxes and books until they came to a small clearing. A battered table and chairs sat in the middle and a row of olive green lockers lined one wall.

He pointed to the locker on the far left. "That's Billy's locker. It's locked, though."

Frisco ran out to his car and returned with a massive bolt cutter. After he cut through the lock, Jo removed it and yanked the handle up. The door opened with a creak. She reached in and pulled out a notebook and a tattered book. Jo carried both items to the table.

The clerk stood next to her. "That's it! That's the notebook he carried with him."

She picked up the book. In the light she could see its faded title. It was a poetry book by Robert Burns. Jo thought about John's discovery earlier in the evening that Billy's tattoo was a quote from the famous Scottish poet.

She opened it to the front page. "It's inscribed to William MacGregor, from his grandfather. It says: *Never forget where you came from.*"

Jo could feel Frisco looking over her shoulder. "Why would MacGregor keep his own book here?"

She murmured, "Good question." Jo thumbed through a few pages and gasped. There was a crudely hollowed out hole in the body of the book, and inside she discovered a thumb drive.

Frisco said, "Holy shit."

Before he could say anything more, Jo closed up the book and looked at Paul. "We will need to take these with us, for evidence. Since these items clearly don't belong to the store, I am sure you won't have a problem with that."

"No, no, of course not." Paul looked flustered.

She continued, "We appreciate your cooperation. I hope you can understand how important it is you don't mention this to anyone else."

Paul's bow-tie bobbed with his Adam's apple as he swallowed and then nodded vigorously. "Won't tell a soul. I promise."

Jo tucked the notebook, thumb drive and poetry book in her bag. They walked back upstairs, Jo feeling a bit dazed. When they reached their cars, she said, "We need to look at this tonight. Do you want to head back to my house?"

Frisco said, "Why don't we head over to mine? I'm only a few miles from here." He hesitated and tilted his head, as if studying her. "But, Jo. You're pregnant and it's late. You should rest. Why don't I take a look at this and we can re-group in the morning."

Jo looked him in the eye. "Frisco, I appreciate your concern." She lightly punched his arm. "But if you ever suggest to me again I should pull back on our investigation because I'm going to have a baby, I'll look for a new partner in the St. Paul PD."

Frisco chuckled. "Fair enough. Follow me to the house. I'll fire up a pot of coffee for me and pour a glass of milk for you."

Chapter Thirty-Five

St. Paul, Minnesota
February

Chip stood in the ultra-luxurious Ordway Suite at the Saint Paul Hotel as FBI Agent Sam Harden adjusted a Kevlar vest around his upper body. "Not too comfy, but I don't care as long as it does the job," said Chip.

"Oh, it'll do the job. This is a ProMax Premium concealable full-vest, covers the front, back and sides. It has both stab and ballistic protection. No one will know you have it on underneath the custom-made tux you'll be wearing."

Chip's cell phone rang out. "It's Jane. Am I allowed to answer it?"

"Sure, go ahead. I have to test your wire before we put it on you."

Chip pressed talk. "Jane, how is Captiva?"

"You won't believe this place, Chip. It's like paradise inside of Fort Knox. There's a private beach and a pool. The kids went shelling this afternoon and brought back the most amazing collection. I can't wait for this to be over and for you to join us. How are you holding up?"

Chip looked at himself in the ornately-framed bedroom mirror and grimaced. "Fine. The FBI has all the luxury suites in the hotel booked. I'm in one and Maureen Finnegan is in another. There are cops at every elevator and stairway. I'm feeling pretty safe at this point."

Chip wondered if Jane could hear this falsehood through his voice. He was having trouble breathing normally and felt claustrophobic. Wearing the heavy, confining vest was like being tightly wrapped with duct tape. There was no flexibility in it. Sweat beaded up on his forehead.

"Guess what? Lots of celebrities are expected to show up tonight, including the comedian Bill Murray. Seems Finnegan was a huge fan of the St. Paul Saints, and Murray's part-owner of the baseball team. He has the title of Team Psychologist. Isn't that a hoot?"

"Cool. What happens next, dear?" asked Jane.

Chip consulted the detailed timetable he had been given. "A cocktail reception, followed by a sit-down dinner. Under any other circumstances, this would be quite the affair."

"Stay calm Chip. Think about drinking Pina Coladas with me by the infinity pool tomorrow evening. Good luck. Love you more than you can ever know," she said with a catch in her voice.

Feeling choked up with tears gathering at the back of his throat, Chip responded with his love and said good bye.

***

Chip could feel Maureen's tension as she gripped his arm. She was dressed in a long, black silk dress. Despite her make-up, she looked weary. The dark circles under her eyes betrayed the ordeal she had been going through since Patrick's death.

"How can I every repay you, thank you enough," she whispered as they prepared to enter the cocktail reception. "You're my hero tonight."

She opened her evening bag and removed a rosary and slipped it into the pocket of Chip's tuxedo jacket. "If you don't mind, just for tonight. It was my grandmother's rosary. When she was worried, she always made me take it along with me."

The room was elegant. Tall pub tables, beautifully draped with white linens, were scattered around the room. The crystal chandeliers reflected off the mirrored walls and soft music was playing behind the chatter of formally-dressed guests.

Maureen and Chip merged into the crowd, stopping to greet guests, offer introductions and accept tall flutes of bubby wine and canapés from roving waiters dressed in white jackets.

"Chip, this is St. Paul Mayor Chris Coleman," Maureen said as she introduced a good-looking, ruddy-faced man." And this is Dr. Julie Sullivan, the president of Patrick's alma mater, the University of St. Thomas."

Chip was enjoying himself. "I see the Irish are out in full force tonight. It's an honor to meet both of you. Thanks so much for coming."

All of a sudden he was aware of Franco's voice in his ear. "Waiter with a towel over his arm approaching Chip from the back. Nab him." He felt a sharp, intense pain in the middle of his back, like being hit with a baseball bat. The force propelled him forward into the mayor, landing them both on the floor.

Two FBI agents swooped in and grabbed the waiter. Bending his arms behind him, they wrestled him down onto the floor. A gun flew out of the waiter's hand and skittered across the floor. The man struggled to break free, but was no match for the two agents, who dragged him into the hallway leading to the kitchen, his trailing feet kicking. It happened so fast that many guests were unaware of the fuss.

Franco appeared beside Chip and helped him stand. "You okay?"

"I think so. What happened?" He felt dazed and confused. His back was throbbing.

Franco located the gun and directed a police officer to retrieve and bag it. In a loud voice he said, "Just a little mishap here folks, we have everything under control. Please step back and clear this room as quickly as possible. Proceed into the ballroom for your dinner."

Officers began to secure the area, as Franco propelled Chip through the gathering crowd and into the same hallway where the cuffed shooter was being read his rights.

Franco briefly consulted with Sam Harden and then escorted Chip down another hallway to an employee bathroom. They could hear the cuffed man yelling and swearing, his voice echoing down the hallway as he was hauled away.

"We'll have a doc here shortly to take a look at you. Make sure you're not injured too badly. The shooter is on his way out of here with the SPPD team," said Franco

Chip felt faint and slid down onto the cold bathroom floor "I don't understand. How did you know the guy was coming at me with a gun? Who is he? Is it Hal? Is it Finnegan's killer?"

"Whoa, take a deep breath and calm yourself. The guy's facial hair threw me off for a second, but I was sure I recognized him. He wasn't carrying a tray and the towel over his arm looked unnatural. Something in my gut told me he was trouble. I didn't see the gun under the towel. It had a silencer. That's why no one heard the shot."

"But who is he?" asked Chip in a shaky voice. "I'm still confused."

"The guy is a local bad boy. I knew I had seen him before. We tried to pin a homicide on him two years ago, but we couldn't make it stick. A big-time lawyer got him off on a technicality. Sloppy police work, I'm afraid."

"So, did he kill Finnegan?"

"Maybe, maybe not. My guess is he was hired to kill you. I bet he thought he could do the job and walk out the kitchen door in all the commotion."

"Do you think Hal hired him?"

"No, not Hal, but I have a strong suspicion of who did."

A doctor arrived and Chip took off his jacket and shirt. Sam entered the bathroom and removed the Kevlar vest and pulled a bullet out of the back, placing it in an evidence bag.

"You're going to have a painful bruise for a couple of days, but it looks like that vest did its job," said the doctor.

"I thought this vest would protect me from injury. This hurts like hell."

"A bullet can't penetrate this vest," explained Sam. "The ceramic lining stops the bullet, but its impact can still pack quite a wallop. Busted one of my ribs once."

"You think you can go back and join Maureen at the dinner?" asked Franco. "We haven't spotted Hal, but he could still make a move tonight. One down, one to go."

"What the hell, it couldn't be any worse than this. All I've had to eat today is a lousy bacon-wrapped date and a bruschetta with lox, but I don't think I could eat a thing right now."

***

Chip was right. The bloody prime rib on his plate made him nauseous. He sat beside Maureen at the head table scanning the diners for Hal and watching police officers check everyone entering or leaving the ballroom.

At the end of the evening Sam escorted him back to the suite. "No Hal," Chip said. "You know, I don't know whether to be relieved or pissed that we went through all of this and still don't know where in the hell he is."

***

The next morning the whole team, including Chip and Maureen, were gathered in the Lowry Suite for a debriefing led by Agent Masterson. A lavish continental breakfast was laid out on the bar and the aroma of freshly brewed coffee filled the room.

"First I want to thank all of you for your hard work and cooperation. Hal Swanson was a no-show, so unfortunately we do not know any more than we did before about his whereabouts or intentions. But, I want to assure you all we won't stop searching for him."

She paused and took a sip of coffee. "Franco, do you want to give us a run-down on your perp?"

"His name, at least the one he is currently using, is Dwayne Moore. He's got a record that is the envy of criminals state-wide, mainly because he uncannily seems to avoid any harsh sentences. He has friends in very high, very influential places."

Franco took a bite of his bagel with cream cheese and a quick sip of coffee. "He could be involved in something Finnegan was researching or he could merely be the hired hit-man. The latter is my best guess. He always seems to be represented by high profile lawyers, and I heard this morning he already has one of the best."

"Let's pack up and get out of there," said Masterson. "Chip has a charter plane to catch at Holman Field, and Maureen wants to get back to her children."

Maureen stood clutching her hands. "I'm full of gratitude for all of you and all your efforts, especially to you, Chip. You took a huge risk for me and my children. The money raised last night was staggering. It will be more than enough to pay for Abby and Sean's college tuitions."

Chip stood and gave her a warm embrace. He placed her rosary in the palm of her hand and closed it with a squeeze. "Back at you, Maureen. May it continue to protect you."

Chapter Thirty-Six

Head Shot
St. Paul, MN
Early November

Dr. JOHN GOODMAN TOSSED in his bed. It was almost midnight, and for a man who seldom had a hard time falling asleep, he couldn't seem to get his mind to shut down.

He flipped over on his back and his thoughts shifted to the phone call he had received earlier in the evening, soon after Jo and Frisco had left for the bookstore. The president of the University of Minnesota had called him personally to formally invite him to interview for the position of Medical School Dean and Vice President for Health Services. The interview was set for the following day, and he would be meeting with not only the president, but also with several board members.

The university's president had been clear in expressing his interest in John for the spot. Even though they hadn't interviewed him yet, he said they considered him their top candidate. His experience as a world-renowned neurosurgeon, as well as a lecturer, had gotten their attention. Recent headlines touting the success with Rick Wilson's surgery had also been noted.

John was torn. He was passionate about his work as a neurosurgeon and couldn't imagine the day when he would no longer perform that role. However, in light of Jo's pregnancy, his priorities needed to change. True, the job would require long hours and some travel, mainly because he would be representing the university's medical school, with all the fundraising that entailed. However, the hours would be regular, with no more middle-of-the night emergency surgeries. Given

Jo's frenetic schedule – tonight being no exception – one of them needed a reasonable schedule.

Less than a year ago, he would never have considered the position at the university. However, after he made the decision to move to Minneapolis to work out his relationship with Jo, the things that were most important in his world had shifted.

The job opportunity did appeal to John. As the dean, he would have great influence on building an already well-respected program into a world-class one. He could direct research that would further progress in neurosurgery, along with other medical sciences.

He turned his pillow over, finding a cool side. He wished Jo was home to talk to about their future. Switching careers was only the tip of the iceberg when it came to all the changes in store for the two of them.

John smiled when he thought about the life growing inside Jo, the life they had created together. Jo and the baby were the most important people in his life.

His first priority was to marry Jo. To accomplish that, he needed to have her home for more than twenty-four hours.

***

Jo Schwann looked up from Billy MacGregor's notebook and rubbed her tired eyes. It was past one in the morning, and the long hours of reading were taking their toll. She stood up from the couch in Frisco's basement and walked over to the detective, looking over his shoulder as he went through the documentary footage on his laptop. He had plugged in headphones, allowing Jo to focus on reading. On the screen, she watched as Rick Wilson interviewed a woman in her kitchen.

Jo tapped Frisco on the shoulder. When he removed the headphones, she said, "Find anything?"

Frisco paused the film and shook his head. "Lots on the dangers of water contamination from fracking, but nothing that would have pointed a loaded gun at Rick Wilson." He jerked his chin in the direction of the notebook she held in her hand. "Glad you can read that chicken scratch of his; I couldn't make heads or tails of it. Did you find anything yet?"

Jo frowned. "Same as you. Wellborne Industries seems to be skirting the edge of the law, but nothing so far that would make Rick and Billy murder targets."

Frisco stood up and stretched. He rubbed his tired-looking eyes with a meaty fist. "All this movie watching is making me hungry for popcorn. Want some?"

Jo's midsection grumbled at the mention of food. Lately, it seemed as if her stomach alternated between feeling queasy and famished. "Sounds great. Thanks."

As the detective climbed the steps up to the kitchen, Jo settled back on the couch and began to read the notebook again. She read for a few minutes and then sat up suddenly, her tiredness disappearing in her excitement.

She was re-reading the passage a second time when Frisco clumped down the steps, arms full of two large bowls of popcorn. "Hope you're hungry...." He placed a bowl on the coffee table in front of Jo. "Did you find something? You look like you just won the lottery."

Jo looked up. "Listen to this." She began to read Billy's words out loud.

Mazlo practically had a hard-on when he read the actual water contamination reports we got from Trevor Wallace. After he finished reading, he told us, "I've got the bastard now."

When Rick asked the professor what group of feds we were going to go to first, Mazlo looked at him funny and then locked the reports in his desk drawer. Instead of answering Rick's question, he said, "I'll handle this from here. You boys did a great job and I'll see you get an 'A' this semester."

The smug asshole couldn't see that Rick didn't care about grades any more. We were into it. We were going to take on The Man. Rick argued with him, but Mazlo's voice went ice cold when he said, "I want all the documentary footage you've got. Don't forget the copies. I want it all."

Well, that pissed off Rick. We decided there and then to bug the guy's office. No way was he going to steal our thunder. Rick sweet-talked Mazlo's secretary into letting us into his office again and we put a voice-activated recorder in the cabinet next to his desk.

Jo looked up from reading. "Frisco, did you happen to find any audio files on the flash drive we recovered from Subtext?"

Frisco went back to his laptop and brought up a file. "This is the only one I haven't looked at yet. Let's see what's on it."

He brought the laptop over to Jo and pushed aside the bowl of popcorn. "Looks like an audio file. Maybe this is it."

The detective unplugged the earphones and turned up the volume. They listened for a few minutes. At first, the only conversations were mundane discussions between Mazlo and his secretary, Amanda.

However, a few moments later, they heard Mazlo tell Amanda he should not be disturbed because he had a video call to make. The distinctive tones of a video call being connected came over the laptop's speakers, and then a voice said, "Wellborne Industries. How may I direct your call?"

Jo felt Frisco shift on the couch next to her and he quietly muttered, "Holy crap. He called Wellborne. Why the hell would he tip his hand like that?"

They both leaned in a little closer to the laptop. Mazlo said, "I'd like to speak to Mr. Wellborne, please. He's not expecting my call, but tell him it's an old buddy from high school."

After a moment, they heard a deep, male voice Jo immediately recognized as belonging to the oil company's CEO and founder. "Jonathon Wellborne, here. What can I do for you?"

They heard Mazlo say, "Mr. Wellborne, it's been a long time. This is Michael Mazlo. Do you remember me? We were in the same graduating class in Duluth, but of course, we didn't travel in the same social circles. You were the captain of the football and baseball teams and I was the captain of the chess team."

Wellborne sounded impatient when he answered, "Of course, of course I remember you. Look, I'm sorry, but I don't have a lot of time to talk right now. What can I help you with?"

"I'm calling about more than a walk down memory lane. I'm now an adjunct professor at the University of Minnesota, and I've been mentoring a student who created a little documentary I think you'll be interested in viewing."

The CEO spoke. "Are you talking about those two punk kids who came in here a couple of weeks ago?"

"Those punk kids gave me some information that just might sink you and your company. Here, let me show you the reports they received from your compliance guy."

There was a pause, and Jo assumed Mazlo was holding up the compliance reports he had received from Rick and Billy to the camera on his computer. He continued, "Look familiar? Tsk, tsk…you really haven't been a very good corporate citizen you know. What with all those levels of chemicals in the ground water around Williston."

Wellborne interrupted, his voice deepening into a growl. "You think I am afraid of you, you arrogant little shit? The government has come after us before, and all they can manage is a few miniscule fines here and there. May I add, with a lot more data than your little watch dogs found by talking with my staff."

Mazlo's voice was confident when he replied, "Ah, but I have no intention of going to the government. I know you'd only get a slap on the wrist, just like before. No, I'd go to the networks and CNN. I'm sure public opinion would hold a lot more sway than the feds' attempts at keeping you in line."

Wellborne's voice had grown deadly. "What do you want, Mazlo?"

"I want in. Oh, not in the oil business. But you see, there are a lot of ways to make money in your neck of the woods."

After a moment the CEO said, "I'm listening."

"Let me be blunt here. My dad, brothers and I have built up quite a little industry, dealing in the flesh trade, particularly here in the Twin Cities. We want to expand our operations to the oil fields of North Dakota." Jo could hear the haughtiness in Mazlo's voice as he continued, "You'll have your oil pipelines and we'll have our trafficking pipelines."

Wellborne snorted. "You don't need my permission to do that. From what I hear, there's plenty of sex trafficking going on here already."

"But that's the point. We want to be the exclusive traders up in the oil patch, and I know you've got that kind of pull. I did some checking on you. I've heard the local police chief plays poker with you every Thursday night. I'm sure he'd be happy to do you a favor or two, being close pals and all."

He chuckled and continued, "So, do we have a deal? I keep the documentary under wraps and you grant us open access."

The oil executive was silent for a moment and then he said, "I'm curious. How does an adjunct college professor become involved in sex trafficking?"

Mazlo's voice was cold when he replied, "Let's just say it's an old family business. I initially went to college to learn how to run our operations more efficiently and hide money. Along the way, I discovered college campuses were a great place to find naïve and beautiful young flesh for foreign customers with discerning tastes. Now, about my proposal. Do we have a deal or not?"

"What about the two kids who made the documentary? They're not just going to roll over."

Mazlo chuckled. "They won't be a problem. I will make sure they won't say a thing. Ever. Now, are you in or are you out?"

Wellborne's voice sounded ancient when he responded. "I'll make the call to the police chief."

Frisco turned to Jo after it was clear there was nothing else of importance on the audio file. "Good God. Can you believe that piece of filth?"

Jo felt sick to her stomach, only this time it had nothing to do with being pregnant. The idea that Mazlo and Wellborne could talk about human lives with such disregard made her ill. Not only the lives of their victims, but all the people who had been trafficked in her hometown, by Mazlo and his family. She suddenly remembered the flyer for the missing college woman's vigil she had seen at Mazlo's house. Jo was now certain he was connected to her disappearance.

"I always knew the Twin Cities had a bad reputation for human trafficking. Our interstate system, as well as our proximity to the Canadian border makes us a prime location. And heaven knows, there is a huge problem with the exploitation of Native American Women in the area. But, to hear Mazlo talk about it and to know he's responsible..." She shook her head. "How does a man lead a double life of adjunct college professor and sex trafficker? We're going to do something about this. And I mean fast."

The detective's face was grim when he said, "Count me in. So, what's our first step?"

Jo sat for a moment, thinking. "We're going to talk to Wellborne. Let's see if he's willing to plea bargain to save his company." When she saw the frown on Frisco's face, she said, "Don't worry. He'll still get his. Thanks to Rick and Billy, we've got enough to damn near bankrupt him."

Chapter Thirty-Seven

Turners Bend
March

CHIP STOOD AT THE KITCHEN WINDOW, his first cup of coffee of the day in his hand. The early morning sky was gray; the temperature on the outdoor thermometer read a minus four degrees. If Dickens was around to pen the opening line for today, Chip thought it might read...*There was nothing happening and everything was about to happen.* It was a time of suspended animation.

After the excitement in St. Paul and the short respite at Captiva, all was back to normal...the new normal where Hal was still a lingering threat and Chip was plagued by constant unease and lagging motivation.

Jane was preparing to leave the house. "I thought you didn't have any appointments today," said Chip.

"I don't, so I thought I'd drive over to Madrid and take a look at the Lely Astronaut A4 that Sunny Day Farms just installed. I've never seen one in operation."

"What the heck is that? Sounds like a video game."

"It's a robotic milking system. A cow decides when she wants to feed, enters a stall and sensors automatically attach the milking machine to her udder. Very high tech and very costly. I think it runs about $200,000 per cow and Sunny Day has a herd of about 120."

"Whoa, that's bizarre. So a dairy farmer can just flip a switch and then head to the Bun for coffee. Speaking of, I think I'll head there for breakfast this morning. I'll just flip the switch on my laptop and see if it will write the next chapter of *Head Shot*."

***

The Bun was crowded and Chip took a seat at the counter next to a guy in a brown uniform, a dead give-away for UPS. Bernice was bustling behind the counter. "What's your newest bakery delight?" asked Chip.

"Cronuts, a *croissant*-donut hybrid. Today's are filled with chocolate. The guy next to you just ate three, and I'm not hearing any complaints." Bernice laughed, gave Chip a cup of coffee and put a cronut in front of him. "Like it or leave it, I don't have time to take your order, Chip, especially when I can read your mind." She spotted a raised cup and rushed off to deliver refills.

Chip ate the cronut in three bites and turned to the delivery man. "Not bad, huh? Name's Chip Collingsworth. Are you new on the route?"

"Most folks call me Smitty. No, I took over this route last year. Not too many deliveries to Turners Bend, although I've been making lots of drops to that weird place out on County Road 17. Guy won't let me on the property. I have to call him and he meets me out near the "No Trespassing" sign. What's going on out there?"

"From what I understand Rod Mueller is an anti-government nut. He took a shot at me once, so be careful."

"I've been delivering lots of stuff with hazard warnings on the boxes, but today I'm dropping a box from Amazon. It's some kind of cookware. Makes me wonder what he's cooking out there. Suppose I shouldn't be talking about what I deliver, but that dude creeps me out, even more so now from what you just told me."

Smitty finished his last swallow of coffee and put a five dollar bill on the counter. "Nice talking with you, Chip. This place has awesome baked goods; maybe I'll see you here again some time."

Chip felt an adrenaline rush, his skin began to prickle and he could almost feel the sparks jumping between the synapses of his brain. He had to find Fredrickson or Agent Masterson quick. He scanned the tables; neither of them was in the cafe. He paid for his breakfast and headed first for the FBI office. Agent Masterson was behind her desk.

"What's up, Collingsworth?" Chip was reminded again that the agent was never much for pleasantries; she always got right down to business.

"Do you know about Rod Mueller and the Republic of Iowa out on County Road 17?" asked Chip, taking the chair in front of her desk, talking fast and sweating despite a chilly draft in the office.

"Oh yes, he's been on our watch list for years. I've got a pretty thick file on him. Why do you ask?"

193

Chip related his conversation with the UPS guy. "I remember you saying someone in Iowa had contacts with Hakim, Baba's brother. I'm just wondering if it could be Mueller."

Agent Masterson sat up very straight and began to punch things into her computer. She stopped and stared at the monitor. "Well, well, well. Chip, you just broke this case wide open. Hakim is a chemical engineer. He's known as the "Master Bomb Maker" of the Wahhabi Muslims in Ethiopia. Looks like our friend Mr. Mueller may be learning how to make bombs from him. I've got a lot of work to do to confirm our suspicions, but if this is the case, the FBI is going to make a little visit to the Republic of Iowa. This is big. I don't have to mention you can't say a word about this to anyone, not Jane, not Fredrickson, not Baba. If you leak this, I'll have your hide. Remember Manning, remember Snowden?"

Chip gulped. "Yes, Ma'am."

***

Back home Chip reflected on his early morning Dickensian musings. Nothing was happening yet, but something was surely going to happen soon, and maybe all hell would break loose in Turners Bend.

Chapter Thirty-Eight

Head Shot

Minneapolis, MN
Early November

DARK CLOUDS SCUDDED ACROSS the November sky, and the Minneapolis skyline blurred in Jo's windshield when it began to drizzle. In spite of feeling exhausted, her mind buzzed like a hive.

Jo planned their next steps to take down Michael Mazlo for his role in the attempted murder of Rick Wilson and the death of the other young people, as well as his role in a sex trafficking ring. She and Frisco would have their hands full.

She knew the evidence they currently had on the adjunct professor was shaky at best, and so they had no choice but to contact Wellborne to find out what else he knew. The audio file they had recovered was dated a few days before the murder attempt on Rick Wilson, and so there was a good chance there had been more conversations between Mazlo and the CEO.

She yawned and looked at the clock on the dashboard. Two in the morning and it was going to be hard to turn her brain off.

When Jo yawned a second time, she reflected John would not be happy with how she was taking care of herself, especially now that she was pregnant. She rested her hand on her slightly rounded stomach.

To be honest, she was looking forward to the doctor's appointment tomorrow, but the timing couldn't be worse. This case was sucking up all her time and concentration. Jo knew her priorities needed to change, now that she had another life to consider.

Her mind unwillingly shifted back to her case, and she spent the rest of the drive home mentally shuffling her priorities for the upcoming day.

***

Several hours later, after a much-too-brief night's sleep, Jo was back in her office, with a bleary-eyed Frisco seated in the chair in front of her desk. Her first phone call of the morning was to Detective Ron Fischer of the Williston police department.

For Frisco's benefit, she had the call on speaker phone. When Fischer answered the call, his booming voice filled the room. "Hello, Jo. What can I do for you?"

Jo smiled and replied, "Good morning, Ron. Detective Mike Frisco of the St. Paul PD is here with me. We've made significant progress on our case since we last spoke, but we could use your help with the next step."

"Whatever you need. Mind getting me up to speed?"

Jo filled him in on what they had discovered the previous evening. She concluded, "Wellborne isn't our killer. The evidence points to the adjunct professor."

The detective's shrill whistle came through the phone line. "Jesus. Why on earth would he do that to his own student?"

"We're hoping to get some answers today, but it looks like he was blackmailing Wellborne to help him establish an exclusive sex trafficking operation in the oil field region."

"What made him think Wellborne had that kind of pull?"

Jo took a deep breath. "Because Wellborne and your police chief are poker buddies."

Fischer was silent for so long, that for a moment, Jo thought they had lost the connection. She said, "Ron, you still there?"

"Yeah, yeah. I'm here. Just trying to wrap my brain around my boss being a crooked asshole and another sex trafficking ring in my territory. For fuck's sake." He paused and when he spoke again, his voice sounded as if it were made of steel. "Tell me what to do."

Jo told him.

***

Detective Fischer called back an hour later. Fischer's voice once again filled the room. "Special Agent Schwann and

196

Detective Frisco, I'm in the office of Jonathon Wellborne. He's...uh, curious about what you have to say."

When Wellborne spoke, his voice had an edge to it. "Agent Schwann. What's the meaning of this? I'm calling my attorney. We've bent over backwards assisting with your case, but this is flat-out harassment. We...."

Jo interrupted. "There are new developments in our case that affect you directly. If you will allow me time to explain, I think you'll see it is in your best interests - and those of your company - to cooperate further."

"This should prove entertaining."

"We know all about the falsified water contamination reports. We also know about your side deal with Mazlo."

"Who? I've never heard of him."

"Oh, I think you have. You went to high school with him, but he was also the adjunct professor mentoring Rick Wilson's fracking documentary. Originals of your contamination reports are locked up in his desk drawer, and we'll have them by the end of the day when we go to his office with a search warrant. We already have Rick Wilson's testimony as to what those reports contain..."

Frisco shot Jo a look at her bluff, but said nothing as she continued. "...but your cooperation will be considered. We both know that those reports will bring down your company the minute we turn them over to the EPA and every other agency involved."

"And just what do you want in return?"

"We want your testimony that Michael Mazlo tried to blackmail you in order to set up an exclusive trafficking ring in the oil region and he informed you of his plans to kill Rick Wilson and Billy MacGregor."

Wellborne's laugh was harsh. "That's ridiculous. Just supposing this Mazlo did try to blackmail me, how on earth would I go about getting him exclusive rights to a sex trade here? I'm just a simple business man, after all...."

"Oh, I think you underestimate your powers of persuasion. We already know about your cozy relationship with the chief of police in Williston."

She paused to let her words sink in. "Just so we're clear, this offer has a shelf-life of about two minutes."

"You've got nothing solid, or else the fine detective standing next to me would already have me in cuffs. This is all a bluff and I'm calling my attorney."

"I assure you, I am not bluffing. You are welcome to call your legal counsel, but that'll take time. By then, my offer will be off the table. Oh, and did I mention that at the expiration of our offer, we'll charge you with accessory to murder, as well as re-opening the accidental death case of your compliance officer? Sounds like you'll be plenty busy in the next several years."

When her comment was greeted with silence, she pressed home her point. "We have your entire conversation with Michael Mazlo on tape and we will have the reports in our hands shortly. I'd hate to be you when the media finds out you pumped poisons in the water supply and made a deal with the devil to cover it up by inviting in a sex trafficker. I'd say you're in a rather delicate situation, wouldn't you agree?"

When Wellborne spoke again, his voice had lost its usual swagger. "Seems you've got me by the short hairs." Jo could hear a heavy sigh from across the miles. "What do I need to do?"

Frisco grinned at Wellborne's words and he reached over for a fist-bump with Jo.

"I have provided Detective Fischer with a list of questions and he will take your statement. Furthermore, we will expect your testimony in court. If we are satisfied with your information, I will pass that along to the proper channels. You will be under close watch, Mr. Wellborne. Do not think about leaving the area until these matters are resolved. Is that clear?"

"Perfectly."

***

After they disconnected the call with Wellborne, Frisco said, "You know, there are a lot of things about this case that just don't set well with me."

Jo raised her eyebrow, "You mean like the fact that an adjunct college professor is a murderer and a sex trafficker."

Frisco snorted. "Yeah, there's that. But, I'm from Duluth. Born and raised. Why don't I know this Mazlo character from back in the day? Duluth's not that big of a town."

"He's older than you."

"True, but I'm guessing he's about the same age as my brother, Donny." Frisco rubbed his hand across his chin. "Now that I think about it, Jonathon Wellborne might have been in the same graduating class as my brother. Didn't Mazlo tell Wellborne they were in school at the same time?"

Jo thought for a moment. "Yes, I'm sure of it. Remember, Mazlo said when Wellborne was the captain of the football and basketball teams, he was the captain of the chess team."

"That's right." Frisco pulled out his cell phone dialed. He put the call on speaker phone. "Donny, it's Mike."

A voice that sounded exactly like Frisco's came over the speaker of the cell phone. "Hey, Mikey! This is a surprise. Everything okay with the family?"

"Everyone's great. Look, I don't have a lot of time to talk, but I need to pick your brain. You graduated with Jonathon Wellborne, right?"

"You mean that slick son-of-a-bitch who took my prom date home?"

Frisco chuckled. "Oh, yeah, yeah...I forgot all about that. Anyway, do you remember a guy named Michael Mazlo from your class?"

"Doesn't ring a bell. Why do you ask?"

"We're investigating a case down here, and he just might be at the center of it. Are you sure you don't remember the name?"

Frisco's brother said, "Let me go grab my year book. It's been a while, you know."

They waited a moment and then he was back on the line. "What did you say that name was again?" Jo could hear pages flipping back and forth.

Frisco said, "Michael Mazlo."

"I don't see anyone in the directory by that name. Was he in some kind of sports or something?"

"Try the chess club."

They waited while Donny flipped through more pages. Finally, he said, "There is a guy named Michael Mazlowski. Could that be your guy?"

Frisco stood up, "Holy shit, Donny. I could kiss you! Thanks buddy. I'll call you later and catch up. Gotta go."

After he had disconnected the call, Jo said, "Are you going to fill me in on the significance of what your brother just told you?"

"The Mazlowski family has been a pain-in-the-ass for every cop on the North Shore. The father is one of them anti-government nut-jobs, and he usually keeps himself and his family holed up out in the woods." He scratched his head. "Can't imagine how that group of knuckleheads managed to spawn an adjunct college professor."

Jo said, "Guess he didn't fall too far from the tree after all. Anti-government, huh? Do you know if he was into paramilitary stuff, too?"

"Wouldn't surprise me a bit. Maybe our adjunct business professor learned how to shoot a gun with a silencer from dear ole' dad."

Jo thought for a moment. "Frisco, why don't you contact your old police department up in Duluth and have them send everything they've got on the family. I'd be especially interested to know if the Mazlowskis have a history of sex trafficking. Someone's got to know something."

The detective pulled out his cell phone. "I'm on it."

Chapter Thirty-Nine

Turners Bend
March

CHIP WAS ALONE IN THE HOUSE. Jane and Ingrid had left early in the morning for an informational meeting about financial aid at ISU in Ames. He sat in his new work space. He and Jane had re-decorated the kids' former playroom and turned it into an office. They removed the jungle-print wallpaper and painted the walls a serene dove gray. Chip splurged on a state-of-the-art, chrome and glass computer desk and a custom, ergonomically-designed office chair.

He sat staring out the window waiting for his creative juices to emerge. He heard the furnace come on and felt a rush of warm air from the vent at his feet. When it cycled off, he listened to the ticking of the battery-run wall clock. *Crap, my creative juicer is broken; I've got nothing.*

The sky was the same gray as the color of the walls. The snow, which in sunlight was a brilliant, sparkling white, today was an ashy gray. Gray on gray on gray. Chip was working himself into a funk.

He spied a snow plow on the stretch of country road that he could see from his window. In anticipation of a visit from Iver, he went to the kitchen and started a pot of coffee, using the last of their Ethiopian blend.

Within minutes he heard the roar of the plow coming up the driveway. The engine slowed to an idle and then stopped. Iver let himself in the back door and stomped his boots on the rug. "Yo," he called out.

"Come on in, Iver. Coffee should be ready shortly."

Chip took a look at his friend as he entered the kitchen. He always got a kick out of Iver's winter wear. He never wore a jacket. Today he had on a quilted flannel shirt, jeans at half-mast, and a fur-lined hat with dangling ear flaps.

Iver sat in one of the wooden kitchen chairs, which creaked under the pressure of his formidable weight. One of these days, thought Chip, that chair is going to give way under Iver and end up a pile of kindling.

"What's the temperature out there today?" asked Chip.

"In the summer we Midwesterners say, 'It's not the heat; it's the humidity,' and in the winter we say, 'It's not the temperature; it's the wind chill'." Iver took out his phone and punched at the screen with his sausage-sized finger. "Dang, I'm lovin' this phone. Look here, Chip."

Chip glanced at the screen Iver held up to him. It read: Wind chill -26.

"I'd call that more than a little nippy."

"Nah, ain't too bad. Gonna get a lot colder before winter ends."

"It's March; winter will end soon."

"Wouldn't count on it, buddy."

Chip poured two mugs of coffee and handed one to Iver. "What brings you out this way today?"

Iver got a sly smile on his face. "Thought I'd let you in on what's going down tonight. You know I hear things and see things, and I can put two and two together." He got up and went to the cupboard, took out the sugar bowl and stirred a spoonful into his coffee.

"Come on, Iver, cough it up. Don't keep me in suspense. What have you heard and seen?"

"Well, it started yesterday when Chief Fredrickson asked me to plow out the road at the Swede Point Park campsite and wouldn't tell me why. I never plow that road 'cuz the camp is closed in the winter. Strange, huh?"

"Yes, it does seem odd. Why would he do that?"

"I was asking myself that same question, when I overheard something at the Bun at breakfast today. Agent Masterson was at a table with two guys I've never seen before. I assume they were FBI. When she left, the two dudes were talking quietly with a lot of jargon, sounded like code words. I did hear 'campground' and twenty-three hundred hours."

"So, do you think something is going down at Swede Point Park at eleven o'clock?"

"I decided to take another run out to the campgrounds. I parked in a secluded spot and watched vehicles arrive and equipment being unloaded. If I had to guess, I'd say it was a riot squad or SWAT team."

Chip had a pretty good idea of what was being planned. He bet Masterson had confirmed Rod Mueller was making bombs and was planning a raid. He wondered how much he should share with Iver.

"Here's what I think," said Iver. "Mueller's place is near that campground. The feds probably have the goods on him. I think Rod is in for a big surprise tonight."

"You may be right, Iver."

"You game, pal?"

"Game for what?"

"I'd hate to miss out on that show. Thought I might just plan to be in that vicinity tonight on my new sled. It's a two-seater. You up for a moonlight ride?"

"On a sled? In this weather? I don't know, Iver. I doubt the feds will let us get near."

"First of all, Chip, my new sled is a Polaris Turbo IQ LXT with a 4-stroke 750cc engine. It powers up to 140 HP and gets to triple digits in 1320 feet over hard-packed snow."

Chip shook his head. "I don't understand a word you just said."

"It's a snowmobile." Iver took a gulp of coffee and continued. "Here's my plan. There's a trail that runs in back of Mueller's place. There's a rise with a clearing that has a good view of his land. Full moon tonight, so we should be able to watch all the action with little chance of being detected. What do you say?"

Chip hesitated. He and Iver had some previous adventures that were wild, but this one seemed a bit crazy. Yet, it was tempting. He hedged. "But I don't have any gear."

"I'm sure Sven has got stuff stored here someplace. He and Hal used to ride. The suit may be a tad long for you, but that doesn't matter."

"What would I tell, Jane? I have a feeling she wouldn't approve."

"Just tell her the same thing I'm going to tell Mabel. The truth. We're going out for a ride to test my new sled."

"I'm in, partner," said Chip, shaking Iver's outstretched hand.

In the basement they located a black snowmobile suit with orange trim and a matching helmet. Chip suited up, put on the helmet, and pulled down the visor. He felt like a cross between the Michelin Man and Darth Vader. A surge of excitement coursed through his body.

"I'm ready to rumble."

Chapter Forty

Head Shot

St. Paul & Minneapolis, MN
Early November

Dʀ. ᴊᴏʜɴ ɢᴏᴏᴅᴍᴀɴ ꜱᴛᴏᴏᴅ in Rick Wilson's hospital room and checked over the latest vital signs from his patient's chart. Satisfied, he turned to Rick. "How's the memory coming along?"

"Still...don't remember...shot." He shook his head in frustration.

Caroline Wilson, Rick's mother, sent John a glance. John felt bad for both of them. The kid still couldn't recall the events that led him to the operating room, fighting for his life. It was possible he would never remember. John couldn't imagine what it would be like to be unable to identify your would-be killer, to always wonder what happened.

He changed the subject. "Your progress is nothing short of amazing. Hard to believe you'll be heading to the rehab facility tomorrow?"

Rick nodded in response. His mother said, "What can we expect there?"

John took the chair opposite Rick's mother, next to the bed. Although the question came from Caroline, John directed his response to both of them, wanting to make sure Rick would have a clear understanding of the road ahead of him. "A team of professionals there will take over your care. After performing a thorough evaluation – taking into account our records, of course - they will establish treatment goals and begin your rehab regimen as soon as possible. The earlier they begin, the better off you will be. The window of recovery is the greatest early on in rehab. The more aggressive they are in the beginning, the better the outcome."

He paused and glanced at Caroline, before he turned his attention back to his patient. "It's not going to be easy. There are days when you are going to want to give up. But I know you are a fighter; you've already come so far. You are young and strong."

Rick struggled to talk. "Can...take it. Whaaa...what will I be...." He swallowed and tried again, "be like?"

John thought carefully about Rick's question before responding, "Your brain will continue to heal itself for the next five to eighteen months. Unfortunately, the parts of your brain that were destroyed by the bullet are gone forever. While the surrounding tissue will make new connections, it's hard to say with any precision. Each case is different. While it's very rare for a person with your extensive brain injury to recover all abilities and function, I wouldn't rule out anything. I've heard about patients, who after being shot in the head, return to near normal functioning."

Caroline spoke up. "What areas will be the hardest to recover?"

John turned to her. "As I've mentioned before, the damage to Rick's brain was confined to the left side of his brain. That area affects speech, reading, problem solving abilities and hand/eye coordination. These are things you and I take for granted every day. We do them without thinking. They'll be the tasks that will be most challenging in the days, weeks and months ahead. But Rick is in good hands at the rehab facility."

As Caroline and her son quietly talked further about the days ahead, John snuck a quick glance at his watch. If he left in the next few minutes, he would have just enough time to get to his interview at the university. He smiled at his patient and stood up from his chair. "I hate to say this, but I have another pressing appointment. I'll check in on you one more time before you're discharged. Let me know if either of you has any further questions."

Caroline Wilson nodded. "Thank you for everything, Doctor Goodman."

John flashed a smile. "It's been my pleasure to know you both."

***

John arrived a few minutes early for his interview at the University of Minnesota. When he walked to the entrance of the Coffman Memorial Union building, he briefly turned around to admire the view across the mall. It was mid-afternoon and the campus was a beehive of activity. The lawns were blanketed with dried leaves and students hurried along the pathways, huddled against the cold breeze that swirled between the buildings on either side of the mall. Autumn always reminded him of his own years on campus, and he experienced a wave of nostalgia.

He smiled at the thought of being a player on this university's stage, depending on how the meeting with the president and board went, of course. John liked the vibrancy he felt as he strolled around the Big Ten campus.

John pulled open one of the large main doors and strode into the first floor of the massive building. Glancing around to get his bearings, he saw sofas and chairs filled with students working on laptops, sending text messages, reading text books or catching a catnap.

Locating the information desk, he asked for directions to the meeting room and took the elevator to the third floor. As he stood in the elevator, he straightened his tie and checked his watch. It had been quite some time since he had met with a board and he wanted to make a good first impression.

He wished he had a chance to talk to Jo to get her thoughts before moving forward with the interview. However, ever since she began the Rick Wilson case, they had few quiet moments together. He had planned on discussing it the previous evening, but Jo hadn't gotten home from Frisco's until after two a.m., and she had left early in the morning for the office.

The elevator arrived and John located the meeting room to his left. He took a deep breath and walked into the room.

***

The day flew by as Jo and Detective Frisco spent the majority of the afternoon at his desk in the St. Paul police station arranging for a judge to issue the arrest warrant for Michael Mazlo, along with search warrants for his house and business office. Frisco sent his new partner, Riley Simmons, to pick up the warrants from the judge's chambers.

While they waited for Riley's return, Jo's cell phone rang. The caller was Detective Ron Fischer of the Williston police department.

"Ron, give me some good news."

"Never thought it would happen, but I'm holding a lengthy affidavit signed by Wellborne. I'll email it right now."

"Excellent. Anything in it that we don't already know?"

"Yeah. Boy, talk about an interesting and creepy discussion. He said Mazlo called him one day, must've been right before your victim, Rick Wilson, was shot. According to Wellborne, the guy was drunk, or high on something. He aggressively pushed Wellborne to do his part in clearing the way for his skin trade. Mazlo told him one of the college kids had confronted him with proof he was blackmailing Wellborne and threatened to go to the authorities."

Jo interrupted. "I'll bet Mazlo was referring to Rick Wilson. That crazy kid must've told him they bugged his office." She shook her head. "He should have gone to the authorities with what he knew instead of going to Mazlo."

Ron continued. "Well, you know kids at that age, they think they're invincible. Anyway, Wellborne was pissed and wanted a guarantee he wasn't going to be exposed. Mazlo insisted he would permanently take care of the college kids himself and then they would be free to move forward with their deal."

"Did Mazlo tell him how he was going to take care of the problem?"

"No. Guess Mazlo was afraid Wellborne might grow a conscience if he was too specific, and Wellborne would go to the police. But, there was no doubt in Wellborne's mind he was going to kill both men."

"And Wellborne's agreed to testify to all this in court?"

"Yup. He lawyered-up. Wanted to renege on his agreement with you. However, I reminded him of the deep shit he was in, not only for the water contamination cover-up, but also for abetting sex trafficking in the oil fields. He had that attitude of his right up until the point I told him he would be going down for authorizing the murder of his compliance officer.

"After that, he couldn't write down his statement fast enough. When his lawyer tried to stop him, Wellborne threatened to fire his ass for interfering. Said he wasn't planning on spending his life in prison for 'some old high school classmate's shit' is how I think he phrased it. It's been an entertaining afternoon, thanks to you folks."

"Good work, Ron. I owe you one."

"Nah. You're doing me a huge favor with this trafficking thing. Lord knows, we've got enough problems without adding more to the list. Maybe now I can bring Micki and the kids home."

Jo smiled at that. "What about your police chief?"

"I had Wellborne sign a separate affidavit stating the chief's involvement with his shenanigans. He'll be in deep shit before the next shift is over."

Ron paused, and then said, "What's going to happen to Wellborne? It galls me to think he's going to get away with all this in return for his testimony."

"Trust me; he won't be getting off scot-free. He'll be lucky if all he loses is his company, at this point. We should have those water contamination reports from Mazlo's office in our hands by the end of the afternoon."

"Let me know if I can do anything else."

Jo thanked him and disconnected the call. She turned to Frisco and was filling him in on the Williston update when Frisco's phone rang.

"Frisco here." He paused, and then said, "Hang on a sec, Frank. I'm going to put you on speaker."

He placed the phone on top of his desk and mouthed, "Duluth PD". In the vicinity of the phone, he said, "Alright, Frank. Tell us what you pulled on the Mazlowski family."

The voice was loud coming through the phone, as if Frank was worried he couldn't be heard and should shout his findings. "The father, Jacob Mazlowski, used to be a member of the Posse Comitatus over in Tigerton, Wisconsin."

Frisco said, "Wasn't that a white supremacist paramilitary settlement that went out of business back in the eighties?"

"Yeah, that's the one. After the federal government cracked down on the group in 'eighty-five, the main leaders were arrested and the group petered out. Jacob moved back to his daddy's old farmstead, just outside of Duluth."

"I've heard rumors. Any recent activity?"

"Jacob and his sons, Jeb and Samuel, have been keeping a low profile for the last couple of years, but there's been recent buzz they're trafficking Native American women and kids. Very well organized, too. We've had a helluva time getting something solid, though."

Frisco added. "Always heard old Jacob was pretty bad-ass. People are too scared to talk. I'm sure he learned from his Posse days how to keep his activities underground."

The police officer continued. "Jeb's been arrested several times for destruction of property and Samuel's rap sheet includes harassment of several local girls, especially residents of the Fond du Lac band of Lake Superior Chippewa over by Cloquet. Both sons have managed to wriggle out of serious jail time, mainly because no one will testify against them in court."

Jo spoke up. "Any record of problems with the third son, Michael?"

They could hear the unmistakable clicks of a keyboard and the police officer said, "Not since he was a minor. Looks like he kept his nose pretty clean after a stint in juvie." A few more clicks and then he continued, "Funny, I can't seem to find anything on him after his eighteenth birthday; it's like he dropped off the planet or something."

Frisco looked at Jo. "Must've been about the time he changed his name to Mazlo."

Jo nodded. "But it looks like he never really left the family business, just went to college to learn how to do a better job of running it." Directing her attention back to the phone, she said, "Anything else?"

"Not at the moment. I'll keep digging and ask around."

Frisco said, "I'd appreciate it. Looks like I'm buying the beer next time I'm in Duluth, buddy."

The officer chuckled, "Well, then don't take so long to get back up this way. I get mighty thirsty, you know."

After Frisco clicked off the call, his new partner walked into the station. The detective motioned for her to join them and they both stood to greet her.

It was the first time Jo had met Frisco's new partner in person. She was very tall, her Nordic roots evident in her white blond hair and long legs. Riley held out her hand in greeting when Frisco introduced them, and Jo had to look up into her face, her head barely reaching the woman detective's collarbone.

"Great to finally meet you, Riley. Frisco has said great things about you." She smiled. "Now, we're all going to have to sit back down or I'll get a kink in my neck looking up at you."

Riley's cool blue eyes danced with merriment and obliged, taking the seat next to Frisco. "Likewise. All I ever hear about is 'Jo this' and 'Jo that'. I'm a big fan already."

Frisco turned to his partner. "Okay. Enough with the love fest. Got the warrants?"

Riley nodded and held up the papers. "Right here

Jo stood up, grabbing her coat from the back of her chair. "Guess it's time to pick up Mazlo."

Chapter Forty-One

Turners Bend
March

Chip had never been the adventuresome type. He was not obsessed with speed like some men he knew. No power boating, no motorcycling, no car racing. Extreme sports were not in his vocabulary. In Acapulco, while others were scuba diving or parasailing or diving off of high cliffs, he was poolside with a margarita in hand. He hadn't tried rock wall climbing, much less mountain climbing. His one brush with speed had landed him in the ditch and Runt in the hospital. The risks he had taken in the past were mainly at the roulette table or unknowingly at the altar.

Yet, here he was, roaring along a trail on the back of a powerful snowmobile in the dead of night in bitter cold weather, and he loved it. He was urging Iver to go faster. "Open it up and see what this baby can do," he said, his voice being lost in the roar of the powerful engine and the rush of wind.

Jane had not been pleased. As she hunted up long underwear and prepared a thermos of hot chocolate, she berated him with names such as "lunatic" and "fool."

"Be sure to take your cell phone in case something happens," she said.

"What could happen?"

"If you have to ask, you shouldn't be going at all. You have no idea how dangerous it can be. Did Iver tell you how he wrapped his sled around a tree a few years ago? Sheesh, men." She stuffed hand warmer packets into the pockets of the snowmobile suit.

***

The night was crystal clear and perfectly still. The light from the full moon cast shadows around the jack pines and birch trees and gave the snow a bluish tint. Chip looked up and identified Orion's belt and

212

Canis Major and Minor, Orion's hunting dogs. Sirius, the nose of one of the dogs, was brilliant…shimmering.

It was about 10:30 p.m. when they arrived at the site Iver picked for viewing Rod Mueller's place. There was a break in the trees, and they had a clear view from above the house and snow-covered fields. Light from the windows formed pools in the snow around Mueller's house. There was no sight of the SWAT team, no action on County Road 17.

"What if it's not tonight? We don't know for sure," Chip asked Iver, as they perched on the sled, visors up and steam from cups of hot chocolate warming their faces.

"I could be wrong, but I don't think so," Iver said pointing to a line of armored vehicles slowing moving into sight. "Show time." He stowed the thermos and took out a pair of binoculars.

Passing the binoculars back and forth between them, they watched the vehicles line up outside Mueller's gate and assault rifles and battering rams being unloaded. Chip spotted a small figure he guessed must be Agent Masterson. She held a megaphone. Miraculously the sound echoed through the still night air and they could catch her words.

"Mr. Mueller. This is the FBI. We have a warrant to search your premises. Please exit immediately."

After a few moments, she repeated her statement and added a warning. "If you don't come out peacefully, we will make a forced entry."

The tinkling of breaking glass pierced the air. Gunfire sounded from the house, and Chip and Iver saw sprays of snow fly up as each bullet landed across the yard in front of the house. The SWAT team moved into place and advanced behind battering rams. From their vantage point on the hill, the scene looked like toy medieval warriors marching into battle.

Iver passed the binoculars to Chip and gestured to a figure moving from the rear of the house, zigzagging from tree to tree, heading for a shed. Within seconds they heard an engine start up and watched an ATV head out of the shed in their direction.

Then it veered off to the left.

"He's heading toward the bike trail that leads to the trestle over the Des Moines River. Hop on," yelled Iver.

They left the trail and headed downhill, dodging trees and throwing up snow on either side of the sled. Momentarily they seemed stalled in a low spot but Iver gunned the engine and soared out, almost tossing Chip off the sled in the process. They were closing in on the ATV when the rider turned his head and spotted them. He threw an object that looked like a duffle or backpack into a wooded area. Swerving to avoid a guardrail along a steep drop-off, the ATV flipped onto its side, the two wheels in the air still spinning.

Iver pulled up alongside the overturned vehicle. With the engine idling both he and Chip jumped off the sled and approached the rider who was screaming in pain. "My leg, my leg."

Chip grabbed a flashlight from the storage compartment on the sled and turned the beam on the man, as Iver put his shoulder to the ATV and turned it upright. The guy's leg was twisted into an unnatural position and his femur was visible through his flesh, blood spilled out, bright red, soaking into the snow like a cherry snow cone. The man became silent.

"He passed out, probably going into shock," said Chip.

"Call 911, we need an EMT and back-up here. Hurry."

Chip fumbled in the pockets of his suit, where he found only the hand warmers. He unzipped the top of the suit and reached the inside pocket where he located his cell phone. As he dialed, Iver unfolded a Mylar emergency blanket and placed it over the unconscious man. He pulled up the woolen ski mask that covered the man's face.

"Well, I'll be damned," he said in a low voice. "It's Hal Swanson."

Chapter Forty-Two

Head Shot

Minneapolis, MN
Early November

Jo SCHWANN DROVE TO Mazlo's red-brick mansion. Both passengers, Frisco and his new partner, Riley Simmons, were silent. A pair of St. Paul's police officers followed in a cruiser as back-up. Jo could feel the adrenaline course through her body as she parked in the driveway. This was an arrest a long time in coming.

Jo saw the curtains shift in the bay window as she walked up the brick walkway. She caught a glimpse of Candace Mazlo's pale face before the fabric fell back in place. Jo rang the doorbell. When there was no answer, she called out, "Mrs. Mazlo. This is Special Agent Schwann. We need to speak to your husband. Open up."

The door flew open. Michael Mazlo's wife stood in the doorframe, her brows furrowed. "My husband is not here. What's this all about? He answered all your questions the other day...."

Frisco interrupted, "I'm afraid we can't comment on that right now. We need to speak to your husband. Where is he?"

She crossed her arms. "If you can't tell me why you are here, then I'm afraid I'm going to have to ask you to leave." She attempted to close the door, but Jo shoved her leg in the opening, grunting when the heavy wood banged into her thigh.

Jo felt Frisco shove past her, the warrant in his hands. "This search warrant says we have every right to be here. Where is he?"

Candace Mazlo's eyes widened in fear. "But I...I don't understand. What are you looking for?"

Frisco gave Jo a meaningful look and shrugged. Jo turned to Candace. "We also have an arrest warrant for your husband. You need to tell us where he is."

The color drained from Candace's face, and she abruptly sat down on a bench in the foyer as if her legs could no longer support her weight. She didn't speak for several moments. Looking down at her feet, she murmured, "He's been acting so odd lately...."

Candace looked up and Jo saw the stubborn set of her jaw. "I'm not saying anything until I've spoken to my husband."

Frisco scowled. "Suit yourself." He turned to one of the police officers and pointed to Candace. "Keep an eye on her. I'm sure we'll have questions for her later."

Jo motioned for Riley and the other officer to begin their search of the house. Jo went to the library where they had first met with Michael Mazlo. She had been searching through the massive desk for several minutes when Riley appeared at the doorway with Frisco at her side. "Special Agent Schwann...you're going to want to see this."

She and Frisco followed Riley down the hallway and descended the thickly carpeted steps at the end. Riley guided them through a theater room, and indicated a brightly lit opening to the left of the movie screen. "Almost missed the door, because it was hidden in the panels. I had to force it open."

Riley led them through the damaged doorway. Florescent lights lit up a large workbench standing in the middle of the room.

Frisco breathed out, "My God."

Jo scanned the small, stark room. Hundreds of photographs covered the back wall, nameless men, women and children. Each had a number neatly printed in the lower right corner. Her eyes were drawn to the picture pinned on top of the others. She recognized the face of Claire Russell, the young woman whose vigil notice she saw when they first met Mazlo.

Riley pointed to the enormous maps plastered on the adjoining wall. There were maps of Minnesota, the Dakotas, the United States and the world. Thousands of pins were pushed into various points on the maps, with the highest concentration being centered around the Twin Cities. "What do you think all those pins are for?"

Jo moved in to take a closer look. Her stomach lurched when she saw tiny tags attached to the pins, each with a six-digit number and a date. She backed up to scan the maps again. "I think these numbers correspond to the victims, and the pins represent where they were sent."

Frisco's voice was hoarse when he said, "It's a goddamn sick inventory system."

Jo turned toward the workbench. There was an empty handgun case lying open on top of several sheets of paper. Once she moved the case aside, Jo was surprised to see floor plans of various buildings, including Mazlo's office building and several at the University of Minnesota. As she flipped through them, she saw the tunnel systems connecting the university's buildings had been highlighted with a marker. "Frisco, look at this. What do you make of it?"

Looking over her shoulder, he shrugged his shoulders. "Looks like escape routes to me. Maybe he knew we'd figure out his real business in human trafficking and thought we'd go after him at work or the U."

"Sounds plausible." Tilting her head to indicate the empty handgun case, she said, "We have to find Mazlo ASAP."

Frisco nodded. "I'll grab his wife." He left and returned a moment later with Candace Mazlo.

Jo pointed to the floor plans on the workbench. "Tell us what those are for."

Candace Mazlo's shook her head. "I have no idea." Her eyes traveled up to the walls covered in photos. "What....what are those?"

"Your husband is wanted for murder and sex trafficking," Jo said. She walked over to the wall, and pulling on a glove, she took down the picture of Claire Russell. She tossed the photo on top of the floor plans in front of Candace. "That's one of the women your husband trafficked."

Candace's eyes widened in horror. "Oh, my God. This doesn't make sense. He's just an ordinary businessman with an import/export company...."

Frisco grabbed her arm. "You have to tell us where your husband is. Now." He nudged the photo away, and revealed the floor plans beneath. "Is he at the university?"

Candace raised haunted eyes to his. She nodded. "He's speaking at a symposium in the Great Hall at Coffman Memorial Union."

She paused and then in a voice barely above a whisper, she said, "Wait; there's something you should know." Mazlo's wife pulled a cell phone out of her pocket and flicked through her text messages. She held up the phone for Jo to read. **Why is the FBI here with the police?**

Tears filled Candace's eyes. "I sent it before you came inside. I'm sorry...I didn't know."

Frisco looked at Jo and let out a puff of air. "He knows we've come to arrest him."

She nodded. "He'll be desperate enough to try anything and he's got a gun." The nauseous feeling in Jo's stomach had nothing to do with morning sickness. "We'd better get down there fast. Call the campus police and tell them to clear the lower levels of Coffman. Have them block the exits, but tell them not to make any moves until we get there."

The detective nodded, his face grim. "I'm on it."

***

John took the elevator to the lower level of the student union, his stomach grumbling. He hadn't had a chance to eat before his interviews, and truth be told, his nerves beforehand would have made food unpalatable. Now that the meetings were over, he was famished.

As the elevator car passed the first floor, he heard shouting and a loud bang. "What the hell...?"

The elevator dinged, announcing its arrival to his floor and he stepped off. He heard a woman yell, "Officer down!"

He turned just as a slightly built man barreled into him. They both fell onto the tile floor and the man sprawled on top of him. He felt something hard dig into his side.

The man pushed off of him as he struggled to extricate himself. He stopped suddenly and his eyes widened. He stammered, "You...you're that doctor."

John was startled. He tried to get up, but the man pushed him back to the ground. "Hey! What gives....do I know you?"

"No, but I know you. You were in the papers. You're the neurosurgeon who saved Rick Wilson."

The man got to his feet and John saw to his horror what had jabbed him in the side when they fell. The man held a Glock pistol. He raised his arm, pointing the gun at John's chest. "You're my ticket out of here."

***

Jo drove through the convoluted streets of the University of Minnesota, while Frisco made all the necessary phone calls at her side. Since they would be arresting Mazlo on campus – which fell under the joint jurisdiction of the Minneapolis Police Department and the University Police - Jo asked Frisco to notify both departments as a courtesy. He sounded irritated by the time he completed the second call.

Frisco sighed. "Both forces will be there for back-up. This is turning into a multi-jurisdictional shit-show. Between us, and the other two forces, we're going to have a crowd."

Jo took her eyes off the road for an instant. "Put yourself in their place, Frisco. An arrest like this could go sideways, especially with so many students around. Given Mazlo's family history with the law, we have to assume he's not going quietly."

"I hear you, but still...too many cooks, as the saying goes."

Jo nodded. "We'll make it work." She wished she felt as confident as she sounded.

She double-parked at the student union building. As they climbed out of the SUV, a Minneapolis PD squad car pulled in behind them. Two officers stepped out and walked toward them. The tall one with a shaving nick on his cheek introduced himself as Officer Keck and the other as Officer Canton. He said, "Not often the feds are involved in campus matters."

"We're not sure what this guy has in mind. A criminal like Mazlo will be dangerous and unpredictable on a crowded campus. Thanks for joining us." Jo threw Frisco a sidelong glance. When she walked past him a moment later, he murmured, "Playing nice with others, I see."

They climbed the steps and walked between the massive columns. As they entered the main doors, a burly campus police officer lumbered toward them. His face was pale and his voice sounded strangled when he said, "We blocked the entrances to the Great Hall, just like you said. The suspect came out and when one of my guys tried to stop him, he shot him. Jesus…he just shot him in the face, in cold blood!"

Frisco clenched his fists. "Shit."

Jo said, "Do you know where the suspect is now?"

The campus police officer nodded, his face grim. "He ran off toward the bookstore." He looked away for a moment. "We screwed up. We cleared the lower levels, but didn't shut down the elevators in time. Some guy got off on the ground floor and Mazlo grabbed him. He's holding him hostage in the bookstore."

Jo closed her eyes briefly, rubbing her temples to relieve the pressure that had taken up residence there. The arrest of Mazlo was rapidly spiraling downward and she needed to figure out a way to gain the upper hand. She opened her eyes again. "Has he made any demands yet?"

The officer said, "No, and he said he'll only speak to you."

"Is there another way downstairs?"

He pointed across the room. "There's a staircase over there."

Jo turned to Frisco's partner. "Riley, take Officer Keck and Canton down the stairs and see if you can see anything." She hesitated for a moment, and then added, "But for God's sake, don't let him see you."

Riley nodded and dashed across the room, the two officers at her heels. Jo watched them disappear down the stairwell.

Next, she turned to the campus police officer. "You need to clear the rest of the building of all non-essential people." The man nodded and reached for his shoulder-mounted radio, calling for additional help.

Frisco said, "What do you want me to do?"

"You and I are going down the escalator." They swiftly moved through the deserted study lounge and stepped onto the down escalator, guns drawn.

She could feel her heart thump in her chest. Hostage situations were always unpredictable at best, with emotions running high. Mazlo would be desperate now, and feeling cornered. She had to figure out a way to defuse the situation and fast. The life of his hostage depended on it.

Crouching down at the base of the moving steps, Jo came to an abrupt halt in front of the college bookstore. Her head swam, trying to wrap itself around the vision in front of her.

Standing in front of a display of gold and maroon University of Minnesota clothing was Michael Mazlo, holding a gun to John's head.

Chapter Forty-Three

Turner Bend
March

Cʜɪᴘ ᴀɴᴅ Iᴠᴇʀ sᴀᴛ ᴏɴ ᴀ ʙᴇɴᴄʜ in the police station, where they had been waiting for almost two hours. It was past four in the morning and all the adrenaline had oozed out of their endocrine systems. They were tired and cold and feeling like miscreants sitting outside of the principal's office. Chief Fredrickson was on the phone in his office. Iver began to laugh.

"What's so funny?" asked Chip.

"We did it again, partner. Every federal agent in the country has been looking for Hal for months, and we ran him down. We should be bounty hunters or private detectives, don't you think?"

Chip failed to see the humor in the situation. Strangely he felt depressed. "I almost wish we hadn't found him. This is going to be hard on Jane and the kids. It's going to be all over the press. There'll be a trial; he'll go to jail for a long time, maybe forever. It would be easier if he had just dropped off the face of the earth and we never heard from him again."

"Guess I hadn't thought about that, Chip. I was just caught up in the excitement of the chase. Sorry...you're right."

Chief Fredrickson came out of his office, shaking his head. "You two hot shots better come into my office. By the way, you look like hell."

As they seated themselves in the inner office, the chief grabbed three mugs from beside the coffeemaker. He pulled a fancy bottle of bourbon tied with a red bow from his bottom desk drawer. It reminded Chip of a similar situation in Franco's office last fall. The chief poured a generous portion in each mug and passed them around, taking a big swig out of his own mug.

"The booze was a Christmas present from a grateful citizen of Turners Bend," he said by way of explanation. He cleared his throat.

"Not for favors granted, in case that's what you were thinking." He replaced the bottle and shut the drawer.

"First of all, I've had calls from Mabel and Jane. I assured your wives you are both fine and will be home for breakfast. I'll leave it up to you to give them the details." The chief sighed deeply. "I suppose I should read you the riot act, but Agent Masterson is on her way, so I'll let her berate you. She'll do a much better job of it. I also got a call from Deputy Anderson at Iowa Methodist in Des Moines. Hal's in surgery. By the time he's out of the OR, a federal detail will be there to take over guarding him. Guess I'll have to drive over later this morning and pick up my sidekick. This is huge for Jim, riding in a copter, guarding a felon. We'll never hear the end of his storytelling about it. "

"What about Mueller?" asked Iver.

"Rod is on his way to the Omaha office of the FBI with the SWAT team. I'll let Masterson tell you all about it. He'll be charged with harboring a fugitive, maybe abetting in a crime. Don't know yet. I've known him all my life. He's a kook, but I doubt he's a terrorist."

The three sat in silence sipping bourbon until Agent Masterson arrived. She took off her Kevlar vest and helmet and settled in the desk chair Fredrickson vacated for her. She drilled her gaze into Chip's face and then switched to Iver's downturned face. "Well, well, well. I don't know if I should thank you two or box your ears. You want to start by telling me how you just happened to be out back of Mueller's place last night?"

Iver told her the truth about what he had seen and heard and how he had figured out what was planned. "What I didn't know, of course, was that Hal was there."

"That doesn't tell me why you two were there."

Iver looked at Chip for support, and Chip hesitated before jumping into the conversation. "We could say we were out for a joy ride and just happened to be there."

"Yes, I suppose you could say that," said Masterson. "But, I suspect that would be a half truth. I'll just assume you were thrill-seeking and sticking your noses in something that was none of your darn business. I can't charge you with anything, but the government doesn't look kindly on citizens taking the law into their own hands.

You should have called it in and waited for us to track down Hal. You know that, right?"

Both men nodded their heads, like contrite schoolboys, and muttered in unison, "Yes, Ma'am."

Agent Masterson smiled, a rarity for her, and her eyes sparkled. She picked up the mug on the desk, smelled it and rolled her eyes.

"Now that's over, here's my off-the-record response. Thanks, guys. Nabbing Hal Swanson the way you did was pretty awesome. Did you know he was on the FBI Most Wanted list? By the way, Chip, your lead from the UPS driver was spot on, although it was Swanson not Mueller making bombs. Hal had been hiding out at Mueller's for months. He's the one who had been communicating with Hakim Dibaba, mainly through Dibaba's *How to Make a Bomb* website. According to Mueller, the bomb was meant for you. Swanson planned to plant it in your car and detonate it with a cell phone. We believe he had a bomb with him and tossed it during the chase. As soon as it's daylight, our bomb squad will go looking for it."

"So Mueller's spilling the beans?" asked Iver.

"Yes, I guess you missed out on the capture. When he saw the advancing SWAT team, he caved...actually waved a white dishtowel out the broken window. The minute he came out, he started to blab about Hal and his bomb-making, claiming his own innocence, while at the same time protesting our violation of his legal rights in the Republic of Iowa. I doubt very much we will be able to pin any terrorism charges on him."

Chief Fredrickson chimed in. "Chip, I think we'll find out Hal is the one who shot at you in the parking ramp and drove you off the road. Franco and I will be able to close those cases soon, and your paranoia can cease."

"Nice to know I don't have anyone gunning for me anymore. What's going to happen to Hal?"

The agent answered. "The list of charges against him is a mile long. Federal agencies will have to line up to charge him. Of course his mental state is in question, but he'll probably be incarcerated for a long time after prolonged trials. It'll be pretty ugly."

"What about Baba? Is he cleared now? He wasn't involved in bomb-making or terrorism. The poor guy has been worried sick and terrified something awful was going to happen to him."

"I'm sad to say he will remain on the watch list. His familial relationships and loyalty to his brother are still problematic. Sorry there's nothing I can do about it. I know it's not fair, but those are the rules."

The agent stood, stretched her back and rotated her shoulders. "I believe the Bun opens at 5:30 a.m. It's been a long night and I'm starving. Would you gentlemen care to join me?"

Iver and Chief Fredrickson consented, but Chip declined. The thought of telling Jane about the events of the night, especially about Hal, made him lose his appetite.

Chapter Forty-Four

Head Shot

Minneapolis, MN
Early November

BEHIND HER, JO HEARD FRISCO swear under his breath. His voice forced her brain to reengage and she looked into John's eyes, willing herself to look away from the gun in Mazlo's hand.

She kept picturing John with a bullet in his head. *Stop...you can't think that way!*

When she re-directed her attention to Mazlo, she could practically see the wheels turning in the adjunct professor's head. She fingered the trigger of the Glock in her hand, trying to decide what to do. Jo saw a trickle of sweat run off of John's brow and down his cheek.

She pointed the gun at the adjunct professor's head. "Put down your weapon, Mazlo. You've no place to go. All the exits are blocked. This will end badly for you. Let him go."

"No, it won't. The doctor is my way out. You will call whoever it is you need to call and get me a helicopter out of here." Jo saw the grim determination in Mazlo's face, and she knew she was looking into the eyes of a man who no longer had anything left to lose.

She took a deep breath to slow down her heart rate and lowered her gun a fraction. Indicating that Frisco should do the same, she forced her voice to be steady. "Mazlo, you know that will take some time."

She tried not to look at John, tried not to give away how much his hostage meant to her. "Why don't you let the doctor go and we can talk about this? No one has to get hurt."

Mazlo's laughter held a particularly nasty edge. "Why would I trust a fed like you? I've seen firsthand the extent of their lies, their tricks. I was there when they rounded up my old man's friends and hauled them off to prison in Wisconsin. Men who just wanted to be left alone to live their lives. My brothers and I ran like scared rats, following our dad through the woods. We lived off the land for days, staying out of sight."

"I didn't know that. It must have been hard for you."

"Damn straight. The feds are deceivers."

Jo tilted her head. "If you think all feds are deceivers, why did you ask for my help in getting you out of here?"

Mazlo's grin was broad. "I found a few of the doctor's text messages to you on his phone. Looks like you have a special relationship. I'd call that extra motivation."

The bile rose in the back of Jo's throat as she realized Mazlo held all the cards.

Jo caught a barely perceptible movement behind Mazlo's shoulder and saw Riley and the two Minneapolis police officers creep up behind Mazlo. She knew she had to keep the man's focus on her, so she tried a new tactic. "Okay, Mr. Mazlo. You're obviously in charge here." She slowly crouched to the floor and put her gun at her feet, kicking it away from her reach.

The adjunct professor followed her movements with his eyes. He didn't seem to be aware of what was going on behind him. She said, "I just need my phone to call for the helicopter."

As she was about to pull her phone out, she saw the gun belt of MPD officer Canton brush up against a mannequin and it wobbled. He caught it quickly before it toppled to the floor, but it clattered before he could set it upright. Mazlo whipped around at the sound of the noise and shot his gun in Canton's direction. The bullet struck the officer in the stomach and he fell to the floor, writhing in pain.

Pushing down her panic, Jo quickly took advantage of the distraction by reaching out for John's arm and pulling him toward her, but Mazlo was quicker. He yanked John back and pointed the gun at his head once more.

He growled, "Stop right there." He waved to Riley and Officer Keck to move in front of him. Once they were in his line of vision, he said to Jo, "Call the helicopter now or I'll start shooting bits and pieces off of the doctor until there is nothing left of him."

Jo cursed. She could hear Canton moaning on the ground and knew Mazlo was capable of carrying out his threat. She glanced at John and saw he had turned pale. Frisco had been right; this had turned into a shit-show of epic proportions.

Her eyes re-focused on Mazlo. "You win." She dialed her boss at the FBI headquarters. After explaining the circumstances, she requested the helicopter.

She disconnected the call. "The helicopter will be here in five minutes. They will wait for you on the mall across the street from Coffman."

Mazlo nodded. "I'll be taking Doctor Goodman with me, just in case the pilot or anyone else decides to be a hero. Just remember that."

Jo turned to face Frisco and the others. "Please step aside and put your weapons down. Let him by; there is no need for anyone else to get hurt here."

MPD Officer Keck said, "Special Agent, with all due respect...."

Jo interrupted him. "At the moment, Mr. Mazlo is in charge."

Keck shook his head, and she could see a muscle jump in his jaw, but he crouched down to set his weapon on the floor. She was grateful he complied.

The group parted as Mazlo backed out of the store. One hand gripped John's arm, dragging him along, the other holding the gun to his head.

Jo watched helplessly as John's eyes pleaded with her. He said, "I'll be fine." He briefly cut his eyes at Jo's stomach. "Just remember who's at stake here." She nodded and felt hot tears prickle in her eyes.

She watched Mazlo feel his way to the escalator and back up onto the step, pulling John with him. When John stumbled, Mazlo yanked him to his feet, jerking him backwards up the moving staircase. The muzzle of the gun was pointed at the back of John's head.

With a last quick look at Jo, John threw his elbow back into Mazlo's stomach, causing the man to double-over. Jo heard

Frisco shout behind her as she dashed up the escalator, taking two steps at a time. John wrestled with Mazlo on the moving stairs, trying to pry the gun out of his hand.

Jo could hear the labored breathing of someone running up the down escalator adjacent to her. She had almost caught up with Mazlo and John by the time they reached the top. As Jo reached for Mazlo's gun, Mazlo's eyes locked onto hers and he gave John a vicious shove.

John landed on top of Jo and they tumbled downward together. She felt the metal steps digging into her back and thighs. John landed on top of her, his knee driving into her stomach. Jo felt a sharp pain in her midsection.

Her head bounced off the metal stair and briefly she thought of the baby. Just before her vision faded, she heard John's voice calling her name. Jo struggled to stave off the encroaching darkness, to call out to John, but suddenly there was nothing but black.

***

John rolled off Jo, flipped open the plastic cover on the emergency stop and pressed the button. He crouched down over Jo's unresponsive body and reached out to check her pulse. When he detected the steady beat of her heart, he shoved aside his fears, and his years of training kicked in. He didn't dare move Jo in case of a neck injury, but gingerly felt for the knot at the back of Jo's head. He cursed under his breath and felt a burning desire to strangle the man who had held the gun to his head a few short moments ago.

He was dimly aware that a tall, blond woman had appeared at his side and was calling for an ambulance. When she turned toward him, she said, "I'm Detective Riley Simmons, Frisco's partner. Help is on the way." She paused, staring at him. "Hey, are you okay?"

John realized he was swaying. The shock of the last half hour was finally catching up to him, and he plopped down on the floor, putting his head between his knees. He took a couple of deep breaths and once he felt in control again, he responded, "Yeah. I'm fine."

He glanced up the escalator. "Where the hell is that ambulance?" He knew the detective had just called for help, but every second Jo lay unconscious was an eternity.

Just then, he heard the faint wails of emergency vehicles headed their way. A few moments later, three groups of EMTs descended the escalator.

One of the EMTs looked at Detective Simmons. "We heard there were several people down. Where are the gunshot victims?"

Riley pointed off in the direction that John had first heard the screams. "A campus police officer is down over there, near the Great Hall." While one EMT crew rushed off in that direction, she pointed in the other direction. "We have a MPD officer there, behind that stack of sweatshirts."

The third crew began to work on Jo. A young, dark-haired woman knelt down next to Jo. Her eyes quickly assessed the situation. "Tell me what happened."

John responded, "The gunman took me hostage up to the top of the escalator and then pushed me on top of her..."His voice cracked as he recalled the feeling of tumbling down the moving stairs with Jo taking the brunt of his fall.

He cleared his throat and finished, "When we fell to the bottom, she hit her head and was knocked unconscious. Also, you should know she's pregnant."

The EMT nodded and wrapped a brace around Jo's neck. She and another EMT then carefully slid Jo onto a board.

Once they had Jo strapped down to the board, the EMT looked at John. "Are you hurt?"

"I'm okay, just a little shaky."

They hoisted Jo up the escalator and John followed. The EMTs placed Jo on the waiting gurney at the top of the steps and rolled her out to the ambulance.

John had to step to one side as the other set of EMTs came through with another gurney, this one with the victim completely covered by a sheet. John wondered which of the shooting victims had died and felt queasy when he realized it could have easily been him or Jo under that sheet.

As John stepped out into the sunshine, he saw Frisco put the man from the escalator into his vehicle. The detective looked over at Jo and raised his eyebrows when he spied John. John shrugged. What could he say? He wished he could tell Frisco Jo would be fine, but at the moment he really didn't know.

He walked over to the EMTs who were loading Jo into the ambulance. He turned to the dark-haired EMT. "Remember she's pregnant. Let them know at the hospital."

The EMT nodded and closed the doors. Since the University of Minnesota's hospital was only a few blocks away, John ran in that direction, his long legs covering the campus grounds quickly. A few minutes later, he entered the emergency room doors and looked around.

Because she had a head injury, John knew Jo would be triaged immediately. He caught a glimpse of her being wheeled to a bay, an intravenous line already started by the EMT. Every fiber of his being wanted to be at Jo's side, but he knew he needed to follow the proper protocols first. He quickly answered the check-in questions at the receptionist desk, then raced down the hall to Jo's bay.

The doctor turned to him. "Are you a relative?"

John nodded. "I'm her fiancé, John Goodman." He shook the woman's hand.

"I'm Doctor Cooper." The doctor stopped and stared at John a moment, her eyes widening. "Wait, I recognize you from your picture from the paper. You're the neurosurgeon who saved that kid's life, aren't you? His remarkable recovery is all anyone's talked about lately. "

John felt color rising in his face. "We were lucky." He looked down at Jo. "What are her vitals?"

Doctor Cooper looked down at the chart. "Her heart rate is a little high, 70. Her blood pressure is 130 over 95, also on the high side. No vomiting, which is a good sign. We've already done a blood draw to check her CBC, Chem 7 and a CMP."

John knew she was referring to Jo's complete blood count, as well as a test for her electrolytes, glucose and complete metabolic panel. They would also check for blood coagulation, to make sure she wouldn't bleed out. He said, "Has she had any eye response to light?"

The doctor nodded. "Yes, her accommodation is normal, and both pupils are the same size. By all indications, she has suffered a minor concussion, but we're scheduled to take her for a MRI in a moment. I was told she was pregnant, so we're doing that in place of a CT scan."

John nodded. "Do you need any other information from me?"

"What type of meds is she on? Any prenatal vitamins?"

"Nothing currently; she was scheduled for her first OB/GYN appointment tomorrow."

Doctor Cooper tilted her head. "How far along is she?"

John felt sheepish, not really knowing the answer. "I'm not sure. Two, three months maybe? She says she's not very regular." He paused, and then continued, "Will she be seen by an OB/GYN soon?"

"Yes, we've already contacted the doctor on consult from labor and delivery. He's waiting on us to wrap up the MRI. I'll go check on that now."

After the doctor stepped out, John studied Jo's face. Bruises and scrapes from the tumble down the escalator were already beginning to appear on her face. John felt a red-hot anger rise within him. He shook his head, trying to clear away the desire to hit something.

He took a deep breath to calm down and sat on the chair next to Jo's gurney. Through the curtained opening, he heard a child crying for his mother to make his arm stop hurting. In the other direction, he heard a man pleading for someone to save his daughter's eye. The sharp scent of fear assaulted his nose, an odor he was all too familiar with.

He wished Jo would wake up and look at him. He couldn't remember being so helpless before this moment. He was used to being the one in charge. He was the surgeon, not relying on anyone else but himself. Even when Jo had been in danger in their first case together, he had been there to make sure nothing happened to her. This time, there was nothing he could do but wait and pray. This time, it wasn't just Jo's life at risk.

John was startled out of his thoughts a few moments later when Doctor Cooper returned. "Doctor, we'll take her down for the MRI now. "

***

John sat at her bedside thirty minutes later, when Jo let out a moan. He grasped her hand. "Jo. Can you hear me?"

Her eyes fluttered open, but she quickly closed them again. John said, "We're at the hospital, sweetheart. You suffered a mild concussion. You need to stay overnight, for observation, but the doctor was encouraging."

Her eyelids flew open and her eyes had a haunted look about them. She croaked out, "The baby...."

John squeezed her hand tighter and made an attempt at a smile. "They're going to perform an ultrasound shortly, but I'm sure the baby is fine." With a sinking feeling, he realized he said the words to reassure himself as much as Jo.

Of course, nothing mattered more than Jo right now. First things, first, he reminded himself.

A frown formed between her eyebrows. "Mazlo?"

John was torn between wanting her to rest and wanting to keep her awake because of the concussion. He decided she needed to stay awake more. "I assume you mean the guy who took me hostage." He smiled briefly. "I spoke with Detective Simmons, Frisco's partner, while you were getting the MRI. She said Frisco raced up the down escalator while I was wrestling with Mazlo and managed to tackle him at the top, like an all-star defensive lineman." He blew out a breath. "He's in custody."

He could tell she was growing sleepy again when all he could see was a sliver of her green eyes. She said, "Why...why were you there?"

"I had a meeting at the university today. I had just stepped off the elevator when Mazlo literally ran into me." He shook his head. "Jesus, I've never been as frightened in my life as I was when I landed on top of you at the bottom of that escalator." He tried unsuccessfully to swallow back his anger once again.

He released his frustration on her, "What the hell were you thinking? You're pregnant, Jo. You can't just keep running after bad guys, like only your life matters anymore...."

He stopped abruptly when he saw the tears coursing down her cheeks. He felt terrible for berating her. This was neither the time nor the place to have this discussion, and he knew she was just as frightened about their baby as he was. He ran his hand through his hair. "Jo, I'm so sorry...."

She squeezed his hand. "No, I'm sorry. You're right; I have to do a better job at balancing this. But when I saw that gun to your head...."

They were interrupted when a new doctor stepped into the room. He was short, not much taller than Jo, and looked to be somewhere in his early fifties. Extending his hand to Jo and then John, he said, "Hello, I'm Doctor Fillmer. Glad to see you're awake." He raised an eyebrow. "I understand you've had a bit of a tumble recently. Let's make sure everything is in order, shall we?" John thought the doctor's voice sounded a little too hearty when he continued, "Ready?"

Jo swallowed and nodded. John held tight to her hand as the doctor sat on a rolling chair next to her. After the ultrasound machine was hooked up, he raised Jo's gown to bare her stomach. The doctor squirted some gel onto the end of the transducer probe and slowly rolled it across her midriff. All eyes were glued to the display screen. John crouched forward, searching for proof their child was alive and well. He could feel Jo's hand tremble in his own and he gave it a squeeze to reassure her.

The doctor moved the probe back and forth, making small noises in the back of his throat. "So far, no signs of lacunae."

Jo looked to John for explanation "He means there is no evidence of blood leaking between the placenta and the uterine wall." He smiled at her. "It's a great sign, Jo."

John's eyes returned to the screen and, looking carefully, he began to see a child's form. A lump formed at the back of his throat as he realized he was looking at their child for the first time. He almost stood up and cheered when he saw the baby move its tiny arm, but suddenly realized he saw something else.

There were two babies on the screen. He looked up at the doctor for confirmation. The doctor smiled. "They're doing very well, I'd say. Their fetal heart tones sound normal."

Jo shook her head gingerly. "Must be this damned concussion. I thought you said, 'they're', as in more than one."

John's grin was so wide it almost hurt. The words escaped from his mouth, "My, God, Jo. We're having twins!"

Chapter Forty-Five

Turners Bend
March

IT WAS NEARLY SIX IN THE MORNING when Chief Fredrickson drove Chip home before he headed to the Bun for breakfast with Agent Masterson and Iver. As they neared his house, Chip called Jane. "Hi, Honey. I'll be home in about ten minutes."

All she said was, "Okay," which set Chip to worrying. *This is not going to be easy, and I'm way too tired to deal with it.*

When he arrived, Jane was at the stove stirring a pot of hot oatmeal. She was dressed in her ratty terrycloth robe, which was once white, and a pair of wool slipper socks. Hair had fallen out of her carelessly bound ponytail. She did not turn when Chip entered the kitchen. She spooned oatmeal into two bowls, added brown sugar and raisins and put them on the table, along with a carton of cream.

Chip removed his outerwear and hung it on a hook near the backdoor. He sat in a kitchen chair across from Jane and watched her flood her oatmeal with cream. She had still not spoken a single word. She placed her elbows on the table, folded her hands and stared at him...waiting.

Chip gulped and started at the beginning. He kept nothing from her; he didn't evade or sugar-coat any of the details. Jane did not interrupt with comments or questions. Meanwhile their oatmeal remained untouched, cold and congealed.

When Jane finally spoke, it was not at all what Chip had expected her to say. She took a deep breath and said, "I'm going to the hospital to see Hal."

"Mom. I want to go with you. I want to see Dad." Chip and Jane turned to see Ingrid standing in the kitchen doorway in her snowman-print, flannel pajamas.

***

The three of them headed for Des Moines with Jane driving. The calm, clear night had turned into a gray, windy morning, and snow blew off the tops of snow banks and drifted across the road, the wind buffeting the car. Chip dozed in the back seat while Jane and Ingrid rode silently up front.

Before they left home, Jane talked with Chief Fredrickson and agreed to give Deputy Anderson a ride back to Turners Bend, saving the chief a trip to the hospital. She also called Methodist for an update on Hal's condition, but was unable to get much information.

When they arrived at the hospital they were directed to a family lounge where they found Deputy Anderson asleep in a recliner. They registered at a reception desk and were told the hospitalist would be paged. They helped themselves to lukewarm coffee and waited until a small dark-skinned man in a white coat entered the room. In a lilting accent he introduced himself as Dr. Sanjay Singh.

"Are you Mr. Swanson's wife?"

"No, I'm his ex-wife. This is his daughter, Ingrid, and this is my husband, Charles Collingsworth." Dr. Singh shook hands with them, bowing his head slightly to each.

"Please let us sit." They seated themselves in leather chairs that surrounded a small low table littered with tattered *People* and *Prevention* magazines.

"When Mr. Swanson arrived early this morning, he had a challenging compound fracture of his right femur and had lost a significant amount of blood. We successfully did an open reduction with an internal fixation by which we essentially pinned the bone back together. You understand, yes?"

They nodded. "Just like with Runt," said Ingrid.

"Runt is our dog, Dr. Singh," explained Jane. "His broken leg was repaired but with an external fixator. How is Hal now?"

"With compound fractures our greatest concern is not the broken bone; it is infection. This morning it became clear he has developed a bacterial infection, which we are culturing. In his weakened condition, his body is not able to fight the infection, and he is in very critical condition."

"May we see him?" asked Jane.

"Because of the circumstances of his injury and the presence of law enforcement people, Mr. Swanson is in isolation in an empty section on the fourth floor. You will have to check with the guard at the door to gain entrance. If you will follow me, I will show you the way."

Chip recognized the agent who was seated outside Hal's room as one of the agents who had first come to Turners Bend with Agent Masterson to investigate Hal's laundering of drug money. He was the one Bernice thought looked like Paul Newman.

The agent stood as they approached. "Agent Warner," he said extending his hand to Chip. "We met a couple of years ago."

"You may remember my wife, Jane Swanson, and this is my step-daughter Ingrid. Would it be possible for them to see Hal?"

"It's supposed to be medical personnel only, with me in the room, but under the circumstances I think I can let them in for a private visit, just for a few minutes."

While Jane and Ingrid were in Hal's room, Chip tried to sort out his own feelings about the man. All he could come up with was pity. Hal made one bad decision after another and ruined his life, lost everything and now faced harsh punishment for his misdeeds. Chip remembered that he himself had been heading down the path of self-destruction. Maybe not the same path as Hal, but an equally bad road...the road to perdition. Somehow in the middle of Iowa he managed to turn his life around. He suddenly felt the need to remind himself of his gratitude. *There, but for the grace of God, go I.*

Jane and Ingrid exited the room, holding each other, grim faced but dry eyed. Two strong, brave women, Chip thought. He didn't know if he deserved them, but he was proud to call them his family.

"Let's get some lunch before we head home," he said, walking down the hallway with his arms around both of them.

They ordered navy bean soup and grilled cheese sandwiches in the hospital cafeteria and crowded around a small table. They picked at their food without much appetite. Chip finally broke the silence. "How was he?"

"He was sedated. We hardly recognized him; he's changed so much. They had him hooked up and wired to lots of machines and monitors. I think he's in pretty bad shape," answered Jane.

"Do you think he heard us, Mom?"

"Yes, Ingrid. I believe he heard us and understood who we were and what we were telling him. I'm sure he did, sweetie."

Chip wanted desperately to know what they have said but knew he had no right to ask. Ingrid, however, told him.

"We told him to always remember he was very much loved at one time. That we will remember the good times, forget the bad times, and hold him in our hearts forever. And he shouldn't worry about us; we now have someone else in our lives to take care of us, and that man is a good person." She stopped and looked to her mother before she continued. "Someone who loves us and Sven, too."

Chip had always wondered about the "lump in the throat" description, but now he experienced it, and the lump was accompanied by watering of his eyes. He reached over and put his hand on Ingrid's cheek and kissed her on the forehead.

They left most of their lunch uneaten and returned to the family lounge to pick up the deputy before returning home. Jim was awake and waiting for them. "The doc is looking for you. Something about lab results."

Dr. Singh arrived and asked them to be seated again. "As you saw, Mr. Swanson is gravely ill. The lab reports show he has bacterial septicemia, a blood infection. The particular bacteria we have identified are a highly-virulent strain. We will treat him with the antibiotics we have, but the prognosis at this point is very poor. I'm very sorry to tell you this."

Chip was always in awe of Jane's command of crises. She took charge and made swift decisions. Chip was to return to Turners Bend with Deputy Anderson and come back to the hospital with Hal's parents, Harold and Ruth. She would call Sven and book him on the next flight from Minneapolis to Des Moines. Hal Swanson, should he die, would not be alone and would not die without final goodbyes from his family.

***

And so it was. Chip returned to the hospital with Hal's parents, Sven flew in from Minneapolis, and thirty-two hours later Hal Swanson passed away with his family by his side, an FBI agent at his door and Chip Collingsworth sitting by himself in the family lounge, holding a cup of stone-cold coffee in a Styrofoam cup.

***

Hal Swanson was laid to his final rest. The interment was private, for family only, and was in the old graveyard beside First Lutheran

239

Church. Chip stood huddled with Jane and the kids, while Rebecca, Hal's sister from Chicago, and her husband Lyle, held on to his parents. The elderly couple looked frail and old beyond their years, bereft and broken.

Rebecca was faced with the task of making decisions about her parents and moving them from the family home into assisted-living. Chip did not want to think about the day he might have to do likewise for his own parents. Charles and Maribelle Collingsworth would not go without a *battle royale*.

Iver had thawed out a small patch and dug a hole for the urn that contained Hal's ashes. It was in the Swanson family plot, alongside Hal's grandparents and various aunts and uncles.

The day was raw, with heavy clouds and a sharp wind that stung any exposed skin. Pastor Henderson made short order of the committal service.

"Into your hands, O merciful Savior, we commend your servant, Harold. Acknowledge, we humbly beseech you, a sheep of your own fold, a lamb of your own flock, a sinner of your own redeeming."

The words couldn't have been more perfect, thought Chip. When he had first approached the pastor about doing a service for Hal, he thought he might get some pushback, even a rejection. But Henderson didn't hesitate. Instead he quoted scripture. "Chip, Roman 3:23 reminds us we all have sinned and fallen short of God's glory. Hal Swanson was baptized, confirmed and married in this church. We bury our own regardless of their sins."

***

The ending of a real life story, Hal Swanson's story, was done. Chip recalled all the times various law enforcement friends had reminded him about the differences between real life and fictional crime tales. Not all criminals are caught, justice is not always done, endings are not always happy. He feared Patrick Finnegan's murder would not be solved and tied up with a pretty bow.

Yet, he wanted a happy ending for Jo and John. He could not leave his crime series, depart from the characters he had lived with for years, without knowing they would go forward with a happy life. And thus, he wrote the last chapter of *Head Shot*.

Chapter Forty-Six

Head Shot

St Paul & Minneapolis, MN
February, Fifteen Months Later

MEDIA VANS CLOGGED WEST Kellogg Boulevard in front of the eighteen-story, limestone-clad Ramsey County Court building. It took Jo Schwann some time to locate an open parking space. Once she did, she had to dodge several snow banks, as well as reporters' speculative questions about the outcome of the Mazlo murder trial. To each question, she replied with her standard, "No comment." The jury had been deliberating for the last two days, and Jo had received word this morning they were ready to present their verdict.

Jo stepped off the elevator and her eyes swept the crowded hallway. She finally spied Frisco and his partner, Riley standing next to Rick Wilson and his mother, Caroline. Once Jo had greeted them all, she turned to Rick and Caroline. "How are you both holding up?"

Rick shrugged and his mother replied, "Ready for this to be over. Just when I thought it couldn't get any worse than sitting through the trial, there was the fresh hell of waiting for the jury to decide. I kept wondering what was taking them so long. Surely they found the bastard guilty." Caroline looked up at Jo, pleading with her eyes.

Jo certainly knew what she meant. The road to justice for Rick and the other victims had been long and arduous. The case had taken an extraordinary amount of time to come to a close, primarily because the first case had been declared a mistrial after the original judge died of a heart attack on the golf course near the end of the trial.

241

Jo offered them what she hoped was a reassuring smile, "Today is going to be the day this jury finds Mazlo guilty on all counts."

As soon as she had uttered these words, the bailiff opened the door and announced the jury was returning to the courtroom. Jo gave Rick's hand a brief squeeze. They filed into the room with the other victim's family members.

Taking her place on one of the walnut benches in the courtroom, she smiled encouragingly at the families of Rick Wilson's roommate and his girlfriend who had attended every day of Mazlo's trial. Also in attendance was the young wife of the campus security officer, who died at Coffman Memorial Union on the day of Mazlo's arrest. In June of last year, the former adjunct professor had been found guilty of second-degree murder in his death, along with attempted murder for the wounding of Officer Canton of the Minneapolis Police Department. Jo had heard Canton had just returned to active duty as a desk sergeant a few weeks ago.

Noticeably absent was Billy MacGregor's mom. In spite of the fact this trial was separate from her son's murder trial, Jo had half expected her to attend anyway. The victim's families had grown close over the previous several months.

However, Jo couldn't blame her for not being here. During the murder trial to convict Mazlo for the murder of her son, Mrs. MacGregor had experienced several heart problems, worsened by the outcome of the case. While his murder trial had proceeded without delay, the jury had found there wasn't enough evidence to convict Mazlo on the first degree murder charge. They had handed down a lesser sentence of involuntary manslaughter. Jo suspected Billy's mother may have had her fill of courtrooms. She made a mental note to stop by and check on her when this was all over.

While they waited for the judge and jury to enter the room, Jo directed her gaze to Caroline Wilson's face Jo noted the deep lines that had formed around the woman's mouth and she was shocked at how much weight the woman had lost over the last several months. Caring for her son and attending the trial for his attempted murderer had taken its toll on Rick's mother.

Throughout her career, Jo had always thought of herself as sympathetic to the families of victims. However, now that Jo was a mother herself, she realized she couldn't begin to imagine the horror of being in this woman's shoes.

She shifted her focus to Michael Mazlo, who sat at a table next to his attorney. He too had aged in the intervening months; his once salt-and-pepper hair had turned completely white. Jo could not muster any sympathy for the former adjunct professor. In fact, she took a certain pleasure in seeing what the trials had cost him and she hoped he would be rotting in a jail cell for the rest of his life. The monster deserved everything the court system could throw at him and more. And Jo was there to make sure it happened.

The bailiff interrupted her train of thought by calling out, "All rise."

The quiet buzz of conversations around the room ceased immediately, and everyone rose to their feet. All remained standing until the judge took his spot at the large rosewood bench. The somber jurors filed in next, taking their places in the jury box. Jo studied their faces, looking for a clue as to their collective decision. Without exception, however, the eight men and four women had turned their gazes to the judge.

Jo felt Caroline tremble next to her. She felt her own heart thudding in her chest and Jo offered a silent prayer that justice would be served. She shook her head. The time for praying was over, because the jury had already reached a verdict it would soon reveal to the rest of the world.

The foreman of the jury, a lanky, dark-haired man, passed the verdict form to the courtroom clerk, who read it out loud. Jo listened as Mazlo was pronounced guilty of murder in the second degree for Rick's roommate, Kyle Marshall and Kyle's girlfriend. Jo heard a gasp behind her and the quiet weeping of both of the young victim's mothers.

She reached for Caroline's hand, which was cold and clammy. Jo held tightly as the last verdict was read, "In the count of attempted first degree murder, we find the defendant, Michael Mazlo, guilty." To her left, Frisco raised his fist in triumph. It was the strongest verdict that could have been levied against Rick's former mentor.

Rick Wilson wrapped his arms around his mother, who slumped against his chest. He said, "We won, Mom. We won."

Caroline calmly looked up at her son with tears in her eyes, and Jo knew she would never forget the woman's expression when she replied, "But did we, really?"

Jo looked over at Michael Mazlo and saw no emotion in his face. She didn't know if it was because he was already thinking ahead to the sentencing or to his future appeals.

***

The stairs in their home on Lake Calhoun emitted a homey creak as John Goodman climbed them with ten-month-old Max tucked into the crook of one arm and his twin sister Emma tucked into the other. He wryly thought about no longer needing to work-out at the gym these days. Although the twins were born a month prematurely, they had grown quickly and were now a pleasant weight in his arms.

Caddy, their dog, followed him down the down the hallway and together they entered the master bedroom. His son, always full of energy, squirmed to get down and John gently set him on the carpet at Jo's bare feet. Max immediately pulled one of Jo's shoes toward his mouth and she quickly diverted his attention. Both children were crawling, and John wondered what would happen once the twins were walking. He knew he and Jo were going to have their hands full when that particular milestone was reached.

Emma, happy to be held, patted her father's cheeks with her chubby little hands and John felt an immense sense of peace at this simple touch from his daughter. He caught a whiff of the baby shampoo in her soft red curls and nuzzled her neck until she let out a squeal of delight.

He paused to admire his beautiful wife as she stood in her bra and panties in their walk-in closet. She leaned over in a futile attempt to alter their son's path to pulling on Caddy's tail. After giving birth to the twins a little over a year ago, Jo was even more beautiful now than when he had first met her. He found himself looking forward to their date tonight, even if it was a fund-raising gala for the med school, and they would spend half the night schmoozing with the wealthy alumni of the university.

Jo's red curls grazed the top of her son's matching ones when she scooped him up and kissed his pink cheek. "Little man, you are your father's son; always distracting me from the task at hand."

Jo's green eyes met her husband's over Max's head. "I'm looking forward to tonight, but did it have to be in the Grand Ballroom in Coffman Hall?" She teased, "Couldn't you have used your influence as dean of the med school to have the event venue changed to somewhere other than the scene of my botched arrest of Michael Mazlo?"

John returned her banter. "The only things they let me do are give speeches and beg for money, you know that."

Jo laughed out loud. "Well, you are pretty good at it."

He looked from his daughter to his son. "I'm excited about the evening as well, but I'm going to miss these little monsters. You're sure Mrs.Carson is up to the task? You know how they get into everything these days...." The woman who was their primary caregiver while Jo and John worked was getting up in years and he sometimes worried the twins were getting to be too much for her.

His wife patted his arm with her free hand. "You worry too much. Mrs. Carson has been caring for children for many years and will continue to do so for a long time yet. Besides, I've seen her in action; nothing gets by her."

"I don't know how she does it. If I spend two hours with them, I'm worn out. Maybe she could give me lessons."

Jo smiled. "John, you are a terrific dad. Trust me, I've seen the best and the worst dads in my line of work, and you definitely rank number one in the best category."

"Speaking of terrible dads, now that the murder trials are finished, what'll happen with Mazlo's father and brothers?"

Jo gently freed her hair from her son's fist. "The U.S. District attorney is trying all four of them together for sex trafficking. The trial is scheduled to begin in a couple of weeks."

"And what about Jonathon Wellborne?"

"Wellborne Industries has declared bankruptcy. They couldn't survive the scandal. Detective Fischer in Williston is now Chief Fischer, by the way."

John studied her for a moment. "Are you glad this is pretty much over?"

Jo tilted her head, considering his question. "Yes. At first, I thought I'd miss it. But now that I'm in the white collar crimes division, I'm relieved. This back and forth between my old and new job at the FBI has gotten old."

"Not sorry you moved to the new department, are you?" He was curious about her response. Although it had been her idea to transfer to a less dangerous department after the scare they had when she was pregnant, he sometimes wondered if she missed the excitement of her former position. He, on the other hand, was delighted she was out of harm's way.

John released the breath he had been holding when she responded with a smile. "Absolutely not. I thought the pace of the job would be slower. I know some white collar criminals are as dumb as a bag of hammers, but there are those that are really devious." She shook her head. "Earlier this week, we caught a case of a former Iowa business owner who is laundering money for a Columbian drug cartel. Those are the cases that keep me on my toes."

He shifted Emma's weight to his other hip and changed the subject. "How's Rick Wilson doing, by the way?" Once his former patient had transferred to the rehabilitation center to recover from his injuries, it had been more difficult for John to keep up with his progress.

"Great, thanks to you. You'll be pleased to know his memory has mostly returned. Although he never saw who shot him, he remembered the majority of the conversations with his former mentor in the days leading up to the shooting."

"How is his speech coming along?"

"Remarkable, considering the amount of damage to his brain. He still slurs every now and then, so he had to repeat himself a few times during the trial. Sometimes he substitutes odd words, but all in all, I would say he was very effective on the witness stand. The jury was obviously moved by his courage."

Jo handed their wiggly son over to John. "Would you mind taking them downstairs so I can finish getting ready? We're going to be late if I don't get a move on."

He took Max in his free arm. "Come on, you two troublemakers. Let's give your momma some room to get ready for her big night with Daddy."

Walking toward the hallway, he heard Jo say, "John?"

He turned to face her. She said, "I don't remember what life was like before we met. Do you?" Her green eyes glowed like emeralds held under a jeweler's light.

He smiled broadly. "Me, either."

Chapter Forty-Seven

AपprIL, AND STILL NO SIGNS OF ANY relief from the grip of winter, no promise of spring to come, just cold windy days and gray, dirty snow. After Hal's capture and death and the completion of *Head Shot*, Chip lacked motivation, felt depression when he should have felt relief. Finnegan's unsolved murder was vexing him.

He searched online newspapers for any updates on the case but found nothing. Mario Franco was avoiding his calls and emails. He wondered if the detective's lead had gone cold.

By popular request he had changed his ringtone to Katy Perry's latest hit. He heard her singing out and grabbed his cell. It was Franco.

"Detective Franco. This is so strange; I was just thinking about you. Any news on the Finnegan case?"

"I thought I'd give you a heads up. Something is going to break on the WCCO six o'clock news show tonight. I'm trying to flush out whoever hired Moore as a hit man. Do you have a way of watching the telecast?"

"I suppose I could live-stream it on my computer. You've got me more than a little intrigued."

Franco seemed to hesitate then lowered his voice before he began. "I'm calling from home and don't want my wife to hear, especially when I'm about to stick my fingers in a meat grinder."

Chip's mind began to race, trying to put pieces of information together. "Can I take it you leaked something to the news station, something that can get you into trouble?"

"Bingo, you're pretty sharp. Must be your crime writer's mind. Remember I told you I had an interview with a woman in detox, named Winona Little Feather?"

"Yes. You said she knew a lot about some kind of criminal activity, but that she couldn't be trusted."

"Well, when Winona's DTs stopped, she implicated some of my co-workers in a sex trafficking ring."

"No shit. You mean she fingered cops from the MPD?"

"Right again."

"Finnegan and Murphy might have been researching sex trafficking in the Twin Cities. Maybe they uncovered the MPD's connection and that's what got them killed."

"That's where my mind is going, too. Tonight that theory is going to hit the headlines. I'm the whistleblower. If I'm right, I'm screwed, and if I'm wrong, I'm screwed."

"What about Dwayne Moore? How does he fit into this scenario?"

"Good question. I said he had friends in high places, one of which may be the MPD Vice Squad."

***

Jane and Chip sat in front of his computer monitor watching the evening news from Minneapolis. The co-anchors were an attractive pair, both with long Italian names. The male anchor led off the newscast with a teaser about a scandal in the Minneapolis Police Department.

"Breaking news only on WCCO. An anonymous source has lodged allegations of corruption in the Minneapolis Police Department's Vice Squad."

The female anchor took over. "Members of the Vice Squad are accused of running a sex trafficking ring, specifically prostituting Native American women. The source also links the deaths of crime writers Patrick Finnegan and Margaret Murphy to the ring. Our police reporter is outside the First Precinct station. What can you tell us, Andrea?"

The camera cut away to a live shot of an attractive young woman wearing a jacket with the WCCO logo on the front. "The Police Chief was unavailable for comment. The department's spokesperson denied any knowledge of the allegations. Rumors of an internal whistleblower are unconfirmed at this point. We hope to have more information for the ten o'clock news."

The male anchor continued. "Viewers may remember the murder of local crime writer Patrick Finnegan last September. His body was found in the ONCE UPON A CRIME bookstore. The homicide division identified it as an active case, so they are not at liberty to comment. Our source revealed Finnegan may have been researching sex trafficking in the Twin Cities."

The female anchor took over. "The death of writer Margaret Murphy was first reported as a suicide. It now appears that may not be the case. Apparently crime writing can be a dangerous occupation."

The two anchors moved on to a story about the threat of Asian carp in the Mississippi river.

"Franco was the whistleblower, Jane. He called me earlier today."

Chip began to pace around the room, so agitated he could not stay still. "Franco could lose his job over this. Finnegan and Murphy must have discovered the Vice Squad was involved in sex trafficking, and they shut them up…permanently."

"Chip, I don't want to believe that law enforcement people would resort to murder to keep them quiet. I know this kind of thing can happen, but in the Minneapolis Police Department?"

"There's a lot of money in sex trafficking. Money corrupts. It's happened in other major cities, so why not Minneapolis? They probably had Moore or some other thug do it and paid him a tidy sum. Poor Franco, he's jumped into the fire. He's done the just and honorable thing, and he's most likely going to get fired for it."

***

Over the next several weeks Chip, along with Chief Fredrickson, followed the story in Minneapolis, piecing together information from as many news sources as they could and meeting at the Bun to discuss events as they unfolded.

Over coffee and cherry pie they talked about crime within police departments. "What happens to crooked cops?" asked Chip as he forked Bernice's flaky piecrust into his mouth.

"Big city departments have an internal affairs staff. They review complaints and misconduct. In Minneapolis the department has a reputation of dismissing charges against officers and not meting out much in terms of disciplinary action, just referring the officers for what they call coaching." The chief signaled Bernice for a refill. "My god, Bernice, what's in this pie?"

"I'm making my pie crust with lard these days; don't tell your doc. And, I put amaretto in the cherry filling. What do you think?"

"I think I'll have another piece."

Chip returned the conversation to his recent findings. "Yesterday I read in the Star Tribune that the city council's Office of Police Conduct Review is investigating the case and the American Civil Liberties Union of Minnesota is also putting up a fuss. What do you think is going to happen?"

"To tell the truth, Chip, I think there will be a discreet cover-up. Unknown to the public the culprits will be dismissed or maybe just demoted to street duty. I doubt there will be any criminal charges filed. Eventually the police will issue some statement about continuing to investigate the murders and their dedication to bringing their killer or killers to justice."

Chip put down his fork. "Really? That's just not right. Something should be done about it. How can they get away with that? What about the women who are being victimized? What about all the illegal money that is being made by rotten cops?"

"You're right, of course. Franco knew despite the evidence he had that nothing drastic would happen. His source probably named names all the way up to the Captain of Vice, but he knew her testimony would not hold up in court. He did it anyway...for his own self-worth...because he's one of the good guys. He expected to be shunned by his fellow officers. It's happened in previous incidences within the force. Snitches are ostracized. "

"How do you know all this?"

"Talked with him last week. Officially he's been on paid administrative leave ever since the MPD discovered he was the whistleblower. The Chief has been trying to protect his reputation by keeping him out of view during the investigation. She's got quite a mess on her hands. Don't envy her. Off the record, he told me he plans to resign his position and resettle his family in another city as soon as he has his affairs in order."

Much to Chip's dismay and frustration, the chief's predictions proved to be right. Two members of the Tre Tre Crisps gang were charged with Finnegan's murder. They had been overheard in a Seven Corners bar bragging about a hit shortly after midnight on the night Patrick Finnegan was shot. They were reported by an off-duty cop who was bartending at the time. Margaret Murphy's case remained open but unsolved.

No one in the vice department was publically exposed or prosecuted. What happened internally was kept under wraps, but it was rumored there was a change in command of the vice squad, and the chief announced she was doubling the force's efforts to stem sex trafficking in the city.

Afterwords

Turners Bend
May

Spring appeared to have finally come to the middle of Iowa. While Chip was reveling in the thawing snow and fresh breezes, a few pessimistic townies kept telling him to wait for the last shoe of winter to drop...a May snowfall. He vowed to think positively, to enjoy the exhilaration he felt at publishing *Head Shot* and heading his writing career in a new direction.

Jane was in a full-scale party planning mode. Ingrid would be graduating from high school in May and Baba would finish vet school soon. Jane had enlisted Lance Williams to help her stage a gigantic celebration. On two other occasions Lance had proven to be a highly successful party planner. Chip laughed to think that he was once jealous of Lance's attention to Jane. Now he was grateful he could step out of the way of the frenzied party preparations and let Lance take over.

Lance and Lucinda had made a trip to world-famous IVF treatment center. Lucinda bought a case of pregnancy test kits, which she used sometimes more than twice a day, reporting to Chip after each test, despite his protests that it was TMI...too much information for his tastes. His literary agent continued to prepare for a pregnancy while waiting for the blue plus sign, spending a small fortune on clothing, equipment and toys, and giving her agent duties short shift.

Chip still was following the case of Finnegan's murder and the trial of the two gang members, but there was no progress being reported. He switched his concerns to Finnegan's family. He periodically called Maureen to check on her welfare. With a substantial contribution from his father, he set up trusts for Finnegan's two children, Sean and Abby. He dedicated *Head Shot* to Finnegan and found peace in doing so.

Giving up on trying for a hip ringtone, Chip had changed his to a favorite John Denver song. He grabbed his cell when he heard the strains of "Country Roads." It was Baba on the other end with bad news, news that set his household tumbling into turmoil.

"Sir, I have news from Afra. My father is very ill and near the end of his life. I must return to care for him and accept my place as the head of our village. It is my duty," said Baba in a voice laced with brave resolve.

The ramifications began to reel through Chip's head. "But you're only one month from graduation. Surely you can wait. We've been trying to get your status changed with Homeland Security, but it still appears if you leave, you will not be able to return. Please, don't do anything rash. Let's explore all the options."

"I appreciate all your efforts, Sir, but I must go as soon as possible. This is my fate; my destiny has been written for generations."

***

Despite many phone calls to Homeland Security, Citizenship and Immigration Services and Iowa's two senators, nothing could be done. Through Jane's efforts the veterinary school had graciously granted Baba an early diploma. His return flight to Ethiopia via New York City and Rome was scheduled.

Ingrid was devastated. "I somehow thought he would be able to stay, that the government would come to its senses and see what a harmless, wonderful person he is. And that he would want to stay here, maybe be mom's assistant. This sucks, this sucks big time. Do something, Dad, don't let this happen."

"Ingrid, your mother and I have tried everything we could think of, but the reality is he is determined to return to his home. We'll keep in contact with him. He'll always be part of us."

The day arrived. Sven come down from Minneapolis and the whole family drove Baba to the Des Moines airport. Chip felt like he was driving a hearse. Sadness shrouded the car and few words were spoken. There had been well wishes and tears at the Bun that morning, and Bernice made a batch of injera for the occasion. Iver tried to give a little speech but got too choked up to continue.

Chip sought special permission to go to the gate area with Baba, but airport security denied his request. Their farewell would have to be outside of the security check point.

Baba handed each of them an envelope. "Please do not read these until you get home. Have S'Mores and hot chocolate and remember all the wonderful times we have had." With those words, he turned from them and passed through the metal detector. They watched as the TSA agent pulled him aside and led him to another area. His name was on the watch list. Even though Agent Masterson had tried to smooth the way for his exit from the country, it would be not be easy for him. Not easy for any of them.

***

Jane insisted on following Baba's request. She made S'Mores and hot chocolate and the four of them sat at the kitchen table with their envelopes from Baba in hand.

Each opened their notes and read them aloud.

Dear Doctor Jane,

I lost my mother so many years ago and now I have found a new mother in you. I will honor you for the rest of my life and try to make you proud of your son Baba.

Dear Sir,

In my country a father is always to be respected, obeyed and honored above all others. You now are my American father, and I am humbled to be your son Baba.

Dear Sven,

Brothers to the end, Dude. Keep the faith and do good works.

Baba

Dear Ingrid,

I will be in Afra, but my heart will always be with you. Wherever you are, whatever you are doing, look to the stars and know that I am thinking of you. Should the fates bless us, we will see each other again.

With love, Baba

Five Years Later in Turners Bend

Chip Collingsworth and Jane Swanson are still living happily in Turners Bend with Runt, Callie and their new puppy, a chocolate lab named Hershey. Chip finished his crime series and is now working on his "Great American Novel," a story about life in a small Iowa town. He was recently elected mayor. He likes to say he won hands down, which is technically true since he ran unopposed.

Ingrid Swanson has finished her degree at Iowa State and is working for an international hunger relief organization in Africa. She is in frequent contact with Baba, who succeeded his father as tribal leader. Stay tuned for news on their relationship.

Sven Swanson has formed an independent documentary film company along with a fellow MCAD alumnus. They aren't making any money, but they sure are having a wonderful time and making headway to their goal of having an entry in the Sundance Film Festival.

After a failed *in vitro* fertilization procedure, Lucinda and Lance decided to adopt a special needs toddler. The happy family now lives in Turners Bend full time, and Lucinda is a stay-at-home mom (can you believe it?). Little Atticus is hearing-impaired and many of the townies, including Bernice, are learning sign language.

Speaking of Bernice, she won $25,000 in a national baking contest. She used the money to open her own bakery, Bernice's Main Street Bakery. Stop by when you're in town and try her rhubarb crispies…they are to die for.

Chief Fredrickson retired. He likes to quip that he has "retired from a life of crime." He and Flora bought an RV and fly down south with the snowbirds every winter. Iver also bought an RV (bigger than the Chief's), and he and Mabel join the Fredrickson's in Sun City from January through March.

Mario Franco is the now the police chief of Turners Bend. His son is the star guard on the Prairie Dog's basketball team…go Dogs!

Five years later life is good in Turner Bend, and the Benders hope the same for you, dear readers.

Discussion Questions for Writing Can Be Murder

1. The mining of frac sand and the fracking of oil are both highly controversial. What are the controversies? How do you feel about his method of producing crude oil?

2. Are the women involved in sex trafficking victims or criminals in the eyes of the law? In your eyes? What do you think can be done to address this problem? Why is the incidence of sex trafficking high at the time of national events such as sports events or political conventions?

3. In this story Chip Collingsworth is struggling with step-parenting. Share any of your own experiences with being a step-child or a step-parent.

4. In *Head Shot* Agent Schwann is struggling with career versus motherhood issues. How can women be successful at both? Share your own experiences and compare them to your mother's experiences.

5. Tolla Dibaba (Baba) ends up on the terrorist watch list even though he is not a terrorist. How effective do you think this and other Homeland Security measures have been in reducing terrorist activities in this country?

6. If you have read the previous books in this trilogy, what do you think about the ending of each of the two stories?

The first two books in the Can Be Murder Series by

Marilyn Rausch and Mary Donlon are:

Headaches Can Be Murder

and

Love Can Be Murder

You can find out more about the authors and their books at

www.rauschanddonlonauthors.com or on the

Rausch and Donlon Facebook page.